Sparrman

A Soldier's Tale

ALBERT SANDBERG

To the memory of
Frank Sandberg
1954 – 2020
A soldier

ACKNOWLEDGMENTS

Thank you Amelia of Amelia Wiens Editing for the insightful manuscript critique.

1

June 1807
Håkansson farm
Överboda countryside

J ohan Israelsson walked along the dirt road leading Agnes, the family's aged
   mare. He held the lead rope loosely in his right hand and carried an ax over
his left shoulder. He had spent the morning cutting and placing pine poles to
extend the farm's fence. Johan could feel the heat of the sun on his back as
they walked. "It's going to be a hot one, Agnes."

Standing five foot seven, Johan is of average height with broad, sloping
shoulders. He wore a homespun linen shirt and hand-me-down woolen
trousers. Because his legs were longer than those of his older brothers, his
mother had lengthened them with two-inch strips of salvaged material.

"Look at that, Agnes, soldiers."

Johan moved Agnes to the side of the road and stood waiting for the soldiers to pass. Twenty soldiers by his count. He recognized a few and nodded to them as they marched past. He was not a fan of the new cylindrical hat with the white plume; he preferred the three-cornered hats like the one his father had worn. Some grinned and returned the gesture; others lifted their heads as if to look down on a peasant farmer. It didn't matter that, just a few months earlier, they too were peasant farmers.

"Soon, Agnes, I will be marching with them."

Agnes nickered and impatiently pawed the dirt, anxious to get back to her stall.

"Okay, old girl, let's go home."

Home is fifteen acres, including thirteen cultivated acres. The farm was once forty acres, but as Johan's older brothers married, his father subdivided the land, giving each newlywed son five acres. So far, five of Johan's brothers have each received five acres. The downside is, his older brothers appear to have taken the best lots.

All the buildings on the original farmyard are squared log construction, most with sod roofs. The exception being the house. Israel had replaced the roofing when, a few years previous, the sod had dried out and cracked during a heatwave. One evening, dirt and grass had rained down on Israel's supper, and he threw his fork down and vowed to tear the roof off. True to his word, Israel got up the next morning, walked outside, and tore off the old roof. He then framed a new roof with rough-sawn lumber and covered it with wood shingles. The project was the talk of the area, many men stopping on the side of the road, in the shade of a large maple tree, to watch and criticize the project's progress and craftsmanship. Only a few neighbors had offered to help.

The house is twenty by thirty feet with a loft. The main floor has two bedrooms and a large open room for cooking and eating. A fifteen by twenty-foot loft held another bedroom. The house always seemed to have the aroma of fresh bread and pastries. Attached to the house's rear is a ten-foot by twelve-foot lean-to. Once used for livestock, it was now a combination cloak and chamber room. Other buildings include the barn, a corn crib, and an outhouse. Wooden fence rails hold their livestock in separate pens: sheep for wool production, a milk cow, several pigs, and Agnes. A chicken coop sat beside the barn for the laying hens, free to roam the dirt yard.

Jonas had just released Agnes into the corral when he heard his mother call, "lunch!" His stomach growled as he made his way to the house's porch. He walked to the end of the porch where the washbasin stood and washed his hands, face, and back of his neck. Johan was drying his face with a linen cloth when his father, Israel Håkansson, and younger brother, Harald, stepped onto the porch.

"How far did you get on the fence?" Israel asked.

"Two sections, maybe twenty-six feet."

Israel nodded, impressed but doing a good job hiding it.

They sat down at the heavy kitchen table. Johan's mother, Frida Goransdotter, made her way around the table, setting plates and cutlery in front of them. Despite bearing children and all the hardships of farm life, Freda had the figure of a woman half her age. More than a few married men had earned a cuff to the head when their eyes had lingered a little too long on Frida. She was also known far and wide for her cooking and baking skills. And a mystery to everyone was how Israel wound up marrying her. He was shorter than her, skinny, had missing teeth, and imbibed a little too often. But they were happy together, and that's all that mattered to them.

On the table were pickled herrings, turnips, knäckebröd (thin, hard rye bread), lingonberry jam, warm ale for the men, and cider for Frida and the children to drink. Johan, at seventeen, was considered a man. Not so much because of his age, but because of the man's work he performed every day. Harald, twelve, and his sister, fourteen-year-old Eva, sipped their cider, smacking their lips at the tartness. Johan looked on with yearning for the cider. He would prefer it over ale but, drinking ale made him a man so, he drank the yeasty brew.

After the meal, Johan lingered at the kitchen table. He wanted to discuss something important with his father. Israel sensed his son wanted to talk, so he shooed out his younger children.

"Can we go swimming?" Eva asked. There is a stream that flows by the Håkansson farm, which feeds the Ume River. Many years ago, somebody had moved boulders into the water to slow the flow, forming a large, deep pool of water ideal for swimming.

"Okay, but watch out for your brother," Frida said.

"I don't need anyone watching me!" Harald whined. He was slight in stature for his age. Frida attributed his slow growth to several illnesses he had in infancy. After the children left, Frida busied herself cleaning the dishes but stayed within earshot of the men.

"Now, what's on your mind, son?" Israel asked, lighting his pipe. At fifty-nine years old, Israel is older than his forty-eight-year-old wife. Frida is his second wife. His first wife, Christina, had died in childbirth, the child being Johan's older sister, Anna Stina. For as long as Johan can remember, his father wore the same set of clothes. Homespun trousers with suspenders over a threadbare linen shirt. Then again, Johan had seen his father's clothes hanging from the clothesline while Israel was working in the field. His father must have an identical spare set of clothing! With that little mystery solved, Johan took a deep breath and made his pitch.

"I want to join the army, sir." He kept his hands clenched below the heavy birch dining table, one knee bouncing nervously.

They both looked at Frida when she gasped. An enamel plate slipped out of her soapy hands and clattered to the floor, where it seemed to wobble faster and faster before settling down.

"No, son, you are only seventeen years old," Israel said. "Maybe in a year or two."

"But Erik Kiällberg was only twelve when he joined!" Johan failed to keep the whine out of his voice.

"He was an orphan, and it was in a time of war, and he joined as a drummer boy! Do you want to be a drummer boy? Banging on a drum while everyone else is fighting?" Israel pantomimed drumming, his nose in the air and shoulders swaying side to side. Under other circumstances, Johan would have found it funny.

"No, sir," Johan said quietly, his head lowered.

"Your father needs your help on the farm, Johan," Frida said as she picked up the plate and turned back to washing as if to put an end to the subject.

"That's right, son, speaking of that, you need to clean out the stalls."

"Yes, sir," Johan said as he slowly stood and walked out the door.

Johan draped his forearms over a fence rail at the horse pen and lowered his head in disappointment. Sensing his mood, Agnes walked over and nudged him. Johan raised his head, smiled, and scratched Agnes behind her ear. It was a favorite spot for Agnes, who tilted her head into the scratch and pulled her lips back in what appeared to be a smile.

He sighed and strode toward the barn door to clean the stalls. As Johan was about to enter the barn, excited yells in the distance drew his attention. Walking towards the lane leading into the farm, Johan could see a cloud of dust rising above what looked like a circle of yelling children on the main road. Deciding he had better investigate, he walked toward the children. As Johan approached, the cries of encouragement became more distinct, and he heard Harald's name and that of a neighbor boy.

"Now what?" Johan muttered, accelerating his pace. Johan hoped Harald was at least winning this time. The last time his little brother was in a fight, he had come home crying with a bloody nose and torn shirt.

Pushing through the ring of children, Johan grabbed the boy on top, not his brother, of course, and dragged him off. The boy swore as Johan let go of him.

"Easy, Ollie!" Johan commanded, recognizing the boy and pointing a warning finger at him. Turning to his brother, who still lay on his back with his forearms covering his face, Johan said, "get up, Harald." Harald peaked through his forearms and then slowly got to his feet, blood dripping out of one nostril and mixing with his tears. Among the group of children was Eva. She had tried to pull Ollie off before Johan arrived, only to be swatted aside by the large boy.

"Eva, come!" Johan said. "The rest of you kids, go home."

The other children were their neighbors if three miles between homes could be considered neighbors.

He nodded at Maria Larsdotter among the children. He felt the familiar stomach flip and a warm surge in his chest when he saw her. They have been friends since childhood, attending the same church and school. They have been playing the flirting game for several months.

Johan strode back the way he had come, followed by Harald and Eva. The children wore their everyday clothes, homespun linen shirts, woolen trousers, a skirt for Eva, and bare feet. They would have swum in their clothes had they made it to the swimming hole. Harald's pants had many patches, he, being the fourth owner of them after his older brothers had, in turn, outgrown them. All their shirts were the same creamy white, their pants and skirt, varying shades of tan. If they were ashamed of their hand-me-down clothing, they did not show it as most of their neighbors were similarly dressed.

Their father had ten children, seven boys, and three girls: five boys and two girls with his first wife, two boys, and a girl with Frida. Harald, Eva, and Johan are the youngest and the only ones still living at home. the only ones still living at home. The children's surnames were their father's first name, followed by either 'son' or 'dotter.' So, all of Israel's sons have the last name Israelsson. All his daughters have the surname Israelsdotter.

Eva took her younger brother's hand as they trudged down the dirt road.

"It's okay, Harald," She whispered, "Mama won't let Papa strap you."

Harald dragged a sleeve across his nose, winced at the pain it caused, and nodded, head down as he shuffled home.

2

The atmosphere was more upbeat for the neighbor children as they walked toward their home in the nearby Sörfors countryside. Maria looked back and watched Johan as he walked away.

I am going to marry that man someday!

"Hurry, Maria!" Called Ollie.

Maria is fifteen years old and the eldest sibling in her family. Next is Anna at fourteen, Olaus (Ollie) twelve, Petter eight, and seven-year-old Magdalena (Magda). They had stopped and stood looking back at her.

"Coming!" She called and, after another glance at Johan, turned and ran towards them.

"Do you think I will be in trouble, Maria?" Ollie asked when she caught up with them.

"I don't know," she said, "it depends if anyone tells on you."

"I won't tattle," Anna said.

"We won't either, Ollie!" Petter and Magda chimed in together.

They were halfway home when they passed the path that led into the Öhn farm. Maria glanced toward the cottage and thought she saw one of the front window's curtain drop back into place. The farm was the local rote soldier's croft, currently assigned to the soldier, Tobias Öhn. Tobias is their first cousin, once removed. He, being the son of their grandfather's brother. A rote consisted of four farms tasked with maintaining a soldier for the province's regiment, in this case, the Västerbotten regiment.

"Look!" She said, "I think there is someone in Toby's cottage!"

"Where? I don't see anyone." Ollie said.

"I saw it too," Anna pointed towards the cottage, "that curtain moved!"

"It can't be Toby," Ollie said, "he's at the army training grounds at Gumboda hed."

"What do we do, Ollie?" Anna asked.

"I'll run back and get Johan. The rest of you go home and tell Papa." Ollie said, "hurry!"

Maria ran like a colt, all elbows, long legs, and bare feet, quickly leaving her siblings behind, "Anna, stay with Petter and Magda!" She called over her shoulder.

"Papa, Mama!" Maria cried when she ran into the Larsson farmyard.

"What happened, Maria?" Her mother, Kajsa Olofsdotter, asked as she stepped out of the house and stood on the porch.

"Someone's in Toby's cottage!" She gasped, slightly bent at the waist with one hand massaging a stitch in her side.

"Oh, Maria, you gave me a fright!" Kajsa said, "I thought something happened to one of you."

"No, well, Ollie got into a fi…" Maria trailed off as she realized her mistake.

"A fight? Who was he fighting?"

"It's okay, Mama; he won!"

"What's that? Ollie was fighting again?" Lars Larsson came out of the house, hitching up his suspenders.

The Larsson home is larger than most, a two-story structure measuring twenty-eight feet by forty feet. It is a timber frame structure with board and batten siding painted red with a peaked roof and wooden shingles. Lars had followed Israel's roofing example. Lars was one of the few, along with Tobias, who had helped Israel build his roof when other neighbors chose to stand by and criticize. Now, most homes in the area were slowly converting to wood shingles. Some of the more prosperous farmers were even putting heavy clay shingles on their roofs, of all things!

"Yes, with Harald Israelsson, but someone's in Toby's croft!" Maria cried.

"Maybe it was one of the other rote farmers," Lars said.

"Where is Magda and Petter?" Kajsa asked.

"Anna's with them; they are coming."

"Where's Ollie?" Lars asked.

"He went to get Johan." Maria said, "c'mon, we have to go!"

"Israel's boy?"

"Yes, hurry, let's go!" Marie said, stamping one foot.

"No, Maria, you will stay here; I will ride there!" Lars said.

"But…,"

"Maria, go inside. Now!" Kajsa ordered.

"Yes, Mama," Maria mumbled, walking into the cottage.

Lars saddled Sofia, their old Icelandic mare, and rode out of the yard. The horse was a wedding gift Kajsa had received seventeen years ago from her aunt Lovisa Öhn and uncle Pehr Raderman. They are also the parents of Tobias and operate a successful horse breeding stable near Trondheim, Norway.

"Go inside," Lars called as he rode past Anna, Petter, and Magda. Lars ignored the chorus of protests from the late-arriving children. Lars was tall and lean with corded muscles. He was considered by those who knew him as a man who could tackle any job and, more importantly, finish it. He also had a playful side, blessed with the ability to look serious when doing so. Even after all their years of marriage, Kajsa still didn't know when he was playing a trick on her until he delivered the punchline.

I should have brought my carbine.

Lars was proud of the French-made 1793 flintlock carbine. He had purchased the gun in Stockholm a year earlier and usually took every opportunity to show it off.

I should go back and get it.

The children, who were still watching him, thought that he had changed his mind about letting them come along. They began running toward him only to stop again and look heartbroken when their father rode away. Little Magda appeared to be on the verge of tears.

Lars kicked Sofia into a trot after deciding that there is probably no one at Tobias's farm and, therefore, no reason to bring his carbine. He did not notice when his children started to run after him nor their disappointment when he rode away.

He met Johan and Ollie at the entrance to the lane leading into the Öhn farm.

Tobias's croft was small, as soldier crofts go, twelve-foot by sixteen with no loft. The walls are tightly fitted square logs. Birchbark and sod covered the pole roof. There is a ten-foot by twelve-foot kitchen/dining room at the cottage's front, one six-foot by nine-foot bedroom, and a three-foot by six-foot area divided into two closets at the back. One closet is off the bedroom, and the other off the main room—two small windows and one door complete the croft. The farm itself is also relatively small, two acres, including the yard.

The croft had a run-down, forlorn look to it, but it was not always that way. Once, it was home to the Öhn family; Tobias, his wife Helen Carlsdotter, and their six-year-old son, Georg. That is until the accident. Seventeen years earlier, Georg had been playing in the barn while his father was cleaning stalls. He had climbed the ladder to the loft, slipped on the top rung, and fell to his death on the frozen dirt. After Georg's funeral, Tobias woke to find Helen's side of the bed empty. He searched the farm and found her hanging in the barn near the spot where Georg had died. Since then, Tobias has maintained a stoical demeanor.

"You see anything, Johan?"

"No, Ollie said you might be coming, so we waited for you."

"Okay, let's go have a look," Lars said, dismounting. They would walk the hundred or so feet to the small cottage.

Johan could see that one of the windows was open from ten feet away, a slight breeze ruffling the curtain.

"Hey!" Lars called. "You in there! Come on out!"

Johan was aware of the situation he and his neighbors were in; he was glad Lars was here to take charge. They were unarmed and did not know if the person or persons inside were armed and dangerous. Then they heard something drop to the floor inside the cottage.

Nodding to Johan, Lars moved forward onto the porch and stood to the side of the door. Johan moved to the other side of the door. Not knowing what to do, Ollie stayed where he was in the yard with a bewildered look on his face. They heard a shuffling sound, and an object fell and rattle to the floor.

"Hey." Lars's voice broke. He cleared his throat and called more forcefully, "hey, you inside there; come on out!"

A low growl replaced the shuffling. Lars looked questioningly at Johan, who looked back with a puzzled look on his face. Lars tried the doorknob and found it unlocked. He nodded at Johan, who returned the gesture. Throwing the door open and going into fighting stances, they were surprised by a streak of grey fur as a large lynx shot between them. They both yelped and leaped back as the lynx loped straight toward Ollie before swerving to one side and galloping out of the yard and into the bush. Ollie had jumped out of the way, fell on his rear, and yelled, "Fek!"

Lars ran out to him and helped him to his feet, "you alright, son?"

"Yeah, what the hell was that?"

"A lynx, and a damn big one!" Lars said. "And, I will forgive you the cursing, this one time."

Johan came up to them and said, "did you ever see such a thing?"

"Once, many years ago, when I was hunting a moose," Lars said. "I wouldn't want to tangle with one, that's a fact."

"Well, we almost did; I felt him brush my leg as he ran by us!" Johan laughed nervously.

11

They stood grinning at each other, as men do when they come through a risky situation unscathed.

"Let's go see what damage he did."

There was surprisingly little damage, a few cups knocked over in the kitchen area, and a puddle of urine by the door. The lynx had been looking for food and had gotten into Tobias's smoked herring barrel.

"I'm not sure if I would eat any of that herring," Lars observed.

"I'll clean up here if you two want to get home; it's getting dark outside," Johan said, eager to ingratiate himself with Maria's father.

"Okay, thank you, Johan. And I want to apologize for Ollie fighting with your brother. I will punish him."

"Thank you, Lars. As poor a fighter Harald is, he makes up for it in determination!"

"Yeah, he does that!" Ollie said, eliciting a glare from his father.

"Come on, boy, there's a diamond willow waiting for you."

"Yes, Papa," Ollie mumbled.

3

After Lars and Ollie had left, Johan looked around for something to clean up the cat piss with before it soaked into the wood plank floor. He spotted a chest in one corner and went over to it. He was struck by the detailed carvings on its surfaces, slowly running his fingers over the designs. At first, he thought it was an ordinary chest that may contain rags but quickly realized it was something more. He stood without opening it and decided to look in the bedroom. He didn't expect to find anything useful for cleaning, but he couldn't resist a little snooping. The room was relatively small, barely room for the bed and little else. A sturdy washstand stood in one corner. It had some of the same carvings as the chest. What drew his eye, though, was the large bearskin spread out on the bed.

Did Toby kill this bear?

Finding nothing to sop up the cat piss with, he walked out of the cottage and headed toward the small barn.

Johan was surprised to see an old rusty chain looped through the barn door handles, the end links secured with a large padlock. The rust color blended with the seasoned board and batten wood, which made the padlock and chain nearly invisible from a distance of twenty feet or more.

Who locks a barn and leaves his house unlocked?

Curious, Johan walked around the structure and found a square opening about one foot by one foot set high in the rear wall. It had a wood door with hinges on top. He suspected it was there for ventilation. Walking around the barn, Johan found an old ladder lying along the base of one wall. The ladder consisted of two oak poles with birch sapling rungs notched into the wood and secured with wooden pegs. Leaves, dead and blackened, covered the edge that rested on the ground. Lifting the ladder, he was not surprised to see portions of the wood beginning to show signs of rot. Johan carried the ladder to the back of the barn and propped it against the wall under the opening.

He stood back and looked at the ladder with apprehension. The rungs were moss-covered and looked slippery. Curiosity got the better of him. He justified his decision on the premise that if he was careful and stepped on the rungs close to the poles, he should be okay. The first rung was already missing, so he stepped on the next rung, grasping the ladder with a firm grip and testing his weight. It held. Emboldened, he slowly made his way up the ladder, the poles bowing inward under his weight. The opening was twelve feet above the ground, so he only had to climb about seven feet up the ladder to see inside.

Johan lifted the door and grasped the lip of the opening, taking as much weight as he could off the ladder. Holding the door open with the top off his head, Johan peered inside the barn. It took a few seconds for his eyes to adjust to the inner gloom, and what he saw when they did, made him gasp. Johan's foot broke through the spongy birch when he moved higher up on the rungs. All his weight transferred to his hands, which slipped off the ledge before he could react. Crashing through the lower rungs and scraping along one pole, he hit the ground hard, his head bouncing off the turf, and the wind knocked out of him.

Johan gasped until he filled his lungs. Laying still, he took stock of his injuries. No broken bones, but his side stung where the pole had scraped the skin, and he felt a goose egg on the back of his head.

What the hell are those things, and what had Toby planned on doing with them?

He decided he would come back the next day or the day after to try to find a way into the barn for a closer look. Rolling over, Johan braced a hand against the wall and pushed himself up with his other hand. He steadied himself until a wave of dizziness passed, and then he fell to one knee and vomited on the ground. Wiping his mouth on his sleeve, he limped out from behind the building. In the gathering gloom of dusk, Johan cast a final glance at the padlocked barn and then slowly made his way out of the yard. As he walked home, he tried to make sense of what he had seen. He had forgotten about the cat piss.

* * *

"Strange stuff. Some kind of drum, hide cloaks, and evil-looking masks! A circle on the floor, in the middle," Johan repeated. He was sitting in a chair shirtless while his mother cleaned the scrapes on his side.

"Drums?" Israel asked.

"Yeah, large and flat and covered in leather."

"How many masks?"

"I...ah, what?" Johan hissed when Frida poured akvavit, Israel's home-made liquor, over the raw scrapes.

"The masks, how many?"

"What masks?"

"Are you touched in the head, boy" Israel asked, exasperated.

"What's wrong with your head?" Frida asked.

"Nothing!" Johan said. "Oh, a bump is all."

"Let me see," Frida said and went behind Johan to inspect his scalp.

"And there was a chain and lock on the doors?"

"Eh?"

"That's a big knot on your head, Johan!" Frida said. "Come, you are going straight to bed!"

Israel lit his pipe and reached for his jug of akvavit, hefting its weight and shaking it to judge how much of his homebrew his wife had wasted. Well, wasted may not be the word he was looking for, maybe overused was a better term. Yeah, how much did she overuse? Ach, too much. He shook his head disapprovingly and looked up to see Harald and Eva staring at him.

"What?" He didn't think that out loud, did he? Shrugging, he poured himself a serving.

"I will go there in the morning." He declared when Anna came back into the kitchen.

"Is that wise, Israel?" Frida asked. "That is Toby's barn; do you have the right to enter his property?"

"Hmm. You have a point there." The decision to mind his own business made, Israel poured another serving, winking at Harald and Eva.

4

Larsson farm
Sörfors countryside

M aria Larsdotter read her book near the parlor's fireplace, in one of the home's two upholstered armchairs. Her grandfather, Olof Raderman, sat in the other chair. The book was the family's copy of Luther's Small Catechism, which is required reading by children in preparation for the annual household examination by the parish priest.

Luther's Small Catechism contained explanations of the Ten Commandments, Apostle's Creed, Lord's Prayer, and the Sacraments. Every year, the priest would visit and test the children's knowledge of the Catechism.

The room was dark with aged spruce walls and pine plank floors. A stone and mortar fireplace radiated heat and some light, and a south-facing window allowed natural light in through its wavy glass panes. Candles set in wall sconces provided illumination to read by in the evenings. Opposite the window stood a finely crafted Mora clock beside a corner bookcase that held more knickknacks than books.

Olof sat quietly and smoked his pipe, patiently waiting for Maria to finish her studies. They had settled into a habit of sitting together in the evenings before her bedtime, sometimes talking, sometimes just sitting quietly in each other's company. Her mother, Kajsa, was in the adjacent room cleaning dishes and would look in on them now and then and smile. Kajsa herself held a special bond with her father since the day he found her after being kidnapped by a wild man. That was a long time ago when she was only ten years old. The crazy man was Lovisa Öhn's first husband, a Sámi man who had suffered a psychotic break, killing two Sámi hunters before kidnapping Kajsa. Olof had been relentless in his search for his daughter and found her after she managed to escape captivity.

Now seventy-five years old and a widower, he lives with Kajsa's family.

"Grandpa, do you think Sweden will go to war?" Maria asked, setting her book down.

"That is hard to say, Maria," Olof said, "I hope not. Why do you ask?"

"Just curious. Is it bad, being in a war?"

"Yes, it's the worst thing a man will experience in his lifetime," Olof sighed, "that and losing a wife or child."

Maria sat quietly, looking into the fire, absently picking at the edge of her book.

"You are worried Johan will join the army?"

"What! No, why would I be worried about him?"

"I notice these things, Maria when others don't."

They were silent for a few moments, each in their thoughts.

"War is a terrible thing, Maria; many of the young boys will not return," Olof said, breaking the silence. "Those that do will not be the same person they were when they marched off to war."

"What do you mean?"

"War changes people, the horrors they witness, the terror of the battles." Olof sighed. "I still have nightmares of fighting in Pomerania, after all these years." He shook his head and scraped the bowl of his pipe.

"But you made it through that war, and so did Uncle Emanuel and Pehr and Erik!"

Olof, his brothers Emanuel and Pehr, and their friend Erik Kiällberg had all survived the Pomeranian war with Prussia forty years previous. Another brother, Jakob, had died in battle.

"Yeah, Pehr didn't fare so well, mistakenly accused of desertion and forced to live away from Sweden. And Erik still has frightful nightmares." Olof said, glancing at Maria. The worry on her face broke his heart.

He cleared his throat and said, "Johan's a tough man, Maria; if he joins the army and if there is a war, I think he will come back stronger than ever."

Maria smiled, and they sat quietly together for several minutes. She got up and placed the book back in its proper place on the shelf beside the clock. She went over to Olof and leaned down to hug him.

"Goodnight, Grandpa"

"Goodnight, Maria."

After Maria left, Kajsa came into the room and stood beside Olof's chair, resting a hand on his shoulder.

"Thank you, Papa," She said.

He nodded and patted her hand as he looked into the fire. He envisioned the battle at Klempenow Bridge in Pomerania. Olof, Emanuel, and Erik had charged into what they thought was certain death. That battle has always haunted him. The dreams were so vivid; he would wake up certain he could smell burnt gunpowder in the room. Shaking his head as if to chase the memory away, Olof said, "maybe it's time to have this young man over for supper?"

"Yes, I think you may be right."

"Too bad, Lars has to be there!"

"Papa!" Kajsa exclaimed, then grinned at the look of mischief on Olof's weathered face.

The next day was cleaning day. Maria and Anna were helping their mother clean the house while Ollie helped his father in the barn. Petter and Magda were getting underfoot, so they had been tasked with carrying water to the barn from the well in one-gallon pails. Olof wandered from house to barn and back, offering his opinion but doing little work. There was always an air festivity and plenty of laughter on cleaning days at the Larsson home.

In the master bedroom, the cleaning progress slowed as the girls looked through their mother's dresses, holding up the ones they liked against their bodies to see if they would fit. The clothing became more practical and smaller as they emptied the closet.

"Those are from before I married your father," Kajsa said. "If they fit and you like them, you can have them."

The girls both reached for the same dress at once and then began a tug of war with it.

"I saw it first!" Anna wailed.

"It won't fit you yet!" Maria said.

"Girls!" Cried Kajsa, "Maria, you take it. Anna, you can have it after Maria outgrows it."

Anna pulled harder, then let go quickly and laughed as Maria fell on her rear.

"Mama!" Maria cried. "She did that on purpose!"

"What's all the racket in here?" Olof growled, coming into the room.

"The girls are fighting over my clothes."

"Ah. It is the oldest who always gets handed down clothes first and then the second oldest afterward. That's the way it is and the way it has always been."

"It's not fair!" Anna said, arms crossed, and bottom lip stuck out.

"You are right, little one," Olof said. "Tell you what, you can have my trousers when I outgrow them!"

"Eww!" Anna said, "they smell like pee!"

"Anna!" Kajsa cried, then grinned when Olof bellowed laughter.

"What's this?" Maria asked, pulling out a long, wooden object from the back of the closet.

"That's my bow! I haven't seen that in years!"

"This is yours? Do you know how to shoot it?"

"Maria, your mother is the best bow and arrow shooter in all of Sweden!" Olof declared from his seat on the bed.

"Papa, I am not!" Kajsa said.

"She could put an arrow through a spruce chicken's head at fifty feet!" Olof said.

"Really?" Maria said. She was admiring the craftsmanship of the curved wood. "Who made it?"

"The Sámi; Lovisa gave it to me and taught me how to shoot."

"Oh," Maria said. "Tell us about Lovisa."

"Yeah!" Anna cried. "Tell us, Mama!"

"Alright, but keep working," Kajsa said. "We have a lot to do before supper."

"Pull me up, girls!" Olof said, holding out his arms. "My stinky trousers and I are needed in the barn."

"Lovisa is married to your grandfather's brother, Pehr." Kajsa began after Olof left the room. "You have never met them; they live in Norway."

"Can we go to visit them, Mama?" Anna asked.

"No, it is a long and dangerous journey." Kajsa sighed. "Lovisa taught me how to hunt and a lot of other things. I miss her."

Kajsa was quiet for a time. Her daughters waited for her to continue. She had stopped cleaning the windowpanes and was looking through the wavy glass at the distant mountains.

"She lived with the Sámi for a time." Kajsa continued. "She is Tobias Öhn's mother."

"Toby?" Maria gasped. "Cousin Toby, from down the road?"

"Yes."

"Is Toby a Sámi?" Anna whispered with big eyes.

"No, Toby is Pehr's son."

"How come they live in Norway?" Maria asked.

"Pehr fought in the Pomeranian War with your grandfather and Manny, oh, and Jakob too," Kajsa said.

"Who is Jakob?"

"Jakob was also your grandfather's brother. He died in the war."

"I'm sorry, Mama," Anna said. They were now sitting on the bed, the cleaning forgot for the moment.

"It's okay, Anna. I never met Jakob. When Jakob died in battle, Pehr was injured and lost his memory."

"Really?" Maria asked.

"Yes, he was captured and left on a farm. After the end of the war, Pehr regained his memory, but the army didn't believe him and accused him of desertion. Pehr ran away, and everyone thought he was dead. I met him in Norway at Trondheim many years later, and Lovisa married him. But they can't come to Sweden because the army still considers him a deserter."

"That is sad," Anna said.

"We don't see them anymore, but they are happy together," Kajsa said. "Now, you two get back to work."

5

On a warm and sunny Wednesday afternoon, Anna and Ollie walked the three miles to the Håkansson farm. Their mission; to invite Johan for dinner. The trip took longer than it should have, mainly due to a small rabbit who had the misfortune to hop across the road in front of them. What followed was a frantic chase through the willows and brambles, shrieks and laughter terrifying the poor creature. Finally, the rabbit went where no person could go, into a thicket of thorny blackberry brush. Ollie skidded to a stop, but momentum tilted him forward, where he rocked off balance. His arms windmilled in a futile attempt to stop himself from falling forward. With an "aargh," Ollie fell forward into the thorns. Fortunately, Anna managed to pull him out before too much damage occurred. The injuries Ollie suffered were several painful punctures to his legs, wrists, and hands. Pinpricks of blood seeped through his pants and beaded on his palms and wrists. The rabbit watched from safety before hopping away to live a long, by rabbit standards, and fruitful, also by rabbit standards, life.

Ollie wanted to abandon their mission and head back home so his mother could make it all better. But Anna would have none of that, telling him to stop being a baby. Eventually, Ollie acquiesced and stumbled along beside her. He winced now and then when his trousers rubbed against the punctures on his legs. The next delay was when they neared the path that led to Tobias Öhn's farm.

They heard the men before they saw them. They were speaking loudly in a strange language, although some words seemed similar to Swedish. They continued walking past the path, all the while staring into the yard, but the barn was not visible from the road. And that is where the strangers must be. Curious and knowing that Tobias was still away from home, Anna and Ollie decided to keep their presence hidden and sneak through the bushes to investigate. Ollie was overly careful as they crept through the underbrush, lest he encounters more blackberry thorns.

They came up behind the barn and stopped thirty feet away.

"Look!" Ollie whispered. "That ladder has been broken recently."

"How can you tell?"

"The moss has rubbed off in some areas, and the exposed wood is clean."

"So?"

"If that ladder has been lying there for a while, the wood wouldn't be so clean," Ollie explained a little too condescendingly for Anna's taste. Just then, she shrieked when a bushy-haired older man stuck his brown face around the barn's corner and stared straight at them. They both leaped up and ran through the brush to the road and then toward the Håkansson farm.

"Wait for me, Ollie!" Anna cried when Ollie began to leave her behind.

He slowed and hollered, "hurry, Anna!" He did not see anyone coming down the road from Tobias's farm, but the strangers could be running parallel to them in the bush, waiting to jump out in front of them. Ollie took Anna's hand and pulled her along behind him.

"Slow down, Ollie!" Anna cried, "I can't keep up!"

Ollie slowed, then stopped while Anna caught her breath. He tried listening for any noise in the bush but did not hear anything. No one was on the road behind them, so when Anna was ready, they walked the rest of the way to the farm, frequently looking over their shoulders.

They walked up to the Håkansson's front door and knocked. Johan's mother, Frida, answered the door.

"Oh, Ollie and Anna, Välkommen!"

"Thank you." Anna said, "but we just came to give a message to Johan."

"Johan, you have visitors!" Frida called over her shoulder.

Johan appeared behind his mother, who gave no indication she was going to move.

"Yeah?"

"Johan Israelsson," Anna said in her most officious voice. "You are cordially invited to dine at the Larsson abode this Friday evening."

Johan was at a loss for words, so his mother nudged him and said, "answer the girl, Johan."

"Ahh, I never ate cordials before. What are they?"

"Bull's testes!" Israel hollered from the table with a chuckle. He had been sneaking sips of akvavit all afternoon, much to Frida's annoyance.

"Ahh." Johan stammered.

"It is not!" His mother said. Then turning to Anna, she whispered, "is it?"

"No, it isn't," Anna said with a giggle. "My father and mother, and Maria, just want Johan to come for dinner." She had given up trying to sound formal.

"Johan would be delighted to attend!" His mother said.

"Ahh." Johan stammered.

"Come in, have a cup of water, or maybe tea before you go back."

"Thank you; tea would be good," Annie said.

"What happened to you!" Frida cried, seeing Ollie's injuries when Anna walked by. He had been standing behind Anna, partially hidden from Frida's view.

"Lost a fight with a blackberry bush," Ollie muttered.

"Hear that, Harald?" Israel said. "You should go ask the blackberries to teach you how to fight!" He chuckled at his wit. Ollie had to grin at this, and, eventually, so did Harald.

"Israel," Frida said. "Don't you have a fence to repair?"

"Yeah." Israel sighed. "Come on, Johan."

"You know he still has dizzy spells," Frida said.

"Ach! Harald, come give me a hand."

"All right!" Harald said, then to Ollie, "do you want to come?"

"Ollie needs to get home and have those cuts looked after," Frida said before Ollie could answer.

"We were chased from Tobias's farm by two strangers," Anna said after Israel and Harald left.

"What! By whom?" Frida cried.

"Two men, at least," Anna said while dipping a cookie into her tea. "We only saw one, though. A big hairy-faced man!"

"What were they doing at Toby's farm?" Johan asked. His headaches have subsided since his fall, but he still experienced occasional dizzy spells. The memory of the strange items locked in the barn came flooding back to him now.

"They were in the barn," Ollie said. "We couldn't see them from the road, so we snuck through the brush behind the barn. One of them looked around the corner and spotted us, so we ran here. They spoke funny."

"We need to go see!" Johan said, looking at his mother for consent.

"I am not letting you go snooping around Toby's farm while he's gone!" Frida said firmly. "And especially not when strangers may be there."

Turning to Anna, she asked, "what do you mean by funny, a strange language? Norwegian?"

"I don't think so. Some words sounded the same as Swedish, though."

"Humph," Frida grunted.

"Well, at least let me walk Anna and Ollie safely home," Johan said.

"Yeah, okay. But do not go on Toby's farm!" she said, pointing a warning finger at him.

"Can I go too?" Eva asked. She had been serving the tea and cookies and now stood leaning against the kitchen sink nibbling on a gingersnap.

"Yes!" Frida said. She took Eva aside and instructed her to make sure Johan stayed away from Tobias's farm.

"I'll try, Mama," Eva said. "Can I have another snap?"

"Yes, you can have another one." Frida sighed, smiling at her daughter.

6

On the evening of his dinner date at the Larssons, Johan stopped at the Öhn farm path. True to his word, he had so far stayed away from the farm. Now he looked at the quiet farmyard and debated whether he should 'check on it' for Tobias. After all, strange men were snooping around the barn a few days ago. But, before Johan could make up his mind, he saw a dust cloud above a rise in the road ahead, and he ran a few yards so he wouldn't be spotted near Tobias's farm when the rider crested the hill.

When the rider came into view, Johan immediately recognized Tobias by his uniform. Johan stopped walking and stood on the side of the road, and raised his hand in greeting.

"Välkommen, Toby!" He called, anticipating a friendly chat. He had worked out in his head how he would tell Tobias about the strangers, but Tobias didn't slow and merely nodded at Johan as he rode by.

"Hmph," Johan muttered. "That's not very neighborly!"

He arrived at the Larsson home at the appointed hour and stood on the porch. Before knocking, he wondered what he was supposed to say when the door was suddenly flung open.

"Välkommen, Johan!" Anna cried, accompanied by giggles from Petter and Magda.

"Ahh, thank you, Anna," Johan said.

"I think I shall call you 'Ahh' from now on!" She said to more giggles.

"Anna, Petter, and Magda, go away!" Maria ordered. "Sorry, Johan."

"Ahh." Johan stammered much to the younger children's glee.

"Come inside, Johan," Maria said, taking his hand and pulling him into the sitting room. Johan stumbled along behind Maria, breathless at the sight of her and the intimacy of his hand in hers. She was stunning in her dress, blond hair braided, and her blue eyes were sparkling.

"Hello, sirs," Johan said when they entered the sitting room where Lars and Olof sat.

"Hi, Johan," Olof said, enthusiastically shaking his hand.

A nod and a quick handshake from Lars drew a frown from Olof.

After Maria left them to help her mother in the kitchen, the silence became uncomfortable.

"So, Johan, Maria tells me you want to join the army?" Olof said, breaking the silence.

The question brought a grunt from Lars.

"Yes, sir!"

"There have been rumors of war," Lars said.

"With who?" Olof asked.

"Norway or Denmark or maybe both, and possibly Russia."

"Hmph. My brother lives in Norway, as you know."

"Will he be safe there?" Lars asked. Johan began to feel left out of the conversation. Still, he held his tongue as he was not as knowledgeable about world affairs as these two men appeared to be.

"Yeah, he should be safe; he has lived there for many years," Olof said. "Although, he may end up having to supply the Norwegian army with horses, to fight Swedes!"

"A tough spot to be in." Lars agreed.

"Dinner is ready!" Maria called from the kitchen. The aromas had Johan salivating since he had walked in the house, and now his stomach grumbled loudly to the delight of Olof.

"You are in for a treat, Johan!" Olof exclaimed, clapping a hand on his shoulder. "Maria is an excellent cook!"

From the kitchen, Kajsa and Maria overheard Olof's praise, and Maria beamed.

Throughout the meal, Johan could not keep his eyes off Maria. She, of course, was aware of his attention but pretended not to notice. But Olof and Kajsa saw this and shared a grin. Then, Petter and Magda giggled and made kissing noises until being banished to the sitting room.

They asked Johan about his family, home, and his plans for the future. The table conversation eventually turned to current events, mostly dominated by Olof and Lars. Not wanting to be left out again, Johan spoke up. "I met Toby on the way here."

"Yeah?" Olof said. "I will have to stop by and see him tomorrow." Olof liked to talk with soldiers whenever he could to relate much-repeated stories of his own army experiences.

"He barely acknowledged me as he rode by," Johan said.

"He was probably anxious to get home after being away so long," Kajsa said.

"His horse looked similar to the mare you have in your corral."

"Yes, they both come from Pehr's stables in Norway," Olof said.

"What does he do with his horse when he is training?" Lars asked.

"Toby puts up his horse at a stable in Umeå."

"Must be nice to have money to waste on a stable!"

"What else is he going to spend it on?" Olof said.

"You have a point there." Lars said, "I will go with you tomorrow, Olof. I should tell him about the lynx."

"I can tell Toby," Olof said, clearly not happy with the prospect of Lars accompanying him. His visit was between soldiers, after all. "No reason to take you away from your work."

"Yeah, you have a point there, Olof," Lars said, sensing Olof's reluctance to have him along on his visit.

"Maria, maybe Johan would like to sit with you in the parlor before your studies?" Kajsa said.

Maria flushed red, covering her blush by wiping her mouth with a napkin. She stood and looked at Johan. "Would you like to sit with me for a while, Johan?"

The question caused muffled kissing noises from the sitting room, followed by Anna's giggling when Johan responded with, "ahh."

"Petter and Magda!" Kajsa hollered, "come clean these dishes!"

"Why us?" Petter whined as they came back into the kitchen. "We never even got to finish eating!"

"And where are we supposed to smoke?" Lars complained.

"You can smoke on the porch," Kajsa said.

"Pour us a cup, Olof," Lars said, rising from his chair. "There's a nip in the air this evening."

Olof grinned, pleased at the thought of a drink of akvavit to enjoy with his pipe.

* * *

Johan had stayed longer than he had planned to, and it was twilight when he walked away from the Larsson farm. He had broken a rather long and shy silence with Maria by mentioning his adventure at Tobias's barn. The story and the mysterious items locked inside the barn enthralled her. One theory was that Tobias prepared a Fettisdagen costume for the festival celebrated between Shrove Monday and Ash Wednesday. People would dress up in scary masks and attire as part of the festivities. Another theory, and quickly dismissed, was that Tobias was a witch.

Johan smiled as he remembered sitting across from Maria. Their faces were inches apart as they speculated on the mysterious items in the barn. He savored her scent, clothes fresh from the outdoor clothesline, soap, and hints of the pastries she had baked for dessert. He felt as if he was walking on air, thinking of how she put her hands on his as they talked.

His reverie was interrupted by muffled chanting as he neared the Öhn farm. Stopping, he slowed his breathing and cocked an ear towards the yard. It was now quite dark; a half-moon offered some intermittent light between clouds drifting across the sky. Over the croaking of frogs and chirping grasshoppers, Johan caught the muffled murmurs again. They seemed to emanate from the barn.

Creeping along the edge of the path leading into the farm, Johan kept looking from the house to the barn. He stared hard at the house's porch.

Was that someone sitting in a chair, looking his way?

He stopped and held himself still, his heart pounding and the beginnings of a headache forming. Emboldened when the shape didn't move, Johan crept further into the yard until he could see the barn. He could see a shaft of light coming from under the doors. From where he stood, Johan could also see a small beam of light shining through what he suspected was a knothole in one of the boards.

Johan crossed to the other side of the path, never taking his eyes off the shape on the porch. He decided it must be a coat or blanket draped over Tobias's rocking chair. Johan had noticed the chair on his previous visit, not giving it a second glance. He worked his way through high grass and between trees to the side of the barn, suddenly stopping when a twig cracked under his feet, and the chanting stopped. He stood still, ready to bolt if the barn door opens.

When the chanting resumed, Johan let out the breath that he didn't know he was holding. His head was pounding now with every beat of his heart. Careful of his footing, he crept to the side of the barn and smelled the aroma of old manure as he stepped on dry, powdery clumps. Johan jumped when the drumming began.

Curiosity overcame fear, and he approached the wall and slowly leaned his right eye to the knothole. He had braced himself for the unknown, so he was not entirely shocked to see three men dressed in cloaks and creepy masks. The masks were of white linen with elongated noses. One of the men held a large drum in one hand and beat it with his other hand. Another man wore a headdress above his mask and was chanting while performing some sort of dance. The third man stood still across from the wall from Johan.

Johan jumped when the chanting changed to yelling. He stared at the headdress man as the pace of his dancing increased, and the pitch of his yelling increased. Looking toward the others, Johan was shocked to see the man across from him was staring directly at his eye. Jumping back, Johan turned and ran to the path leading into the farm. His fear intensified when he glanced at the house and saw that the shape on the porch had changed. It was now clearly the shape of an empty rocking chair!

With a gurgle escaping his throat, Johan ran to the road and then turned toward home, all the while sure he could hear running footsteps behind him. He skidded to a stop when he saw a figure standing in the middle of the road ahead of him. He was about to turn to his left and run when the figure strode toward him.

"Johan! What the hell are you doing out here?" Israel called.

Johan almost collapsed with relief, trotting toward his father on rubbery legs. He glanced over his shoulder, but the pursuing footsteps, if they were not his imagination, had stopped, and the road behind was empty.

"Do you know how worried your mother is?" Israel demanded.

"Sorry, sir, but -"

"I don't want to hear your excuses!" Israel turned and began walking back home. He was determined not to show Johan the relief he felt that his son was safe and not on his way to join the army. Johan trailed behind his father, occasionally looking back over his shoulder.

Was Toby the man in the mask who looked directly at him?

If so, did he recognize me?

And what was he doing?

Is he a witch?

Is there such a thing as witches?

My head hurts!

These thoughts occupied his mind all the way home and well into the night. His dreams, which should have about Maria, instead were filled with the terrifying images of masked men chasing him through the county side. Dreams that ended with Johan bolting upright in his bed soaked through with sweat. He vowed to avoid Tobias and his farm from now on.

7

On February 21, 1808, Russian forces invaded Swedish ruled Finland. One month later, on March 14, Denmark, allied with Norway, declared war on Sweden. March 14 was also Johan's eighteenth birthday and, on that day, Johan walked out his front door and didn't stop until he arrived in Umeå, where he joined the army.

In the months leading up to his birthday, Johan and Maria discussed his wish to join the army and marriage. Maria was against Johan entering the army, but if he did, she wanted to wait until any threat of war was over before marrying. Johan was persistent in his wish to marry soon after his birthday. Eventually, Maria accepted that Johan would be a soldier and agreed to marry him on the condition that her father gives his blessing.

Johan's parents first heard the news that he joined the army when Israel went to the Larssons looking for him after he failed to come home for supper. Maria had told Olof about Johan's plan to join the army that day, and Olof, in turn, informed Kajsa. And Kajsa broke the news to Israel when he came to their front door.

SPARRMAN • A SOLDIER'S TALE

When Johan returned from his initial training with the Västerbotten regiment, he went straight to the Larsson farm. Resplendent in his uniform, Johan asked Lars Larsson's permission to marry his daughter.

"Anna? No, she is too young." Lars said.

"No, not Anna!" Johan stammered.

"Well, Magdalena is even younger; what kind of man are you, asking for a child bride!"

"Lars!" Kajsa yelled from inside the house. She was hiding around a corner wall with Maria.

"Well, Johan, you know I think you are a good man, but I worry you will go to war and not come back," Lars said, all joking aside. "Then what is to become of Maria?"

Maria gasped, then ran to her room in tears. She had never considered the prospect of her father rejecting Johan's request. Although she initially wanted to wait until the threat of war was over before marrying, she had succumbed to the excitement and anticipation of a wedding.

Johan walked the rest of the way home in a daze. He even forgot to take the roundabout route by Tobias's farm he had used since that night of the strange barn ritual. But he need not worry; Tobias was on maneuvers at the training grounds in Gumboda hed.

Over the winter, Johan had more than once caught Tobias staring at him in church. Johan quickly looked away each time. Tobias never approached him, and Johan wondered if he was even in the barn that night.

Was Toby the shape that was sitting on the porch?

Or was he the man in the barn who looked in his direction?

Could he recognize Johan in the dark, or from only seeing an eyeball through a knothole?

Johan wondered if he would ever know the answers to these questions.

His reception at home was not altogether unexpected. His mother, of course, welcomed him home with open arms, but his father only grunted and said he had work to do as he stalked out the door. Harald and Eva were happy to see their older brother; Harald peppered Johan with questions about the army until Israel called for him to help in the barn.

After supper that first evening home, Johan cleared his voice and said, "Papa, I have something to tell you."

When Johan hesitated, Israel said, "well, spit it out, boy!"

"The army assigned me a new name."

"Eh?"

"My soldier's name is Johan Sparrman."

"What are you saying, boy?" Israel demanded. "Are you ashamed to bear your father's name!"

"No, no, of course not!" Johan said quickly. "The army changed it! They said there were too many soldiers named Johan Israelsson. They had to assign me a new last name to avoid confusion."

"Hmph!" Israel grunted, walking out of the cabin.

"You dishonor your father, Johan," Frida said.

"I didn't have a choice, Mama!" Johan cried. "I can change it back once I leave the army."

"That may be many years from now; he may be gone by then."

* * *

Five days later, Johan left home to rejoin his regiment for the next phase of his training. His stay at home consisted of working in the fields during the day and visiting Maria in the evenings. His father was still sore about Johan joining the army but seemed to be slowly coming around. Johan felt obliged to work harder than he ever had on the farm, to accomplish as much as possible before he had to return to the army. Evenings with Maria were what got him through the days of hard labor. The anticipation of each visit building all day so that he would bolt out the door and run most of the way to the Larsson farm after supper.

"You don't know where they will send you, Johan?" Olof asked. He was sitting in the parlor with the young couple the evening before Johan's leave ended. Olof either was oblivious to Johan and Maria's wish to be alone, or he did not care.

"No.," Johan replied, "but we should get our orders any day."

"Yes, I suppose."

"Who would you prefer to fight, Olof?" Johan asked.

News on both fronts, Finland and Norway, had reached the countryside. The topic occupied Lars and Olof's conversations most evenings after dinner when they sat in the parlor, smoking their pipes. Both men considered themselves experts on the subject.

"That is an interesting question you pose, Johan. The Russians are a battled hardened army. But I do have a brother in Norway…" Olof paused to puff on his pipe for effect while Johan patiently waited for him to continue. "For your sake, I would hope it is the west, against the Danes and Norwegians."

"Grandpa, don't you have somewhere else you would rather be?" Maria asked.

"What? No, there is nowhere else I would rather be than visiting with Johan." Olof said with a wink to Johan.

"Papa!" Kajsa yelled from the kitchen. "Get in here, now!"

"Eh?" Olof grunted.

Kajsa came to the parlor door and stood glaring at her father with fists on her hips.

"Ahh. I think your mother wants me to leave you two love birds alone." Olof said, causing Maria to blush fiercely. "So long, and god be with you, Johan." He said, holding out his hand to Johan.

Johan stood and shook his hand. "Thank you, sir."

"You be sure to come back, Johan," Olof whispered in his ear before walking out of the room.

The rest of the evening was a blur to Johan, and yet one that he will never forget. They cuddled and kissed, occasionally separating whenever her mother started making loud noises in the kitchen. It was her way of dampening the young couple's ardor when things seemed to be getting out of hand.

The next morning, Johan was back at the Larssons to say goodbye to Maria before going back to Umeå. When Maria walked Johan out the front door, they were surprised to see Lars waiting for him with a buggy.

"I will take you to Umeå, Johan," Lars said.

"Ahh, okay." Johan stammered.

He said goodbye to Maria, her brothers Ollie and Petter, sisters Anna and Magda, mother Kajsa and Grandfather Olof.

"So long, Ahh," Anna said, "keep your powder dry!"

Kajsa frowned and looked at Anna, wondering where she had picked up that saying.

It was clear that Maria wanted to go along with them, but there was barely enough room for her father and Johan as it was. But she did follow them out to the main road and stood watching them until they disappeared from view. Even then, she stood there. Olof started to walk out to her, but Kajsa put a hand on his arm, stopping him. She smiled at the glistening in his eyes.

The ride was silent, to the point of being uncomfortable until they arrived at the barracks and Johan alit from the buggy.

"You take care of yourself, son," Lars said after clearing his throat. "We will be waiting for you."

Before Johan could respond, Lars snapped the reins, and Sofia trotted towards home.

8

O n a sunny summer's day, a doe ran through the Finnish forest, leaping gracefully over deadfall trees and veering around obstacles in her path. The fear was apparent in her bulging eyes and blowing nostrils as she ran for her life, pursued by relentless predators. The predators were four brothers, Swedish soldiers who were foraging for food when they came across the deer grazing in a small meadow. The brothers dropped everything and charged after the doe, whooping and hollering with glee as they ran.

They are the Tröger brothers, Matthias, Karl, Jakob, and Nils, soldiers in the Hälsinge regiment. They are also "wild." Well, not wild per se, just a little simple-minded, possessive of high pain tolerances, boundless energy, and utterly fearless.

Once, before they were soldiers, the Tröger brothers were chopping firewood on their farm when Matthias accidentally chopped Karl's left-hand index finger off at the second knuckle. Karl's three brothers found this hilarious and then completely lost it when Karl picked up his severed finger and tried to stick it back on. Seeing their reaction, Karl jammed the severed finger in one nostril and then began dancing a jig. Their mother looked out the front door of their modest cabin to see the cause of all the commotion. When she saw Karl dancing and waving his injured hand, she strode across the farmyard, shaking her head and muttering, "God have mercy on poor idiots."

In the same forest, Johan and Tobias were also out foraging when they heard the brother's shouts. From three hundred yards away, they spotted the deer running towards them. Tobias, having grown up with nomadic reindeer herders, knew what to do. After quickly giving directions to Johan, they moved behind a rock ridge. There was a well-used animal trail that went through a gap in the ridge, and that is where they laid in wait. Johan hid behind a tree watching for Tobias's signal.

When Tobias nodded, Johan leaped out from behind the tree, waving his arms and yelling. The yells turned into a yelp when Johan saw how close the deer was to him. The deer skidded to a stop, snorting and eyes bulging. Before it could turn and run, Tobias slammed into it, wrapping his left arm around its neck just below the jaw and slicing his knife deeply across her throat with his right hand. He hung on with his legs wrapped around the deer's body and his head pressed against her head. One bulging eye stared at Tobias as he whispered into her ear. The deer stood on shaky legs, blood flowing from the gaping wound before slowly collapsing. Johan stood frozen in place, watching this happen.

The Tröger boys arrived on the scene in a clamor. Two bent over with hands-on knees, one leaning against a tree, and the other had fallen to the ground; all were gasping for breath.

"Holy shit," Karl Tröger cried when he recovered enough to speak. "That was the darndest thing I have ever seen!"

"Yeah, thanks for stopping our deer!" Matthias added.

"No friends, it is I who should be thanking you for chasing my deer to me!" Tobias said, standing and facing them, bloody knife still held in one hand.

They stood staring at each other, sizing each other up. The Tröger brothers, already impressed with this man, were further impressed by his bravery.

"You are right, comrade!" Nils said, stepping forward and extending his hand. "We will share the deer! I am Nils Tröger, and these are my idiot brothers, Mathias, Karl, and Jakob."

Nils was the oldest and leader of the clan. Mathias was next in age but was considered the smartest of the group, not a significant achievement by any means. Karl, the third born, was the comic which, in and of itself, was a considerable achievement amongst these comical men. Jakob, the youngest brother, was also the strongest. Jakob would usually lift the axle while one of his brothers changed a wheel on a cart or the one who would carry the heaviest logs.

"I am Tobias Öhn or Toby, and this is my friend, Johan Sparrman," Tobias said. He held up his bloody hand in the way of apology for not shaking Nils's hand.

"Ach!" Nils cried. He grabbed Tobias's hand and shook it vigorously, deer blood squeezing out from between their fingers in droplets. His brothers moved forward, shaking hands as Nils stood licking the blood from his fingers. Karl and Jakob turned and shook each other's hands, which Matthias and Nils found hilarious. Tobias looked dubiously at Johan as if to say, 'these men are lunatics.'

Johan and the Trögers watched with admiration the skill with which Tobias quickly dressed the animal. Tobias asked Johan to start a small fire as he removed the tenderloins. He cut the deer in half below the lowest ribs and asked, "do you want the rear or front?"

"What's the difference?" Nils asked.

"There's more meat on the rear, but the front has the ribs, and the organs will go with it."

The brothers looked at each other, puzzled, before Nils said, "we will take the rear." He was not fond of eating organs. The two deer halves would amount to one meal for each of their respective regiments, both halves dressing out at about 30 pounds apiece. After lighting the fire, Tobias hung the tenderloins over the fire on green saplings. Johan rooted around in his forage bag, coming up with several wild onions, which he placed by the fire.

While the meat cooked, Johan and Tobias cut a thick green sapling and trimmed the branches off. They then tied the deer's front legs together and slid the sapling through so that they could carry the load on their shoulders. The Trögers watched this and followed their example.

"Now, my friends, let's eat!" Tobias announced. He cut the two tenderloins in three pieces each, sliced the onions, and told everyone to help themselves. The Trögers were noisy eaters. Johan and Tobias glanced sidelong at each other as their new friends smacked their lips, suck the juices off their filthy fingers, belched, and groaned as they savored the meal. They were also fast eaters. They had finished their portions before Tobias and Johan were halfway through theirs. It was somewhat awkward as the Tröger boys watched hungrily while Johan and Tobias leisurely ate.

Having finished his meal, Johan stood and made sure the fire was out before saying goodbye to his new friends.

"Adjö, my friends!" He said, shaking their hands.

"Adjö!" Came the replies.

Johan and Tobias stood watching the Trögers walk away. The brothers were jostling each other as they walked, all talking at once. Karl punched Jakob on the shoulder harder than Jakob felt was appropriate and returned the favor, running ahead to avoid retaliation. Soon, all four Trögers were running, hooting, and hollering as they went. Nils and Mathias carried the deer and tried their best to keep up with the other two, but the deer started to sway, and they had to slow their pace.

Johan and Tobias grinned, shaking their heads as they watched.

"What did you say to the deer?" Johan asked, suddenly remembering.

"What?"

"When you killed the deer," Johan said. "You were whispering in its ear."

"Oh, that. I was thanking the doe for the meat and the strength it would give us." Tobias replied.

"That is good," Johan said, nodding.

In Johan's first weeks with the army, their interactions were of two men hesitantly looking at each other in passing, each with suspicious looks on their faces. Finally, Johan decided to confront Tobias and clear the air.

"Toby, I would like to talk to you," Johan said. He had found Tobias one evening smoking his pipe alone by a fire after dinner.

"Okay."

"I have a confession to make to you."

"I am not a priest, Johan," Tobias said.

"No, you're certainly not!"

"Hah!" Tobias guffawed. "Okay, Johan. Tell me what's on your mind."

"Last summer, while you were away, Lars, Ollie, and I were told someone was in your cottage, so we went to look."

"Yeah, Lars told me. Thank you, that lynx could have done some real damage if you hadn't let him out."

"Well, after we let it out, Lars and Ollie left, and I stayed to clean up the mess." Johan hesitated, and Tobias waited patiently, enjoying his pipe.

"I went to the barn to look for a cloth to clean up the cat piss with and found it locked."

Tobias raised an eyebrow and scrutinized Johan, putting him ill at ease.

"Aah, I climbed the ladder and peeked through that vent door in the back."

"What did you see?" Tobias asked casually.

"Costumes and drums."

"Yeah?"

"That's not all." Johan continued. He took a deep breath and said, "I was walking by a while later and heard some chanting."

"I thought that was you," Tobias said. He was seemingly preoccupied with cleaning the bowl of his pipe. He held up his hand when Johan was about to speak.

"I have felt my son's presence for many years after he died. I asked a Sámi shaman to come and help my son complete his journey. I did not want him to be alone, caught between the living and dead."

Johan stared at Tobias and tried to determine if he was making the story up or not.

"I saw an eyeball peeking through a knothole in one of the barn boards but couldn't leave to investigate. That was you?"

"Yeah. Did it work?" Johan asked.

"I hope so." Tobias mused, "I don't feel his presence anymore, so hopefully, his spirit is at peace."

Since that talk, Johan and Tobias had become close friends. Tobias took Johan under his wing and helped him through his training.

9

September 14, 4:30 A.M.

In the predawn gloom, Johan and Tobias were drinking coffee by the light of a cooking fire. Sleep had not come easy, and the smell of percolating coffee enticed the two soldiers from their tent. The evening before, they heard gunfire in the north where the Swedish General, von Döbeln's unit was positioned. The fighting had been intense between the Swedes and the Russians from the amount of gun and cannon fire. They could only hope von Döbeln was victorious. A loss would compromise the Swedish army's position from that direction.

Tobias, at fifty, is one of the oldest soldiers in the Västerbotten regiment. Still, you wouldn't know it by the way he carries himself. He has a slight build, five foot seven with corded muscles. Looking at Tobias, men would instinctively know not to mess with him, rightly realizing that no matter how hard you hit him, you would still lose. Johan, on the other hand, is one of the youngest soldiers in the regiment.

They are recent arrivals in Finland, part of the reinforcements that landed at the port village of Vaasa the previous week. Unlike the Trögers, Johan and Tobias have not yet experienced battle. The summer offensive had not gone well for the Swedish army. They had retreated northward and were pursued relentlessly by the Russians, who are battle-tested and have superior numbers. The war with Russia began in mid-February when the Russian army crossed the Finnish border with a considerable force. Finland, under Swedish rule, was caught unprepared for war. With the arrival of reinforcements, the Swedish army halted their retreat. They braced for battle in what many suspected may be their last stand.

Today, Johan and Tobias know that, for the first time, they will face enemies on the battlefield. The Russian army was advancing in force toward their position from the west. Positioned between the Savolax and the Västmanland regiments were the Västerbottens. Other units with them were the Upplands and Hälsinge regiments, the Österbottens battalion, and the Finnish Pohjanmaa regiment. In all 5,500 Swedish and Finnish men. Across a meadow and a small stream, 6,000 Russian jaegers, hussars, cossacks, musketeers, artillery brigades, and Polish lancers would gather for the coming fight.

Johan and Tobias were among friends and relatives in their regiment. Among those were Jon Emanuelsson, Gunnar Johansson, and Petter Pehrsson. Tobias and Jon were cousins, their fathers being the brothers Pehr and Emanuel Raderman, respectively. Johan was thankful to be among friends in this violent place.

Their new friends, Matthias, Karl, Jakob, and Nils Tröger of the Hälsinge regiment, have been in Finland since the beginning of hostilities with Russia and had survived many skirmishes and battles, mostly unscathed. The exception being Karl Tröger, who took a musket stock to the forehead during hand-to-hand combat when they had stumbled upon a group of Russian soldiers in a Finnish barn. He was saved from further injury when Jakob bayoneted the Russian as he prepared to impale Karl with his bayonet. Since then, Karl had a dent in his forehead and suffered from debilitating headaches; headaches intensified by bright sunlight. Today would not be a good day for Karl as it promised to be bright and clear. The pleasant morning with birds singing in the trees behind Johan and Tobias belied the chaos that is to come.

Johan took his pipe out and was packing tobacco into the bowl when he heard gunfire to the west. That would be the fifteen-year-old Swedish artillery officer Count Wilhelm von Schwerin's rear guard engaging the Russians. Lighting his pipe, Johan puffed, coughed, and exhaled the sweet-smelling smoke. He was new to smoking, but he found it relaxing, and he liked the way it made Tobias look wise when he smoked his pipe. He hoped it had the same effect for him. But it still made his head swim now and then.

"Well, there it is, Toby," He said.

"Yeah, you will not die this day, comrade."

"Nor will you, my friend."

Soldiers began emerging from tents, preparing for the order to reinforce the rear guard should it come. They knew the commanders would send some units forward and hold others back in reserve. Jon, Gunnar, and Petter approached them, buttoning their coats. They nodded to Johan and Tobias and then went about checking their muskets.

Artillery fire erupted in the distance. Officers were barking orders on their left and their right. In the false dawn light, they could make out the shapes of soldiers marching across the meadow in double time. The sounds of shouted orders, feet and hooves pounding the ground, canteens rattling, and swords slapping thighs filled the air. Johan rightly surmised that they were soldiers of the Savo battalion. He could not see the soldiers far to his right, but he guessed they must be Hälsingers. If it is them, he wished the Trögers luck.

* * *

5:00 A.M.
Lillträsket Bridge

Half of three battalions under Count von Schwerin's command made up the Swedish rearguard a mile away at the Lillträsket bridge. Among these soldiers were Karl and Jakob Tröger of the Hälsinge regiment. The Count had positioned his men on the east side of the bridge. The Trögers had heard of von Schwerin's bravery at the battle of Ömossa eight days earlier and held great respect for the young man.

The Count placed two six-pound cannons with a direct line of fire at the bridge deck. Karl and Jakob stood behind log breastworks to the left of the batteries supporting the artillery. As with all battles they participated in, a corporal stood close to the Trögers. The move was necessary due to the Tröger boy's overzealousness during the fighting. This time, Corporal Anders Sjöberg knelt behind them, resting a hand on the shoulder of each. As the first hints of twilight lightened the sky with reddish-orange hues, the Russians arrived.

"Hold!" Corporal Sjöberg called, repeating von Schwerin's order down the line and squeezing the Tröger's shoulders for emphasis. He had felt them tense when the Russians came in view. The order to fire came when the Russian artillery appeared.

"Aim for the artillery crews, boys!" Corporal Sjöberg yelled, slapping the Trögers on their shoulders. With whoops of glee, Karl and Jakob opened fire and reloaded in what the corporal would guess was record time as he backed away from them. It was safer to give them some room. He had to grin at the unbridled joy in their laughter as they fired a deadly barrage of musket fire at the Russians.

The Count held his artillery fire until the bridge was full of advancing Russians. When he gave the order to fire, grapeshot tore through the Russians with devastating effect. The blasts are comparable to giant shotguns at close range. Anyone left standing would then face a hail of musket balls from the musketeers. With each new wave of attackers running onto the bridge, the Swedish gun crews would open fire with another deadly round.

Karl and Jakob were laughing hysterically, almost to the point of sensory overload. Clouds of acrid gun smoke floated over the battlefield, musket and cannon blasts, shouted orders, and screams of the injured or dying filled the air. The Russian artillery and musket fire also took a toll on the Swedish defenders. Many Swedish officers were either killed or wounded due mainly to their exposed positions while directing the battle. During a lull after another devastating round of grapeshot, Jakob stood, turned, dropped his pants, and bent over, exposing his bare buttocks to the enemy. He wiggled side to side as Karl fell over laughing hysterically.

Across the river, the Russian Major General, Kulnev, tapped his best marksman, Gösta Mårtensson, on the shoulder. Gösta nodded and aimed at the offending rear end. He already gauged the distance and windage from all the shots he has taken during the battle. Most were kill-shots on Swedish officers, so he knew he had to aim above and to the left of his target. Gösta was Swedish by birth, but circumstances of his own making had forced him to flee the country at a young age. His face had the texture of weathered oak with an oft broken nose and a poorly healed knife slash running from his jawbone, across one eye, and ending above the brow. At forty-four years old, he had the powerful physique gained from a lifetime of manual labor.

Jakob felt the punch to his left cheek that knocked him forward and facedown into the dirt. Funny, he thought, a bee sting never knocked him over before. Karl immediately stopped laughing and went to his brother's aid. Checking the wound, he determined it was not life-threatening, then his anger took hold. He leaped up and began crawling over the log breastworks before corporal Sjöberg and another soldier dragged him back to safety.

"Stay!" The corporal yelled into Karl's face before turning to look at Jakob. Then, the corporal's head exploded, a mist of blood and gore splattering Karl. Karl let out a primal scream and leaped onto the breastworks, firing his musket before a musket ball hit him with enough force to throw him back behind the breastworks. Across the river, Gösta grinned and said, "three arses in a row, sir," which greatly amused the Russian commander.

Jakob lay on his stomach behind the breastworks, investigating the new hole in his butt with a dirty index finger, when Karl landed heavily beside him. They lay face to face, Karl's eyes staring back at him, eyes that slowly lost their light, and Jakob stared back, too stunned to react or to say anything.

After several hours of intense fighting, the Swedish musketeers were running low on ammunition. Without their support, the artillery units had to retreat. Jakob stumbled along in a daze, stopping now and then to tilt his head back to wail skyward. His comrades, sensitive to his sorrow, prodded him along whenever he stopped walking. As wild as he and his brothers acted at times, they were well-liked by their fellow soldiers.

Several musketeers were pressed into service, moving the cannons. They slid poles through the cannons and lifted/pushed as the cannon crews rolled the wheels. Every hundred yards or so, von Schwerin halted the retreat and ordered the cannon crews to fire into the pursuing Russians before continuing the retreat.

It was at one of these stops when a musket ball hit von Schwerin in the abdomen. With their commander down, the Swedes were soon in disarray, and the Russians quickly surrounded them. The Count fought through his pain and dragged himself to his feet, rallying his men for a charge through the Russians blocking their route. The Swedes responded to their commander's courage and broke through, continuing their retreat. Jakob was so impressed by von Schwerin's courage that he placed himself in harm's way to protect his commander from enemy fire. When von Schwerin stumbled and fell, Jakob picked him up and carried him, limping as he marched forward. Even with his injury, Jakob's strength didn't waiver as he carried the slight fifteen-year-old with ease. He had no time to grieve his brother's death or worry about his wound now that his commander needed him.

The retreating soldiers had to leave their dead where they lay, the attacking Russians ruthless in their advance. The Swedes continued their retreat, stopping every hundred yards and firing their cannons at the Russians. That is until they ran out of ammunition, and then they were in full retreat. Their situation was looking dire until reinforcements arrived and covered their retreat. Some of the soldiers ran to take von Schwerin from Jakob. They quickly backed away when he threatened to rip their throats out with his bare hands if they touched his commander. Jakob carried his commander another twenty yards before collapsing from exhaustion, his unconscious form carried by the same soldiers he had threatened.

10

7:30 a.m.
The Battle of Oravais

As dawn broke, numerous mounted officers and aides rode hard toward the rear guard. The Västerbottens remained at the ready for the inevitable frontal assault; some wolfed down what little breakfast was available. They did not know when their next meal may be. Even so, some soldiers vomited in nearby bushes. It often happened, the vomiting, before every battle. The soldiers learned to watch for it lest they slip on the bile.

When the sun rose above the tree line, Johan and his comrades were pressed into service, fortifying their positions. Some took apart local barns and used the logs to build bulwarks, while others chopped trees for the same purpose. At about 10:00 a.m., Johan noticed Russian battalions arriving on the other side of the meadow. They had begun to erect fortifications of their own near the tree line. He was alarmed when several artillery units were wheeled cannons into position. To Johan, all the Russian batteries looked as if they were pointed directly at him. The dark holes of the cannon barrels sent a shiver up his spine.

At 11:00 a.m., von Schwerin's rearguard arrived in disarray, followed closely by the pursuing Russians and more artillery. Once von Schwerin's men cleared the meadow, Swedish artillery opened fire on the advancing Russians. The Russians responded with their barrage of cannon fire. For an hour, the deafening artillery battle shook the earth and laid waste to anything in its path. Johan and Tobias crouched behind bulwarks with their heads down, and their arms covered their ears. They jumped with every cannonade. Tobias wasn't sure, but he thought he had heard Johan whimpering. When the bombardment finally died down, Russian infantry advanced on the Swedish positions to the right of the Västerbottens.

Johan and Tobias slowly rose from their positions and peered over the breastworks.

"Are you okay, Johan?" Tobias asked.

"Yeah, y-y-you?"

"I am okay."

Tobias looked at Johan with concern; his hands shook slightly, and his eyes were wet. Before Tobias could reassure Johan, the order came down the line to advance. Tobias reached over and clasped Johan's shoulder. He smiled at him, and then they climbed over the logs and marched forward with the rest of the Västerbottens to meet the Russians. Johan was surprised at the display before him. He gaped in awe at thousands of Russian soldiers advancing from the opposite treeline, each company with its colorful banners. Drummers beat their drums, mounted officers with swords held high barked orders as their horses pranced forward. The Swedish army, after a failed summer offensive, could not match such pageantry.

Artillery fire from both sides deafened the advancing soldiers. Johan would later say that he could feel the sound travel through his chest as he marched forward. Clouds of acrid gun smoke blanketed the battlefield like a heavy fog as the two armies advance on each other. It seems to Johan that the musket balls flying by his head sounded like a hundred wasps.

To their right, Russian units appear to have bogged down in the marshy ground near the creek. The Västerbottens and units of the Savolax infantry forded the stream and charged forward against far superior numbers. They encountered devastating fire from Russian guns.

Soldiers beside Johan fell at an alarming rate, but no call to retreat was bugled. So, he kept moving forward, now in full bayonet charge with his regiment's remaining soldiers. He dearly wanted to look behind to see if his friends are okay, or maybe for reassurance, but he dared not. Johan could hear his comrade's battle cries as he charged at a Russian soldier. He drove his bayonet into him, propelling the man backward until he fell. Johan put a foot on the soldier's chest and pulled his bayonet free before charging toward another Russian. The savagery of the Västerbotten's charge was so fierce, the Russians, even with superior numbers, retreated into the woods. Before the Västerbottens could follow them, Russian units, who had finally freed themselves from the soggy ground, opened fire on the Västerbottens from their right flank. Johan and his comrades were forced into a complete and disorderly retreat back towards the creek. Those who had survived the bloody onslaught crawled over the log bulwarks while Russian musket balls slammed into logs and Swedish soldiers.

Johan leaned against the bulwarks and breathed heavily as his heart gradually slowed. The ringing in his ears didn't block out the screaming of the injured. He jumped each time he felt the impact of musket balls hitting the other side of the logs at his back. The violent shaking started without warning. Johan cannot remember ever experiencing his body shaking this hard, not even when he fell through the ice on a small lake as a child. He nearly froze to death before his father carried him to safety. Just when Johan began to worry that the shaking would never stop, it gradually slowed. Johan was surprised to feel tears fall from his nose; he didn't remember crying. A strange calmness suddenly came over him. Resolve replaced the near-crippling fear he had felt in battle. Resolve to fight his enemies and avenge his fallen comrades.

Johan wiped his eyes and looked to his right. He saw general Adlercreutz and two adjutants staring at him from two hundred yards away. The general nodded at him before turning and conferring with his men. *How long had they watched me?*

1:00 p.m.

Johan's ears rang as he looked to his right and left. He had hoped to see Tobias amid the chaos. Medics and soldiers were doing what they could for the injured and dying. A few dazed soldiers staggered along the line, fully exposed to enemy fire until fellow soldiers pulled them down to safety.

Johan got to his feet and walked at a crouch behind the bulwarks to the south. He knew his regiment should be in that direction since the recent battle has moved him in a northerly direction. As he walked, he saw the toll the fight has taken. Among the dying are the severely injured and others who appear to be in shock. To his relief, the majority of the soldiers seemed to be calm and resolute.

"Do you know where the Västerbotten regiment is?" He asked one soldier.

"No, I hear what's left of your regiment are scattered." The soldier replies, "why did you counter-attack against so many?"

"No one told us not to." Johan shrugged.

The man studied him for a few seconds and then nodded.

"Who are you with?" Johan asked.

"Upplands regiment."

"Ah, adjö, comrade," Johan said as he continued walking down the line.

"Keep your head down, Västerbotten."

A little further on, a corporal ordered Johan to assist with a wounded soldier. A crude field hospital in an old barn sat a hundred yards behind the front lines.

"Grab an arm." The corporal ordered. The man screamed when Johan and two others lifted him off the ground. His left forearm appears mangled below the elbow. Johan could see a bone sticking out of the skin.

"What happened?" He asked.

"Cannon."

No other explanation appeared to be forth-coming, so Johan concentrated on making the trip to the barn as smooth as possible for the injured man. The man screamed again, but Johan suspected the pile of amputated limbs laying twenty feet to the side of the barn was the cause of the man's scream. Johan struggled to suppress his rising bile.

I do not want to be here!

They placed the man on a bloodstained table, still slippery from the last patient. The heat was oppressive in the barn. He could see a roaring fire in a brazier near the rear wall.

Why would they have such a fire on a warm day?

"You!" The medic commanded Johan as he pulled a leather strap tightly around the man's upper arm. "Hold him down; do not let him move!"

The man's screams reached a new volume when the medic turned and produced a large knife. He swiftly cut through the meat on his upper arm down to the bone. Sweat flew from the medic's forehead whenever he shook his head to keep it out of his eyes. Johan had to use all his strength to hold the man still. The medic set the knife down and picked up a saw. Mercifully, the man passed out when the sawing started. Johan breathed deeply and tried not to vomit. His resolve tested when a man handed the medic a sizeable flat blade that glowed red from the brazier. The stench of burning flesh filled the air as the doctor cauterized the wound. The man came to with a piercing scream before he passed out once again. Johan raced to the door and barely made it outside before he vomited what little he had in his stomach.

As he staggered back toward the bulwarks, Johan hoped he never sees that barn again. He would rather face the enemy than witness another amputation. He walked back to the Upplands soldier and sat down beside him.

"Got anything to eat?"

"Some jerky." The man said. He produced a strip of dried meat from his shirt pocket and held it out to Johan.

The sight of the dried meat made Johan gag. It reminded him of some of the amputated limbs he had seen lying by the barn.

"It's clean!" The man said. He appeared insulted by Johan's reaction.

"Yeah, sorry, I was at the medic's barn."

"Ah." The man nodded, understanding. "I am Bo Svärd."

"Johan Sparrman"

"Try some water and then eat the jerky without looking at it. It may be a while before you have a chance to eat again."

Johan nodded and followed Bo's advice. He managed to eat half the jerky before he handed the rest back to Bo.

"Thank you, comrade," Johan said, then dug in his tunic for his pipe and tobacco. He was on the verge of tears when he found his pipe broken in two.

"Stay close, my friend, until you find your regiment," Bo said. He clapped Johan on the shoulder and handed his pipe to Johan.

* * *

2:00 p.m.

The call had come down the line for the Upplands Regiment to prepare to attack.

"I guess you will fight beside the Upplanders today, my friend!"

"It will be an honor, Bo."

The order to advance came, drummers and fifers repeated the order, standard-bearers led the way, and Johan climbed over the bulwarks for the second time that day. They charged toward the center of the Russian forces catching them by surprise. Soon, Johan could hear more regiments joining the charge. The ground shook beneath his feet as he ran alongside Bo. Johan thought he heard the Tröger's gleeful laughter amongst the cacophony of the attack. Have the Hälsingers joined the charge? Somehow, Johan felt more confident knowing his wild friends were nearby.

The Russians were retreating, pausing now and then to engage the Swedes before being pushed back once again. Battle cries could be heard all down the Swedish line as they rejoiced with each victorious skirmish. Johan felt the exhilaration of a successful battle for the first time.

"That'll teach the bastards!" Bo yelled.

The charge continued as all but two of the Swedish regiments chased the Russian army back towards the Lillträsket bridge, where it had all begun. Johan saw several Swedish soldiers in front of him turn an abandoned Russian canon around and fire it at the fleeing Russians.

"We will chase the heathen bastards back to Russia!" One sergeant bellowed to great cheers.

By 5:00 p.m., they had driven the Russians across the Lillträsket bridge. They were about to follow when an officer gave the order to halt. Confused, Johan strained to see across the river. When the dust and smoke cleared, he was shocked to see hundreds, if not thousands, of Russian reinforcements marching from the south to join the battle.

"Oh, shit!" Bo said.

Being low on ammunition and faced with new Russian units, it was the Swede's turn to retreat.

The retreat was not orderly as the battle raged, and some Swedish units became trapped behind Russian lines. As darkness fell and without ammunition, the trapped Swedes continued the fight in the forest well into the night with only their bayonets. Johan and Bo among them.

"This way, Johan," Bo whispered.

"I can barely see you, Bo."

"Just don't bayonet me."

"Shh! Someone's coming!"

They crouched beside each other in the near blackness of the night and waited as the soft footfalls came closer.

"Ivan?" Bo whispered.

"Nyet."

Bo drove his bayonet into the Russian catching him high in the thigh.

"Stab him!" Bo hissed as the Russian gasped. Johan drove his bayonet forward, aiming below where he thought he had heard the gasp. Johan felt the blade slide into the body, deflected off a rib, and he knew he had just killed a man. In the total darkness, his senses heightened so much so that he could feel the man's quivering muscles and slowing heartbeat through his musket as the man died.

"Shit!" Johan cursed. "That was..."

"Let's go."

Bo had removed the dead man's baldric, the strap that held his sword, and they each held onto an end so they wouldn't get separated. They could hear the occasional scream and the scuffling and grunting of several struggles nearby as they made their way through the forest. Johan and Bo could not help their comrades in the darkness. For all he knew, some of the fights may be among comrades. In the black night, it was either kill or be killed. Then the rain started.

Off to Johan's left, he thought he heard laughter. Tröger laughter. Suddenly, Johan was pulled sideways by the baldric strap. He could hear grunting, and the belt jerked in his hand.

"What's happening, Bo?"

"Hit him!"

"Where? Is he on top of you?"

More struggling and a choking noise were all he heard. Since Bo did not respond, Johan guessed that the attacker was strangling his friend. With surging adrenaline, Johan kicked hard at the outline of a head. He felt the satisfying impact and sharp pain as the toe of his shoe connected with the man's head. When the dark shape slump over, Johan reached down and said, "here, take my hand, Bo." He felt his hand grabbed and then suddenly pulled with enough force that Johan fell over the figure on the ground. The man started punching Johan wherever he could. After the initial shock, Johan hit back.

They rolled over and over, each trying to gain the upper hand. Johan managed to get on top and press his foreman across the man's neck while holding one hand down by the wrist. He bent his head low to avoid the punches from the other hand. He put all his weight down on the man's throat. The man reached up and grabbed a handful of Johan's hair and pulled hard. Johan kept the pressure on the throat, feeling the man's struggles fade. Finally, the man stopped moving, but he kept pressing down on his neck until he was sure the man was dead.

"Bo?" He whispered as he crawled towards his friend. "I'm sorry, I thought you were a Russian."

"Hmph."

"Are you okay?"

"What the fek did you hit me with?" Bo cursed.

"The toe of my shoe." Johan said, "if it makes you feel any better, I think I broke my big toe."

"No, doesn't help a damn bit."

"Shh." Johan hissed.

They remained quiet as several pairs of feet marched past, maybe twenty soldiers. They had no way of knowing if they were friend or foe. They found the most challenging part of remaining undetected was to hold still while clouds of mosquitoes swarmed over them. Most annoying were the ones that got into their noses and ears. As a child, Johan worried that mosquitoes biting his eyelids would penetrate his eyeballs, and he would go blind. He knew it wasn't possible, yet crouched in this terrifying situation, the fear returned. He fought the urge to wipe the mosquitos from his face.

"Let's go," Johan whispered when the footfalls faded away. He wiped a hand across his face, and it came away slick with blood.

Bo stood and swayed. "A minute." He said, steadying himself with a hand on Johan's shoulder.

"Here, let me help." Johan took Bo's arm and draped it over his shoulder, "Why didn't you answer me?"

"Because the bastard was squeezing my throat with one hand."

They walked for an hour; several times, they heard screams, some frighteningly close, grunts, gurgles, and hushed whispers. The rain dampened the leaves and grass and muffled footfalls. Their nerves frazzled, they finally came to the meadow, where they had begun their charge. Looking to his left,

Johan could smell the saltwater of Bothnia, so they waded across the creek and turned right. Up ahead, he could hear men cursing in Swedish.

"Hey, we are soldiers of the Västerbottens and Upplands regiments!" Johan called.

"Välkommen, comrades." A voice replied without enthusiasm.

Among the relative safety of fellow soldiers, exhaustion suddenly hit Johan with full force. He sat heavily, Bo almost falling over him.

"What's wrong, Johan?" Bo asked, settling down beside him.

"I jjjust nnneed a rrrest." Johan stuttered, then the violent shivering returned in full force. Not knowing what to do, Bo put his arms around Johan and tried to warm him. He cursed when a soldier tripped over them.

"Get off the fekking road, idiots!" The man cursed.

"Ttttröger?"

"What?"

"Ttröger?" Johan grit his teeth to still the shivering.

"I am Matthias Tröger; who are you?"

"Johan," Johan breathed deeply, "Johan Sparrman."

"Johan!" Matthias shouted. He reached down and grasped Johan's shoulder. "And Toby?"

"No, I haven't seen Toby since we charged the Russians," Johan said, his shivering had subsided somewhat. "I thought I heard you and your brother's laughter during the charge."

"Yeah, that was us, me and Nils."

"What about Jakob and Karl?" Johan asked.

"Karl died at the bridge, and Jakob took a musket ball to the arse."

"Oh, no, Matthias, I am sorry," Johan said. "And Nils?"

"We got separated in the forest."

"Ah." Remembering these two have not met, Johan said, "this is Bo Svärd, he who you tripped over."

61

"Hi Bo, sorry about that; I can't see a damn thing out here."

"It is nothing, Matthias," Bo said, "it is good to meet a friend of Johan's."

"We better go before we get left behind!" Matthias said.

They continued through the night, wet, exhausted, and hungry.

11

Tobias was also in the forest, at one point, within five feet of Johan and Bo. Not knowing if they were friend or foe, Tobias moved in a different direction. He was alone. The group of Västerbottens he was with separated during the retreat. Tobias had given up looking for Johan. The last he saw of Johan; he was charging into the Russians. Tobias had lost hope of seeing his friend again.

He heard a noise and turned in that direction when a man slammed into him. They both fell to the ground, the attacker driving a knife into the ground beside Tobias, narrowly missing his head. He grabbed the man's wrist and rolled him over on his back. Tobias managed to drive his knee into the inside of the man's thigh. He cursed in Swedish.

"Who are you?" Tobias demanded.

"Västerbottens."

"Who is your sergeant?"

"Andersson. Sergeant Andersson."

"That is my sergeant too! I am Tobias Öhn."

"Toby? Its Petter, Petter Pehrsson!"

They let go of each other's wrists and grasped each other's shoulders.

"Which way?" Tobias asked.

"Follow me."

They could hear screams and struggles all around them as they crept through the forest. Tobias felt the musket stock's impact slam into his head; stars burst in his vision, and his ears rang before he lost consciousness and fell forward.

Sometime later, Tobias opened his eyes. Pain shot through his head, and it took a few minutes for him to remember where he was. He put a hand to the back of his head and felt the crusted blood.

"Petter?" He whispered.

Nothing. Tobias cautiously felt in all directions until his hand touched clothing. It was Petter, bayonetted in the back. Tobias felt for a tree and used it to pull himself up. It took a few minutes for the dizziness to pass, and then he vomited. His head pounded relentlessly.

I have to get out of here!

He pushed off from the tree and walked forward. He hoped it was in the right direction. Suddenly, a small flame erupted in the area directly in front of him as someone lit a torch. Tobias froze and strained his ears, trying to identify the men in front of them. They were ten feet away under the canopy of a large spruce tree. One of the men looked his way and then back towards his comrades. Tobias realized the man's night vision must have dulled by looking into the flames. They were Russians. Tobias slowly moved to his left and knelt behind a tree. Another fire flared to his right.

I'm in the middle of their camp!

Someone could discover him at any minute; soldiers roamed about and urinated beside trees like the one in front of him.

Maybe I should shoot into one of the groups and run as fast as possible through the camp and into the forest.

No, if I don't get shot, I will probably run into a tree with my compromised night vision.

He vowed not to be taken without a fight, not knowing how these men treat prisoners. Suddenly, Tobias noticed a glow in the distance. It was moving towards him. At about a hundred yards away, Tobias was shocked to see a small boy beckoning with one hand to come to him.

Georg?

No, it can't be!

The boy, who now Tobias believed was Georg's spirit, had an aura around his little body. Georg turned and looked over his shoulder at Tobias and waved him on. Tobias glanced at the two groups of Russians visible in the glow of their fires. Georg beckoned for him to go between the two groups. As silently as he could, Tobias crept forward and followed Georg. He could see more fires up ahead and wondered what he was doing as he crept behind Georg right through the bulk of the Russian army!

Georg stopped, turned back towards Tobias, and made a lowering motion with his hand. Tobias knelt, and Georg continued the gesture until Tobias lay flat on the ground. A column of Russians emerged from behind a thick stand of spruce and marched by in single file within a foot of Tobias's head. He let out his breath and noticed Georg. He was sure it was his dead son now, who waved him forward once again.

After more stops and starts as they weaved through the forest and avoided Russian soldiers, Tobias finally emerged in the valley. Moonlight peaked through the clouds and reflected off the Bay of Bothnia and dimly illuminated the valley. Georg stood at the creek and waved him on. Taking a deep breath, Tobias left the cover of the forest and ran low towards Georg. When he reached the stream, Georg was now on the other bank.

"You have to go now, Georg," Tobias said.

The boy's glowing increased as he lowered his head and shook it.

"You have to go, Georg! You can't stay here." Tobias continued. "Do you remember your friend, Isaak? He is there; you can play with him." Isaak had been Georg's best friend. He had drowned the summer before Georg died.

"I will be there soon; we will be together again, but you have to go now."

Georg finally nodded and then turned and walked away with his head down, dimming until he disappeared completely. Tobias fell to his knees and sobbed as he had when he found Georg dead eighteen years previous.

It was not the first time Georg has appeared to him. Tobias recalled that he had appeared in the barn several years ago when Tobias leaned precariously over the barn's loft, trying to attach a rope to a beam. That time, Georg had startled him so much that Tobias jumped back onto the loft's deck. He wasn't sure, but Tobias thought that the ghost of his son had saved his life that day. He had felt Georg's presence several times afterward, but he never appeared again, until now. Those instances occurred before Tobias had enlisted the Sámi shaman to help Georg's spirit's ascension. Until now, Tobias had thought the ritual performed in his barn had worked.

"You there!" A soldier called. "Raise your hands and walk towards me!"

Tobias complied, relieved the soldier was Swedish.

"I am a Västerbotten soldier." He said as he waded across the creek toward the soldier.

"Keep your hands up until I can see you."

"Are you with the Hälsinge regiment?" Tobias asked, recognizing the uniform.

"Yeah."

"Then, you must know the wild Tröger brothers?"

"Yeah, I do." The soldier lowered his musket. "You can lower your hands, comrade."

Tobias did so and followed the soldier toward the Swedish bulwarks.

"Who were you talking to?" The man asked.

"Huh?" Tobias asked, momentarily puzzled. "Oh, I was thanking God to have made it through the fight."

"You were talking for a long time."

"Yeah, I may have promised not to do certain enjoyable things anymore."

"Ah, that is a shame." The soldier laughed. "I am Oscar Kristiansson."

"Tobias Öhn, Toby."

"The Västerbottens, what's left of them, are to the right, about a hundred yards down the line."

"Yeah, we had a rough go of it."

"We all did," Oscar said.

12

September 15

When dawn broke, Johan, Bo, and Matthias found themselves part of a disorderly column shuffling along a muddy road. Johan looked around but did not see anyone wearing a Västerbotten uniform. There were several soldiers of the Upplands and Hälsinge regiments, which made for an awkward situation. Bo joined a group from his unit, and Matthias continued walking. Johan stood wondering who to stay with, then came to a decision.

"Adjö, Bo, I want to go see if Nils made it back."

"Adjö, Johan, and good luck to you, my friend!"

Johan hurried along as fast as he could on his sore toe. The kick hadn't broken his toe, he determined, but it was tender. He caught up with Matthias and walked alongside him. As they walked, Johan related what happened in the forest. Matthias's story was much the same.

"After Nils and I got separated, I wandered through the forest, avoiding the Russians. Once, I came across a large group of them; they were setting up camp, lighting fires." Matthias hesitated and then said, "I think I saw a ghost."

"What?"

"A ghost." Matthias said, "it looked like a small boy."

"No!" Johan breathed, "what did you do?"

"I circled the encampment and made my way out of the forest. My body was tingling already, but the sight of that boy sent goose pimples up my scalp!"

"Nobody else saw this ghost?"

"No!" Matthias said a little too loudly, then whispered, "he seemed to be invisible to the Russians, walking right by them."

"Huh."

"Funny thing though, I think there was someone following him, the ghost, I mean."

"Was he -"

"Matthias!" Nils yelled. Matthias looked around for his brother, spotting him waving his arms a hundred feet ahead of them. "Nils!" Matthias shouted and then ran gleefully towards his brother. Johan could see them swinging each other about, their fellow soldiers grinning at them. "Johan!" Nils yelled and picked him up in a bear hug when he caught up to them. They walked three abreast, the two brothers talking a mile a minute. Johan thought about Matthias's story as they walked and then dismissed it. His imagination had run wild when he was in the pitch-black forest, and he suspected the same went for Matthias.

"Have you seen Jakob?" Matthias asked.

"No, I am told he is in a wagon at the head of the column."

After the initial excitement of meeting each other had passed, exhaustion once again settled over them. The soldiers trudged along and looked down at their feet as they tried to keep their eyes open. Johan's ears were ringing, and his head seemed to buzz, and his knees and big toe ached. He could not remember being so tired. The urge to just move off the road and curl up to sleep was almost overwhelming. If it wasn't for Matthias and Nils, he might have done just that. But they needed each other, so he reached deep down within himself and continued walking.

An hour later, General Adlercreutz called a halt at a large open field that looked relatively dry. Johan and the Trögers dropped to the ground and lay on their backs. A pistol shot followed by a horse's squeal, a curse, then another shot.

"Well, I guess we will eat soon," Nils said, but Matthias and Johan were already asleep.

Johan woke several hours later. Soldiers milled about, but Matthias and Nils were gone. He felt something warm under his shirt and reached his hand in to investigate. Johan discovered a piece of greasy, cooked meat. Probably horse meat, he thought. Despite the overpowering reek of human feces, Johan ate the morsel and savored every bite. The meat was tough, with very little fat. It required a lot of chewing, which produced a lot of saliva. When he finished eating, an overpowering thirst gripped him.

He rose and had to close his eyes until a wave of dizziness passed. The field had turned into a muddy mess infused with human feces and urine. Parched, Johan looked around in search of a source of water. Soldiers lay on the ground, stood in groups, or were hunched over the ground evacuating their bowels in diarrheic streams. Some urinated dangerously close to soldier's heads as they lay sleeping. Civility was at a decline.

"Johan!" Matthias called. "Come on."

Johan started walking toward the brothers. "What news have you?" He asked when he came up to them.

"Jakob's in a bad way," Nils said. "His arse is infected; stinks something awful, I mean more than usual. The doctor is going to cut off one cheek."

"That's too bad; I hope he's going to be okay," Johan said.

"Will they let him fight again, being a half-assed soldier?" Matthias asked. The two brothers looked at each other, then burst out laughing.

"Half-assed soldier!" Matthias chuckled at his wit and shook his head.

"One of the corporals said we have to cross the river at Nykarleby today. It's fifteen miles away." Nils said once they fully recovered.

"Nykarleby?" Johan asked. "Why Nykarleby?"

"The rear guard reports the Russians are gaining on us," Nils said. "We need to put the river between us if we don't want to be overrun and slaughtered."

"Ah, destroy the bridge, then?"

"Yeah."

"A lot of people are sick," Matthias said. "A doctor told me it's dysentery."

"Rödsot?" Johan gasped, looking around in horror. He had heard how infectious and deadly dysentery was.

"Yes." Matthias sighed.

They all knew this would slow them down, and with the Russians hot on their heels.

"You got water?" Johan asked.

"Yeah, here." Nils said, then seeing Johan's look of apprehension, said, "it's clean; I got it from the creek we passed, upstream of the crossing."

Johan gulped water, immediately feeling a surge of energy.

"Thank you for the meat." He said, rightly assuming it was one of them that placed the meat in his shirt.

Matthias sidled up to Johan and whispered, "I have more for later."

13

The Russians stopped to camp in a farmer's field a few miles outside a small village. A corporal sent out soldiers to cut fence posts for their fires while others gathered sheaves of rye for their tents. The farm's owners looked on with a combination of disgust, sadness, and fear. The man had draped one arm protectively over his wife's shoulder. The corporal looked at Gösta and was about to issue an order to him, but after seeing the look on Gösta's face, he thought better of it. He turned to another soldier, barking the order unnecessarily loud to cover his fear of Gösta.

The smell of cooking beef drew Gösta to the cooking fires. He couldn't remember the last time he had a good meal. The Russians had confiscated cattle and horses from local farms and plundered villages on their march across Finland. They had terrorized families, looted anything of value, and sometimes burned the houses and barns in their path. Gösta smiled at the memory of one village house they had barged into a month or so before. The husband had protested the intrusion and got bayoneted by a Russian soldier. Gösta raped the screaming wife while the other soldiers walked away in disgust.

After his meal, Gösta lit his pipe; a fine piece looted from a Finnish shop. Everything in that shop was of good quality. He had stuffed every pocket with the most expensive pipe tobacco he could find. Once again, he cursed at the cloying aroma of the tobacco; he much preferred his usual cheap brand, but he hasn't been able to find any of late. A dragoon rode by and disturbed his evening smoke. There was a body of another dragoon draped over the horse. Curious, Gösta tapped his pipe on one of the rocks by the fire until the bowl emptied. He got up and strode over to where the rider was talking with an officer.

"We were patrolling along a trail east of here, riding beside a rock cliff, when peasants ambushed us. Comrade Kozlov died in the attack." The soldier reported.

"And?" The officer, Captain Oleg Popov, demanded. "What of the ambushers?"

"They got away." The soldier said nervously. "I could not find a way up the cliff."

"Where's his horse?" Popov asked, indicating the dead dragoon.

"It rode off while I was trying to find a way up the cliff." The soldier replied nervously. He wasn't going to admit that he was hiding behind a boulder while a farmhand had stolen the dead dragoon's horse.

"Okay, go get something to eat and then make a formal report." Popov walked over to the commander's tent, Gösta trailing along at a distance. He could hear the commander bellowing at the captain. It was not a strain for Gösta to hear the words.

"Bring me the local priest, now!"

Captain Popov came out of the tent red-faced. As he strode past Gösta, he pointed his finger at him.

"You! Come with me!"

Gösta cursed under his breath and followed the captain.

They walked to the corral, and Popov ordered his horse saddled and brought to him and a horse for Gösta. They mounted and rode toward the village church, Gösta kicking his horse to catch up to the fuming Popov.

The captain skidded to a stop in front of the church, slid off his horse, strode to the church's door, kicked it open, and entered. Gösta could hear him berating the priest as he caught the other horse's reins and led it back to the church's front steps. The door banged open, and Popov came out, dragging the priest by his collar.

"Get up there!" He ordered the priest, indicating Gösta's horse.

When the priest stood looking bewildered, Popov grabbed him and threw him face down over Gösta's horse, in front of Gösta. The priest groaned as they rode away at a gallop. Gösta suspected the saddle horn was digging into the priest's stomach. He took pleasure in jumping the horse over small obstacles in his path.

They rode up to where the commander stood at a portable table poring over a map with a couple high ranking officers. Popov walked up to the desk, saluted, and informed the commander of the priest's presence. The commander grunted and walked around the table towards Gösta. Gösta grabbed the priest by his collar and unceremoniously dumped him off the horse. The priest landed with a grunt and struggled to his feet.

"Members of your parish killed one of my soldiers and stole his horse!" The commander bellowed. "You will bring them to Captain Popov before we decamp in the morning. If you fail, we will burn your church and the entire village!"

After the priest stumbled away, the commander turned to Popov, who now stood beside Gösta, and said, "execute the peasants responsible."

"Yes, sir," Popov replied.

"If they don't show, torch the town."

The next morning, Gösta had just finished eating his breakfast when he heard the commotion. The priest led a horse and two men into camp. A procession of villagers followed, and the ones in front were prodding the two men forward. Captain Popov met them.

"These are the men?" Popov asked, nodding toward the two men.

"Yes, they have confessed." The priest said. "This is the horse they took."

The captain nodded to a soldier who stepped forward and took the horse.

"Which one of you killed my soldier?"

"I did." One of the men said quietly, his head down, legs shaking.

"And you stole the horse?" Popov said to the other man.

"Yes."

"Okay. The rest of you go home!" He hollered at the villagers.

"What are you going to do with them?" Someone in the crowd yelled.

"That's none of your concern, now go home!" He signaled to the gathered soldiers who stepped forward, muskets raised.

After the villagers left, Captain Popov spotted Gösta and waved him over.

'Shit!' He mumbled and walked over to the captain.

"Yes, sir."

"Bring the prisoners."

Gösta prodded the prisoners forward with his musket.

"Come with us," Popov said to the priest.

"Where are we going?"

"To the church."

"What are you going to do?"

The captain kept walking, ignoring the priest's question. When they got to the church, Popov ordered the priest to produce two shovels, ignoring the priest's protestations. The priest came back from a small shed with the shovels.

Popov went to the prisoners and cut their bindings with his dagger. "Pick up those shovels and start digging."

"What are we digging?" One asked, "sir."

"Your graves."

The two looked at each other. One of the men looked down at his shovel. Gösta, reading his thoughts, raised his musket, cocked it, and pointed it in their direction. Popov replaced his dagger in its scabbard and pulled out his pistol. When they dug down four feet, Popov told them to kneel in the graves. Resigned to their fate, the men knelt, one shaking noticeably, and a dark stain spread at his crotch.

Popov nodded to Gösta, who walked behind them and shot one in the back of the head. Not the one who wet himself, Gösta was taking great pleasure in prolonging that man's terror. The man began weeping openly. Gösta took his time reloading and then shot. A loud report, but nothing happened.

"Oops, forgot the ball!" Gösta said with a grin.

"Get it over with, soldier!" Popov yelled. He cursed when the sour smell of excrement wafted up from the man.

"Yes, sir," Gösta said once again, taking his time loading his musket. The man was openly balling now.

"Oh, for fek sakes!" Popov cursed and shot the man in the head with his pistol.

The priest, who had been standing on the church steps, walked shakily toward the graves.

"Bury them, pastor," Popov said as he walked away.

"Fek," Gösta muttered and then followed Popov.

14

J ohan, Matthias, and Nils found themselves assigned to the rear guard of the retreating army. When they crossed the river at Nykarleby, the general ordered the rear guard to burn the bridge. The rest of the column continued toward the village of Sundby.

"Do you think this will help?" Johan asked. He was looking down at the shallow water under the bridge.

"It will slow them down some, but it won't stop them," Nils said.

After the bridge was in flames, Johan, Matthias, and Nils stopped several hundred yards down the road to watch. The rest of the rear guard continued their march. When the Russian forward units arrived, the bridge had burned out and collapsed into the river. They watched as Russian soldiers went along the bank in both directions.

"They are looking for a place to ford the river," Matthias said.

"You have any horsemeat left?" Johan asked.

"No, it's all gone."

"The land is barren," Nils said. "There's nothing left to forage, and we are running out of horses."

"Look!" Johan said. "That soldier is wading across the river. The water's barely up to his knees!"

"Damn!" Matthias cursed. "We better catch up with the rear guard and let them know."

Upon news of the failed delaying tactic, the army's plan to bivouac at Sundby was quickly changed to Kokkola, twenty-five miles farther. The commanders surmised that Kokkola offered better defensive positions than Sundby.

Johan, Matthias, and Nils staggered into Kokkola two days later. They were exhausted and starving. They had seen several dead soldiers on their journey, all with soiled trousers, soiled with feces and blood. There was nothing they could do for them. Burying was not an option as they did not have the time nor the tools.

Over the next several weeks, the rear guard set up ambushes to harass the Russians and participated in several skirmishes. All the while surviving on starvation rations and avoiding fellow soldiers ravaged by dysentery. There was nothing they could do for them.

One cold and grey afternoon, Johan huddled around a fire with Matthias and Nils. The cold seeped into their backs as they warmed their fronts. Hunger was a constant companion for them. To make matters worse, Swedish supply ships carrying food and clothing were in sight on the bay, out of reach because of the ice along the shore that extended several hundred yards into the bay. Ice too thin to walk on and too thick to force a boat through.

When Johan turned around to warm his back, he spotted a column of soldiers heading toward the camp. They were Swedish soldiers coming back from the prisoner exchange set up by their commanders.

"Here they come," Johan said. "Let's go see if we know any of them."

"Yeah!" Nils and Matthias said together. The Trögers had lost some of their earlier exuberance. Partly due to their ever-present exhaustion and hunger and partly due to their brothers' deaths. Jakob, the strongest of the brothers, succumbed to dysentery a few days earlier.

They were shocked to see the condition of the released prisoners. Johan and the Trögers, who considered themselves starved, were ashamed of that thinking when they saw these prisoners. They wore rags, some with no shoes; they looked like walking skeletons.

"Those sons of bitches!" Nils cursed. "And after we cared for our prisoners with honor!"

"Gunnar?" Johan whispered, spotting a man who resembled his friend in the column. "Gunnar!" He yelled. Several soldiers looked his way. Johan walked up to his friend, matching his pace, which was no more than a shuffle.

"Gunnar?" Johan said. "Is that you?"

Gunnar Johansson slowly turned to look at Johan, uncomprehending for a few seconds, then he rasped, "Johan?"

"Yes, it is me," Johan said, fighting back the tears.

Gunnar stumbled, and Johan caught him. He held him as Gunnar began to sob.

"You there!" A corporal yelled at Johan. "We have to process these soldiers before they can disperse!"

"Yes, sir!" Johan replied. "I will help him."

The corporal was about to deny him, then saw Gunnar's condition. He nodded and turned forward again. Nils and Mathias rushed forward and helped a couple of the weakest soldiers walk, soon joined by others. Before long, almost every released prisoner was leaning heavily on a fellow soldier. As they walked, Johan saw many of the soldiers watching the procession were openly weeping at the sight of these prisoners. He felt the itch of lice that must have transferred from Gunnar's head to his, but he didn't care; he would deal with them later.

Many of the prisoners would contract dysentery and, in their weakened state, succumb to the infection. Due in large part to Johan's care, Gunnar survived the affliction.

* * *

During a brief truce, Johan and the rear guard stood between the Pyhäjoki River and the Russian army's advance units. The bulk of the Swedish forces were several miles away on the other side of the river. After weeks of brutal cold, an unseasonal thaw had developed. The soldiers welcomed it, but it did make for sloppy roads. Suddenly, they heard loud booms and crashing from upstream. Johan looked in that direction and was amazed at the sight before him. A wall of fractured ice flowed down the river, ripping up ice and boulders in its path. Johan watched in horror as the wall of ice and stone crashed through the bridge, demolishing it and carrying it down the river. Their only means of escape, gone.

The soldiers watched helplessly as the wall of ice flowed past.

"Shit!" Yelled Sergeant Björk.

They have one day of truce left before they become sitting ducks in front of the Russians. That is, of course, if the Russians honor the ceasefire. Scouts were sent up and down the river in search of river crossing possibilities. Johan and Nils were part of the Westward scouting party. They carried with them several coils of rope.

"What will you do after the war, Nils?" Johan asked as they walked along the bank.

"I want to buy a farm, a farm with good soil, and I will build a nice house." Nils said, "a house big enough for a large family and room for my mother."

"You have given this plenty of thought?"

"Yes, every night I think about it."

"Do you have a woman in mind?" Johan asked, "to give you that large family."

"No, but I will find someone. She will have to be strong and a good cook." Nils said, "what about you, Johan?"

"I am engaged, and we have some land waiting for us to build our house on."

"You are lucky. Will you have many children?"

"I hope so, my fiancé is beautiful, and with my good looks, we will have handsome boys!"

Nils punched Johan's shoulder hard and then ran before Johan could retaliate. But Johan gave chase and tackled Nils, both falling onto the grassed bank. They wrestled until exhausted, not long given their malnourished state.

Nils glanced at the river and saw that they were at an area where the water was shallow with several large boulders strewn across the riverbed.

"This looks like as good a place as any, Johan," He said.

"Yeah. Do you want to try going across?"

"Me! Why me?"

"I, uh," Johan hesitated, trying to come up with a reason. "Because I can't swim," Johan said, but, of course, he could swim. He just wanted to avoid the slow, ice-cold crossing. With a rope tied across the river, it would make for a faster crossing.

"You can't swim?" Nils said, with a hint of skepticism.

"No, sink like a rock, I will."

"Alright, Johan, I will go."

Nils sat on the ground and took off his shoes and hose. He then tied one end of the rope around his waist, and Johan played out the rope as Nils waded out into the current using a pole for balance. The flow was quite strong here, forming small rapids downstream of the boulders.

"Christ, that's cold!" Nils said through chattering teeth, a small wet spot formed at the front of his trousers. "And the rocks underwater are slick. Make sure you have a good grip on that rope, Johan!" Johan looked over his shoulder and saw two Russians on horseback a few hundred yards away, watching their progress.

I hope they honor the truce.

Suddenly the rope jerked Johan into the river. He landed on his stomach and was quickly pulled downstream. Johan held tightly to the rope while trying to avoid rocks and boulders as he was swept along. He tried looking for Nils, but the water frothed and hit him in the face. Finally, they came to a less turbulent area of the river, but it was too deep for Johan to stand up. He could see Nils fifty feet in front of him. He looked unconscious and was face down in the water.

Johan swam towards Nils but was suddenly pulled toward shore. He looked up and saw a Russian soldier on horseback in the water, pulling them by the middle portion of the rope. The horse climbed onto the bank, and the soldier kicked his horse forward, dragging Johan and Nils onto the bank. The other Russian raced down to Nils and slid off his horse. He took off his coat, rolled it up, and laid it on the bank. He then laid Nils face down with his midsection on the rolled-up garment. The man then sat on Nils's rump and began pushing on his lower back. Some water eventually spurted out of Nils's mouth, and he started coughing. The Russian turned Nils on his side, picked up his coat, and put it back on. Johan reached them as the man was buttoning his jacket.

"Thank you!" Johan exclaimed and stuck out his hand.

The Russian ignored the proffered hand and nodded slightly to Johan. He mounted his horse, threw a roll of cloth on the ground, then rode away, followed by the other cavalryman. Nils had a deep gash on his forehead, which Johan wrapped with the Russian's bandage and tied it tight. With no way of starting a fire, Johan helped Nils to his feet and helped him walk along the bank. He was on the verge of collapse by the time other soldiers, a frantic Matthias among them, came to their aid.

They quickly built a fire, stripped Johan and Nils down, and rubbed them vigorously with rough, itchy blankets. Johan stood shivering uncontrollably, much as he does after a battle.

"Those are the smallest dinks I have ever seen, other than on a baby!" Matthias exclaimed. "Like a couple of frightened turtles!"

The other soldiers laughed raucously at Matthias's comment, but not the shivering Johan and Nils.

"Don't do that again, brother!" Matthias said, hugging Nils from one side. "You are my last brother, and Mama will strap me if I don't bring you home!"

Matthias and another soldier made it across the river at the spot where Nils had tried to cross. They secured ropes spanning the river, tied at both banks and to several boulders in the river. Nils was carried across while Johan and the rest of the rear guard had to wade.

"Watch that soldier," Nils hollered from his stretcher with a grin. He was pointing at Johan, who had just started to cross the river, gripping the rope tightly. "He can't swim."

The last soldier to cross, a solid, stocky man, untied the rope as he progressed. The rearguard then traveled along the river to the road where the bridge once stood. Across the river stood the Russian advance guard. Johan scanned the massed Russians looking for the two cavalrymen that helped Nils and him but did not see them.

Were they medics?

Without ceremony, the Swedes turned and continued down the road away from the river. Hopefully, they can distance themselves from the Russians before the truce runs out and the Russians cross the river.

15

Larsson Farm
October

Harald Israelsson ran into the Larsson farmyard, scattering chickens before him.

"Slow down, Harald!" Lars Larson hollered at him from the barn door.

Harald skidded to stop in front of the barn.

"Sorry, sir." Harald gasped. "Is Maria home?"

"What do you want with Maria, in such a hurry?" Demanded Lars.

"Toby's home!"

"Is he?" Lars said. "What does that have to do with my daughter?"

"He was with Johan, in Finland!"

"So?"

"Ahh, she may want to know because of -" Harald stammered.

"Spit it out, boy!" Lars demanded, "because of what?"

"Because they are to be married, Lars!" Olof said, coming out of the barn.

"Hmph." Lars stared at Harald for a few seconds before nodding towards the house. "She's inside."

"Yes, sir," Harald said, then bolted towards the house.

"Walk!" Shouted Lars.

Harald skidded to a stop then walked stiffly to the porch. He climbed the porch and was about to knock when the door swung open, and a hand reached out and yanked him inside. Harald was thirteen and slightly built. Childhood illnesses had slowed his physical development. He was not strong, but he could run like the wind.

"Tell me!" Maria demanded.

"Toby has come home; I think he is ill!" Harald said.

It was all Maria could do not to shake the boy.

"What about Johan?"

"I, I don't know."

"Ach!" Maria cried. "Why didn't you ask him?"

"I didn't talk to him." Harald shrunk back from Maria's aggressive questioning. "I saw him riding into his yard and came straight here to tell you. He does not look well."

"Wait, I will ask my Mama if I can go," Maria said.

"Go," Kajsa called from the other room. Maria felt a flush of embarrassment, knowing her mother had overheard.

"Thank you, Mama."

"Ask your grandfather to take you in the wagon."

"That will take forever."

"I don't want you two going there alone, bothering Toby!" Kajsa said, coming into the front room. "Your grandfather will know how to talk to him; after what he's been through himself."

"Okay, Mama." Then to Harald, "come on, let's go."

They found Lars and Olof inside the barn.

"Mama said I could go to Toby's if grandpa comes with us," Maria said.

"No!" Lars said. "You have no business bothering Toby."

"But Papa!" Maria pleaded. "I want to know what happened to Johan."

"You will know soon enough," Lars said. "Now, go back inside and help your Mama!"

"But Papa!"

"Go!" Lars raised his voice and pointed toward the house. "Now."

"I will go with you, Harald," Olof said. "Come, help me hitch up the buggy."

"We have work to do, Olof," Lars said.

"I won't be long; this is between soldiers," Olof said. He did not know that Lars felt slighted at the remark. His son-in-law had never served in the army.

* * *

Olof steered Sofia to the hitching post in front of Tobias's cabin. Harald leaped off the buggy, tied the mare to the post, and started to follow Olof.

"Wait here," Olof said as he walked to the front door.

"Aww." Harald groaned.

After a few seconds, Olof knocked on the door and heard a muffled 'come in.'

"Toby?" Olof said, entering the front room.

"Back here."

"Are you okay?"

"No, I got the shits something fierce!"

"Can I get you anything?"

"Water." Tobias croaked.

"I've seen this before, Toby," Olof said. "I will put some salt in it. Do you have any sugar?"

"Yeah, in the cupboard. Why?"

"It seems to help."

After Olof came back into the room, he gave Tobias the drink and pulled a chair beside the bed. The room smelled of sour feces.

"I will go empty this," Olof picked up the full chamber pot. He gagged at the smell and the sight of blood mixed in but managed to fight down his rising bile. Going out the front door, he passed the pot to Harald. He told him to empty it in the outhouse and set it by the front door afterward. Harald looked at the chamber pot with disgust, then pulled his shirt sleeves down around his hands and carefully picked up the pot. His progress was excruciatingly slow as he shuffled toward the outhouse; concentration etched on his face as he tried not to slosh the pot's contents. Olof resisted the urge to yell at him to hurry. It would be funny, though. He sighed and went back into the cottage.

"What happened over there, Toby?" Olof asked when he sat back down beside the bed.

"There was a battle; we counter-attacked and got caught in a crossfire," Tobias said, his eyes closed. "Our regiment scattered in all directions; most of us forced into the forest. It became dark, so dark I could not see my hand in front of my face."

Olof nodded and asked, "do you mind?" Lifting his pipe. Tobias nodded and said, "go ahead."

"Where's that pot?" Tobias asked. "I need it close by. The shits come without warning."

"I will go get it."

Olof walked out to the porch and picked up the pot.

"What did he say?" Harald asked, "is Johan okay?"

"He hasn't got to it yet."

Olof took the empty chamber pot back into Tobias's bedroom and set it by his bed.

"I will get some clean water."

He walked back out to the porch and handed Harald a large crock telling him to take the buggy and get fresh water. "Rinse it out first."

Olof heard the unmistakable diarrheic evacuation sounds coming from the bedroom when he walked back into the house.

"Is it okay to come in, Toby?"

"A minute." Some shuffling noises then, "Okay, Olof, come in."

Olof tried not to show his reaction to the smell as he picked up the chamber pot.

"I will put this out for Harald to empty."

"Yeah, I should be good for a while."

"Now, tell me what happened next," Olof said after opening a window. He moved a chair closer to the bed, sat down, and lit his pipe.

"It was hand to hand fighting in the forest. I could not tell who I was fighting with; the darkness was absolute. Once, I had a hold on this man's knife hand wrist, and he held mine. We were both trying to gain an advantage when I was able to knee the inside of his leg. He cursed. In Swedish."

Olof kept his silence, allowing Tobias to tell his story at his own pace.

"I asked him who he was, and he said 'Västerbottens.' To make sure it wasn't a Russian trick, I asked who his sergeant was. "He said, 'Sergeant Andersson.' That is my sergeant too!" Tobias said. "I knew this man; it was my friend, Petter Pehrsson! We let go of each other and committed to fighting side by side. It was a relief not to be alone anymore." Tobias paused to drink some of the water Olof had mixed.

.

"We tried to make our way back to the meadow, but we could hear screams and struggles all around us. We weaved our way through the noise when someone hit me on the head with a musket stock. When I came to, Petter lay beside me, dead."

Olof nodded. He could relate to what Tobias described. Not that he went through the same situation, as far as darkness goes, but the hand-to-hand fighting was something he had experienced in Pomerania.

"I wandered through the dark forest and found myself in the middle of a Russian camp."

Olof grunted at this, leaning forward despite the odor, anxious to hear the rest of the story.

"They lit campfires. It would only be a matter of minutes before they discovered me. I knew I had to get out of there, but I didn't see a way out."

Tobias went silent, staring at the ceiling, tears forming at the corners of his eyes.

"What happened, Toby?" Olof urged.

"My son guided me through the encampment and back to our lines."

"Georg?" Olof said. "Your son is dead!"

"It was him!"

"What about Johan?" Olof asked, uncomfortable with the talk of ghosts.

"We got separated during the counter-attack. I never saw Johan again." Tobias said. "But most of the army retreated north. I was with a group that made it to the troopship in the bay. We were defeated and in disarray. I was never so exhausted in my life! I can only imagine how the others felt who had to march north."

"Thank you, Toby, for telling me," Olof said. He did not look forward to telling Maria what he learned. "I hear Harald coming. I will stop by tomorrow to check on you."

"Thank you, Olof," Tobias said. "Oh, Emanuel's son, Jon? He also made it to the ship."

"That is good to hear. So long, comrade."

"Adjö, my friend."

Before Olof left, he went to the barn and found some old barn paint and used a rag to paint a red cross on Tobias's door. A warning to others of the infectious disease within.

16

Early December
Tornio, Swedish-Finnish Border

J ohan was struggling to find the words to put down on paper to Maria. At
a loss, he searched for Ulrik Dahl, who was, in reality, Ulrika Dahl, as most
soldiers were aware. During the campaign, life left no room for privacy, and
it wasn't long before soldiers discovered her true gender. But she fought
bravely alongside the soldiers, and they, in turn, showed her the respect of a
comrade in arms. She had dressed like a man and joined her husband's
regiment at the outbreak of war. He, unfortunately, was killed in the battle at
Oravais.

They halted their retreat at the village of Tornio as both armies ceased
hostilities during the coldest of the winter months. The Swede's winter
quarters were a series of drafty wood plank buildings at the village's edge. A
series of boardwalks connected the buildings. Due to the lack of milled
lumber, they built the boardwalks narrow, too narrow for two people to walk
by each other. Most of the soldiers would turn sideways and sidling by each

other when meeting. But there were those few, the aggressive types, who would walk straight down the center, forcing the person they were meeting to defer and step off the boardwalk. Occasionally, two such bullies would meet, neither giving way until they bumped into each other. What ensued was predictable; chest to chest with chins thrust forward, circling as they glared at each other, then realizing that they had passed each other—a final glare and then both walking away.

Johan walked out of the cabin that housed his and eleven other soldier's sleeping quarters and, after making sure the boardwalk was clear, made his way to the canteen. He found her sitting at a table with several boisterous men. He caught her eye, and she used the excuse to escape the group. The men had begun conversing respectfully enough but had gradually deteriorated into vulgar language that she found offensive.

"What is it, Johan?"

"Could you help me write a letter to my fiancé?"

"You don't know how to write?" She asked wide-eyed.

"Of course, I do!" Johan said. "It's just that I'm having trouble finding the right words.

"You have heard that we are going back to Umeå?"

"No, I haven't. All of us?" Johan asked. He couldn't keep the excitement out of his voice.

"No, just us displaced soldiers." She said. "Västerbottens, Upplanders, and Hälsingers. The rest will winter here."

"I don't know who is better off," Johan observed. "Us walking to Umeå in the bitter cold or those left to wallow in these lice-infested hovels."

"They are not that bad; you just have to clean them now and then."

"I suppose."

"Do you still want to write that letter?" Ulrika asked. "The mail will probably travel with us."

"No, I guess not."

"We will walk together, you and I." Ulrika declared and then walked away, leaving Johan to wonder what she meant by that comment.

As it turns out, the mail would leave before the soldiers.

The next day, Johan was hunting with the Trögers when they sensed the reindeer before they heard them.

"Shh!" Matthias hissed, waving his hand in a downward gesture.

Johan and Nils immediately stopped and knelt behind nearby trees. They had been walking along the supply route. The trail was not well defined, traffic limited to infrequent supply trains from Sweden proper. A two-inch skiff of snow covered the path, and drifts crusted in open areas. Anticipation spiked when they spotted the reindeer in the distance. They would be heroes for supplying fresh meat to the camp! No more salted pork or fermented herring. Well, at least for a little while.

"Damn!" Nils yelled, causing alarm and admonishment from his brother.

"Quiet!" Matthias said. "You're going to scare them off!"

"Those are Sámi reindeer," Nils said.

In the distance, they could see a man walk to the front of the reindeer and start waving at the three hunters, letting them know these were not wild reindeer and not to shoot at them. Johan strode to the middle of the trail and waved acknowledgment to the Sámi man. They stood to the side of the trail as the reindeer approached. There were, in fact, two Sámi, one young and the other older. They each had a team of eight reindeer pulling huge, fully loaded sleighs.

Matthias raised a hand in greeting.

"Hej!" The older Sámi man said in fluent Swedish. "You are Swedish soldiers?"

"Yes," Matthias answered, "you're Swedish is good!'

"A Swede lived with us for many years; he taught me."

"Was his name Toby or Tobias?" Johan asked, his excitement building.

"Yes!" The older grinned widely, "do you know Toby?"

"He is my neighbor, near Överboda. And a comrade."

The powerful older man grinned broadly, grabbed Johan in a bear hug, lifted him, and spun him around as if he were a long-lost brother.

The man released him, and Johan said, "I have some bad news for you, though. Toby was lost in battle a few months ago, taken prisoner or dead."

"No, his sister visited him a month ago at his farm."

"Dárjá?" Johan asked, grabbing the older man by the arms. Nils and Matthias hooked arms and began dancing a jig. The reindeer became nervous, eyes large, and hooves stamping.

"Yes, she is the only sister he has." The Sámi man said as he watched the jigging with bemusement.

"Thank you, stranger, Toby is our friend, and we thought he was dead." Nils had grabbed the man's hand and was pumping it vigorously.

"I am Nikko and this is my son, Kálle."

"I am Nils; this is my brother, Matthias, and our friend, Johan."

"It is good to meet you, Nils, Matthias, and Johan, but now we must continue on our journey before our skis freeze to the ground," Nikko said. "We have food for your camp and mail to pick up." And then they were gone, flying down the trail, snow billowing in their wake.

"Come on!" Nils hollered, racing after the sleighs. Matthias whooped and ran after his brother. Johan grinned and shook his head, and then it hit him; I need to write a letter to Maria after all! And he was running too. Soon catching the Trögers and then passing them, much to their shock. Well, they can't have this! No one can outrun the Trögers! Now it became a race. They were only a few miles from camp, and if it were any further, they might have even caught up with the Sámi sleighs!

Nikko and Kálle were untying the packs on their sleighs in front of the storehouse under the supervision of Sergeant Björk when they spotted Johan, Matthias, and Nils charging towards them. They all stopped to watch as Nils tackled Johan, fifty yards out, both men skidding face first in snow as Matthias passed them. Johan quickly kicked at Nils's arms until he was free from his grip, losing a shoe in the process, and ran after Matthias. And he almost caught him. Both men fell into the snow beside the sleighs, followed shortly by Nils.

"I need to send a letter." Johan managed to say between gasps.

Sergeant Björk stood over Nils and boomed, "not a very honorable way to win a race, soldier!"

Nils looked up, panting, and managed to say, "time of war, sir! Had to improvise."

The sergeant stared at him for several seconds, then said, "quite right." He turned to Johan, saluted, then held out his hand to help him up and said, "I declare you the winner of the first annual Tornio idiot's race!"

"Thank you, sir." It was all Johan could think to say.

Nils tossed the shoe to Johan, "your prize," was all he said.

The Sámi left an hour later, loaded with mail and four soldiers who were too sick to make the journey on foot. They had declined to stay overnight, stating the reindeer had several more miles left in them. Johan noticed the look of disgust on the faces of the Sámi when they saw the camp's condition, a look they quickly hid. Johan scribbled a note to Maria, saying he is on his way to Umeå, and handed it to Nikko.

* * *

The next day, Sergeant Björk led twenty soldiers out of camp. The soldiers included Johan, Matthias, Nils, Gunnar Johansson, and Ulrika Dahl. Nikko had promised to leave caches of food along the trail for them. They were skilled hunters and could shoot their bows from the backs of their sleighs with great accuracy at any moose, rabbit, grouse, or ptarmigan that happened across their path.

Twenty soldiers with full packs, except for sergeant Björk, would take turns, again except for the sergeant, pulling the sleighs that carried their tents, blankets, and cooking utensils. The journey would take them two hundred miles along the coast and across the ice, following the Sámi's supply route. They would average fifteen miles each day. The hope was that the army would meet them along the way. Their first town of any size was Luleå, four day's march and mostly on ice.

True to her word, Ulrika marched beside Johan. Gunnar tried to walk beside Johan, but Ulrika wedged herself between them until Gunnar sighed and moved back in the column. Johan and Gunnar formed a strong friendship after Johan helped Gunnar recover from his captivity.

"Tell me about this girl you are going to marry, Johan." She said on the second day.

"She is the most beautiful girl in the world!" Johan said. "I've known her most of my life."

"She is a neighbor?"

"Yes."

"Maybe you should practice before you get married, so you know what to do."

"Practice what?" Johan asked, not comprehending. The soldiers in front and back of them were listening intently.

"You know, relations between a man and a woman."

The blush started in his cheeks and quickly spread to his scalp, ears, and neck.

"Ahh."

Ulrika was watching him with an amused look on her face. She had a rough, windburned face, not pretty and yet, not homely either. Plain and stocky.

"No, I will stay faithful to my fiancé," Johan said when he regained some composure. "Besides, where would I find a woman to practice with?"

He immediately regretted that comment when she viciously dug an elbow into his side and moved back in the column. She pushed Gunnar to the side and took his spot beside a terrified soldier. Gunnar moved back beside Johan and asked what that was all about.

"I have no idea, my friend."

"Your first lesson in dealing with women, Johan!" Björk called from the front of the line.

"Which is what, sir?"

"Damned if I know."

Johan looked at Gunnar, who merely shrugged. Overhearing the exchange, Ulrika growled deep in her throat, further terrifying the soldier marching beside her.

The first cache of food left by the Sámi was five miles into their second day's march. Grouse and rabbits cleaned and hidden away from scavengers under a stack of firewood.

"They must think we march twenty miles in a day," Matthias said.

"Normally, we would if we weren't so worn out and malnourished," Björk replied.

Matthias glanced at the sergeant's ample girth.

We?

Sergeant Björk stood five foot five, pot-bellied, and sported a bushy handlebar mustache on his ruddy face. The word was, he was furious when the commander denied him a horse for the trip. The cooks had butchered a lot of horses to feed the starving army during their retreat. Those remaining were poorly fed and would struggle on such a trip.

They stopped to eat and enjoyed the best meal they had in some time.

The next cache, as expected, was twenty miles after the first. They arrived midday on the third day to find a front quarter of moose covered with firewood. The soldiers, following their sergeant's lead, gorged themselves on the meat. Ulrika saved a bone and some meat scraps for soup. When the sergeant began snoring after the meal, the soldiers decided to set up camp. When he woke several hours later, Björk bellowed at the soldiers to take down the tents and prepare to march. Since there were only four hours of daylight in early December, the time of day did not matter to them, and the snow provided sufficient illumination for travel. Still, the sergeant's demands irked the soldiers; he is the only one who had slept.

They marched another ten miles before the sergeant called a halt. He was not looking well and had to stop a few times to empty his bowels. The exhausted soldiers made camp and crawled into their tents after helping the sergeant into his tent. When they woke, they discovered the sergeant was in no condition to march. They would have to pull him on one of the sleighs.

Ulrika seemed to have forgiven Johan and stood beside him, watching a soldier struggling to pull the sleigh.

"Is it the rödsot, Johan?" She asked.

"Yeah." Johan sighed. Their march will be more difficult now and worse if more soldiers come down with the dreaded disease. They all knew the survival rate of dysentery victims while on a campaign was extremely low. Their breath rose in clouds on this brisk morning. At least there was little wind to make the -20° Celsius weather even colder.

They walked ten miles and arrived at the village of Luleå. The residents did not receive them well. News had spread throughout Sweden that the army had abandoned Finland to the Russians. There were rumors soldiers were bringing disease with them. Where the soldiers hoped to obtained food and warm accommodations, barred doors met them instead. Worse, when they checked on their sergeant, they discovered he had soiled himself, and the waste had frozen between his rear and the sleigh.

The soldiers forced their way into a barn and posted armed guards at the entrance. Johan started a fire in the barn's rear, and Ulrika made a pot of moose soup – just bone marrow and bits of meat and fat scraps boiled in melted snow. The cleaning of Sergeant Björk fell to two soldiers of the lowest rank. They always seemed to get the worst assignments.

When they woke the next morning, Björk was dead. The only option was to burn the body. It was another bitterly cold day, this time with a wind chill off the frozen bay when they cremated the sergeant on his sleigh. Nobody said anything. They hope their reception would be better in the next village, a two-day march to Piteå.

17

After six weeks, Tobias had fully recovered from his bout with dysentery. He would rejoin his unit after Christmas. Olof continued to visit him every other day, and lately, Olof's brother, Emanuel, would accompany him. The three would sit, play checkers, drink coffee, relate war stories, and discuss Umeå and Stockholm's latest news. Erik Kiällberg had stopped by a few times, but it was more to see his old friends than concern for Tobias.

Emanuel was gathering firewood from beside the cottage when Nikko and Kálle drove their sleighs into the yard. The sight of so many reindeer harnessed to the sleighs struck Emanuel with awe.

"Nikko?" He called, "Is that you?"

Nikko stared at Emanuel for a few seconds before recognizing him.

"Manny!" He whooped and ran to meet his old friend. They had met many years ago when Nikko and several other Sámi hunters searched for Kajsa after being kidnapped.

Olof and Tobias, hearing the commotion, had stepped out onto the porch.

"Olof, Toby!" Nikko hollered, running once again to meet them.

"Nikko, old friend!" Olof called. Being the father of Kajsa, Olof held great affection for the Sámi that had helped in the search for his daughter.

"Välkommen!" Tobias said, "come inside; coffee is on."

Emanuel followed Nikko and Kálle in, hesitating on the steps and looking back at the reindeer.

"They will be okay, Manny," Kálle said.

"What brings you so far from home, Nikko?" Tobias asked.

"Oh, just a minute." Nikko began digging through his pockets and pouches, finally coming up with a folded piece of paper. "A soldier at Tornio gave me this letter addressed to Maria Larsdotter, care of Tobias Öhn."

Tobias and Olof swung their heads towards each other, Olof whispering, "Johan."

Tobias reached for the letter, looked at Olof, unfolded the paper, and then refolded it quickly. "It is signed by Johan." He said, handing the letter to Olof, who slipped it into his pocket.

"I am relieved that he survived the fight at Oravais and, I suppose, all the other battles since," Tobias said.

"As am I!" Olof said. He looked at Nikko and said, "he is to marry Kajsa's daughter."

"Congratulations, my friend!" Nikko said, "what is her daughter's name?" He held great affection for Kajsa, as did most of the Sámi involved in searching for her those long years ago.

"Maria, she who is learning to shoot Kajsa's bow!" Olof said proudly.

"Hah!" Nikko laughed, slapping his knee. He was clearly pleased with the news.

"How did Johan look?" Tobias asked. "Is he healthy?"

"Yes, he is very healthy!" Nikko answered. "He was racing through the snow with two funny men."

"Trögers?" Tobias asked, sitting up straighter.

"I don't know, what did they say their names were, Kálle?"

"Matthias and Nils."

"Hah!" Tobias cried. "My friends!" Then, "only two?"

"Yeah, that's all we met," Nikko said. "Are there more?"

"Yes, two more. Karl and Jakob." Tobias said, visibly slumping in his chair.

The men were quiet for a time, the soldiers among them paying respect to presumed fallen comrades.

"How are you, Toby?" Nikko asked. "You look skinny."

"I had a sickness. I am good now."

"And Lovisa, have you heard from her lately?"

"No, Sweden is also at war with Norway, so it may be a while before we see her again."

"I do not understand these wars," Nikko said. "Why do men have to fight all the time."

"Land," Emanuel said.

"Land! We traveled over so much empty land; it was days before we saw humans again!" Both Nikko and Kálle were shaking their heads now.

"Do you want some moose meat, Toby?" Nikko asked.

"Yes, that would be good! Thank you."

"We better get going, Toby," Olof said, nodding at Emanuel. "Maria will want to read this letter."

"Give my regards to Kajsa," Nikko said. "How is Erik?"

"I will; Erik is well. I will convey your greetings."

"So long, my friends."

* * *

"Maria!" Olof called when he and Emanuel entered the Larsson home.

"Yes?" She called from the kitchen.

"I have something for you."

Maria walked into the front room and saw the two of them standing there, grinning like children.

"I already saw Manny this morning," Maria said.

"Eh?" Olof seemed a little confused, then, "Oh, no. I didn't mean Manny. Here!" Olof started looking in all his pockets. "I'm sure I had it here somewhere."

"What?" Maria was getting impatient.

"Ah, here it is!" He said, pulling the folded paper out of his rear pants pocket, sniffing it surreptitiously before holding it out to Maria.

"Eew!" Maria cried. "Did you fart on it?"

"No, of course not!"

"Does it smell like pee?"

"No…" Olof sniffed the letter again. "Of course not! Take it! It's a letter for you."

Manny stood watching the two of them, chuckling at the exchange.

"Is it…."

"Yes, from Johan."

The men winced when Maria shrieked and leaped for the letter, snatching it out of Olof's hand and hugging it to her chest. She walked into the parlor for some privacy, passing her mother on the way.

"It's a letter from Johan!" Maria gushed.

Kajsa stopped Olof and Emanuel when they started to follow Maria into the parlor.

Olof, Emanuel, Kajsa, and Anna waited patiently in the kitchen for Maria to come out and tell them what the letter said. Ollie, Petter, and Magdalena were in the barn helping their father clean stalls. Anna made coffee and put out cookies, sneaking one.

"Do you think 'Ahh' changed his mind?" Anna asked, nibbling on her cookie. "About marrying Maria?"

"Anna!" Kajsa said. "Do not call Johan names!"

"Sorry, Mama."

"What's taking her so long?" Olof asked. "It is only one page!"

"Give her time, Papa."

"Nikko sends his regards."

"Nikko! I haven't seen him in a dog's age!" Kajsa said, looking out a window. She went quiet, thinking back to a different time.

"Mama!" Maria cried, running into the kitchen, waving the letter. "Johan's coming home!"

"When?" Olof asked.

"It doesn't say."

"Let me see," Olof said, holding out his hand.

Maria hesitated, then handed it over, knowing the letter did not contain anything embarrassing. It looked as though Johan had scribbled it in a hurry.

"They left four days ago. I would say two weeks' march. What do you think, Manny?" Olof said.

"Yeah, that sounds about right."

"He will be here on the fourteenth!" Maria cried.

"No, Maria," Emanuel said. "He will arrive at the barracks in Umeå about that time. No telling when he will be allowed leave for a visit home."

Maria slumped and looked about to cry.

"We will go to Umeå, Maria," Kajsa said.

Maria jumped into her mother's arms, weeping and thanking her.

Olof and Emanuel smiled at Kajsa, nodding their approval.

"Can I go?" Anna asked.

"Yes, we will all go!" Kajsa said.

"Well, I don't know," Emanuel said with a grin. "I will have to see if I am available around that time."

Kajsa smiled at him, and then a worried look came over her face. She will have to talk Lars into making the trip.

* * *

"No!" Lars said. "There is no need for all of us to go galivanting around Umeå like a bunch of rich tourists. We have work to do!"

They were at the kitchen table, about to eat their supper, when Kajsa broached the subject. Maria lowered her head and fought back the tears. Her mother warned her this might happen, yet the words still came as a shock. Olof looked at her, the tears dropping onto her lap, breaking his heart.

"I will take her myself, Lars!" Olof said forcefully. He usually deferred to Lars, being a guest in his house, but at this moment, he would not.

Lars stared at Olof, who stared right back. Kajsa held her breath as she looked at these two strong-willed and proud men, her husband and her father. After a tense moment, Lars said, "fine! Now, where's my supper!" Maria beamed through her tears at her grandfather, fighting the urge to jump up and hug him.

"How come I can't go?" Anna cried.

"Anna, Johan is Maria's future husband," Lars said. "And you are needed here!"

"Hmph!" Annie pouted, arms crossed, and bottom lip out in a full pout. "Just because 'Aah' loses the war in Finland, Maria gets to go to Umeå!"

"Anna!" Lars yelled, slamming his palm down hard on the table, rattling plates and cups, "go to your room, now!"

Seeing the anger in her father's face, Annie ran to her room balling.

"Leave her be, Kajsa!" Lars commanded when she started to rise.

The meal proceeded in awkward silence. The clinking of plates and utensils not entirely covering the sounds of sobbing coming from the girl's bedroom in the open loft. After supper, when Lars and Olof retired to the parlor to smoke their pipes, Maria snuck some food and a cup of water to Anna.

"Thank you, Maria." Anna said, "what is a tourist?"

"A tourist?" Maria thought about it for a while then said, "someone rich, I guess."

"Hmm." Anna pondered that and then asked, "did you bring cookies?"

Maria smiled and produced a ginger snap from her pocket.

18

Rödsot. It is the Swedish word for dysentery. It is the disease Tobias recovered from, with Olof's help and, it is that Olof began showing signs of during the night. He spent most of the early morning in the chamber room before slowly making his way outside toward the outhouse, carrying the full chamber pot with him.

"Are you okay, Olof?" Lars called, coming onto the porch. He got up to investigate when he heard someone moving around the house and then a door opening and closing.

"Stay where you are, Lars!" Olof cried. "I have the rödsot!"

"Ahh." Lars sighed. He knew the disease was often fatal for the old.

"I will stay in the barn," Olof said as he shuffled into the outhouse. The last thing Olof wanted to do was spread the disease to his daughter and grandchildren.

It was not long before Lars could hear the unmistakable noise of diarrhea. He walked to the barn to light a fire in his stone forge. Lars had built the forge several years ago to repair his tools and fabricate metalwork for the farm. It will quickly heat the barn, but he will need more wood to keep the fire going day and night.

Lars tied his handkerchief over his nose and mouth and helped Olof to the barn after he shuffled out of the outhouse. Olof carried the chamber pot with him and, at first, refused Lars's assistance but, after swaying on his feet, accepted his help.

"It comes over me without warning; the shits do."

Lars didn't have a response for that, so he just grunted.

"Tell Maria that I am sorry."

"For what?"

"I don't think I will be taking her to Umeå anytime soon."

Kajsa, hearing voices coming from the yard, got out of bed and went to the window just as Lars and Olof disappeared into the barn.

What are they doing out there at this early hour?

She went out to the kitchen and stoked the fire, putting a pot of water on the hook to boil. She then went to the chamber room for her morning toilet and was immediately struck by diarrhea's sour smell. She was next puzzled by the missing chamber pot.

Someone must have emptied the chamber pot and left it in the outhouse.

She looked in on her sleeping children before heading out to the outhouse, grumbling all the way. The diarrhea odor was strong in the outhouse too, and the chamber pot was missing. She went over what she knew, sitting down on the wooden bench with the hole cut into it. Lars and her father are up to something in the barn, she could smell diarrhea in the chamber room, and the chamber pot is missing.

Oh, no!

One of them is sick!

She knew Tobias had recently recovered from rödsot, and the fear came over her in a full-body flush. Relieved that her bowel movement was solid, she grabbed a handful of moss, wiped, and hurried back to the house. She

107

went into her daughter's room after scrubbing her hands clean in the washbasin and checked their temperatures by putting the back of her right hand to their foreheads.

"What is it, Mama?" Maria asked, coming awake and rubbing her eyes.

"Are you feeling okay, Maria?" Kajsa asked. "No diarrhea?"

She giggled and said, "no, Mama."

"What's going on?" Anna mumbled, also rubbing her eyes.

"How are you feeling, Anna? No diarrhea?"

Maria giggled again, setting Anna off in giggles and waking Magdalena.

"What's so funny?" She asked, stretching and then yawning mightily.

"Mama said diarrhea!" Anna said gleefully.

"What's that?"

"The poops, hot, runny poops!"

"Eew!"

"Maria, the water is heating, make the porridge once it boils. I will be right back."

"Where are you going?"

"To the barn. Stay in the house!"

"Tell me," Kajsa said. Lars had come out of the barn and shut the door behind him.

"It's Olof; he has the rödsot," Lars said.

"Oh!" Kajsa gasped. She had suspected as much but hearing it said still came as a shock. She moved to go past Lars. He grasped her by her shoulders. "No. You need to look after the children. I will see to Olof's needs." She struggled for a few seconds then Lars enveloped her in his arms. Kajsa sobbed in his embrace. She nodded her head and said, "okay." Lars let go, and Kajsa went back to the house.

She sat at the table and stared at the bowl Anna had set in front of her. Maria hoisted the porridge pot onto the table and began ladling porridge into the bowls.

"What's wrong, Mama?" Maria asked. The children went quiet when they sensed something was wrong with their mother.

"Your grandfather is sick." Kajsa said, "he is in the barn. No one is allowed to go in there!"

The gravity of the situation weighed on the children. Magdalena looked like she was about to burst into tears.

"Eat." Kajsa ordered, "Magda, pass the butter." She knew that giving Magdalena something to do would stem the tears. When Kajsa finished her porridge, she refilled the bowl and put her boots on.

"I'll be right back. Stay inside."

"Olof fell asleep and seemed to be having a bad dream, thrashing about and calling Manny's name," Lars said when he came to the barn door and accepted the bowl of porridge. "He woke up briefly and asked me to go get Manny."

"Manny?" Kajsa asked.

"Yeah. I think Olof's worried about his brother; they were both around Toby when he was sick."

Kajsa nodded and said, "Yes, and Erik too."

"Manny's alone; I'll go check on him."

"No, you stay here." Kajsa said, "I'll go see him, and I'll also check on Erik and Kerstin."

"I'd rather you didn't go, but I guess we don't have a choice."

* * *

109

Kajsa's first stop was Emanuel's house. She drove the wagon into his yard and stopped perpendicular to the porch.

"Uncle Manny!" She yelled from her seat, startling the two horses and having to haul on the reins to stop them. She pulled the brake handle and tied the reins around it. Alighting from the wagon, Kajsa walked up the stairs and across the porch.

"Uncle Manny, are you okay?" She hollered again, banging on the door with the bottom of her fist, keeping an eye on the horses.

"Don't come in, Kajsa, I have the sickness!" Manny called.

"Are you alone?"

"Yeah." Emanuel was a widower living with his son Jon who was currently with the army in Umeå.

"I'm coming in, Manny." Kajsa called, "and you're coming with me. My Papa is also sick."

"Ahh." Emanuel groaned, "alright, but cover your face."

Kajsa helped Emanuel to the wagon and onto the bed. She covered him with a blanket.

"Holler if you need the pot. I'm going to Erik's to check on him." Kajsa said.

"That is good, Kajsa, don't go slow on my account."

Kajsa drove into Erik's yard much the same way she did at Emanuel's, this time setting the brake before yelling.

"Erik Kiällberg! Kerstin Svedborg!"

Kerstin came out onto the porch, leaning heavily on a railing post, and said, "Stay where you are, Kajsa! Erik is sick, and I am not feeling well."

"Oh, no!" Kajsa said, "Kerstin, you and Erik are coming with me. We will look after you."

"No, I don't want your family to get sick!" Kerstin said.

"We are looking after my Papa and uncle Manny already, Kerstin; two more are not going to make a difference."

110

"Okay, Kajsa, I am grateful." Kerstin said, the relief evident on her face, "I will prepare Erik."

"Can you help me over to the outhouse, Kajsa?" Emanuel asked while they waited.

"Of course, I'll drive the wagon closer."

It was early evening when Kajsa drove the wagon up to the Larsson barn door.

"How is Papa?" Kajsa asked when Lars came out of the barn.

"He is worse, I'm afraid."

"Oh, no!"

"I'll help our friends in and see to the horses. You should go check on the children." Lars said, "I haven't seen them all day, except for Maria and Ollie. Maria brought broth, and Ollie's been hauling water and dumping pans."

* * *

Lars woke up the next morning and stoked the fire. He turned up the oil lamp and went to check on his 'patients.' His first stop was his father-in-law. Even before checking his pulse, Lars knew he had passed in the night.

"Is he gone?" Emanuel asked. He lay a few feet away, his eyes closed.

"Yes, sorry, Manny."

"Aah." Emanuel groaned.

"How are you, Manny?"

"I shit myself, Lars. I'm sorry."

"Don't be sorry, Manny, can't be helped." Lars said, "I'll check on the others and come back to help you."

"Okay." Manny turned his head and looked at the covered form of his brother. "So long, comrade."

111

"Erik, how are you doing?" Lars asked.

"I think I feel better, not by much, but better." Erik was the only one who managed to drink some of Maria's broth and to keep it down.

"Kerstin?"

Nothing. "Kerstin?" Lars repeated, unable to keep the panic from his voice.

"Mmph."

"How are you, Kerstin?"

Kerstin's face was pale and sweating, her lips chapped and her eyelids dark. A powerful smell of sour feces emanated from her. She didn't respond to Lars.

"How is she?" Erik asked.

"Not good, Erik. I am sorry." He got up to get the water and a cloth to wash and cool Kerstin's face.

"Lars?" Erik said.

"Yeah?"

"Where's your handkerchief?"

"Oh, shit!" Lars hurried over to his cot and quickly tied his handkerchief over his lower face.

When he returned, Erik had moved beside his wife.

"I will clean her, Lars," Erik said. He was weak, but there was no way anyone else was going to clean his wife's private areas as long as he was still alive. Lars nodded and went to the barn door. He did not look forward to telling his wife that her father died in the night.

Lars entered the house and stoked the fire. He put water on to boil and went to crush some coffee beans. Kajsa, awakened by the noise, got up and walked to the kitchen.

"Sorry, Kajsa, I was trying to do this quietly."

"It's okay, time for me to get up anyway. How is everyone?"

Lars stopped grinding the beans, and his shoulders slumped. He turned and put his hands on Kajsa's shoulders. "I am sorry, Kajsa. Olof passed away during the night."

"Oh!" Kajsa turned and went to sit at the table. "I have been expecting this." Kajsa had cried most of the night, knowing in her heart that her father was not going to recover from this disease.

"I will send Ollie to get the priest," Lars said.

Kajsa nodded. She knew that her father, and anyone else dying of this disease, would have to be cremated.

19

Johan and Gunnar stood on the road leading into Piteå. They stayed hidden amongst the spruce and poplar trees, looking at two men behind a barricade on the road.

"What do you think, Johan?"

"Let's go talk to them."

They shouldered their muskets and emerged from the bush, and walked down the road toward the barricade. It took a few minutes for the men to notice them.

"Stop!" One of them shouted, "do not come any closer!"

"We are soldiers of the Västerbotten regiment, on our way to Umeå," Johan called from sixty feet away.

"Are you traveling with rödsot?"

"We have two sick."

"Then you are not welcome in our village."

Johan considered this as Gunnar stared at him.

"What do we do, Johan?"

"I think we need to respect their decision, Gunnar," Johan said. "We have enough food, and we have our tents. There's no need to enter the village."

The soldiers were in good condition, well-fed as the Sámi continued to leave food caches along the way. But, Bjorn and Stig had contracted the disease. They were the two soldiers tasked with the cleaning of sergeant Björk.

"Go around then?"

"Yeah."

"We will go around!" Johan yelled and waved to them.

One of the men waved back, clearly relieved.

When the rest of the soldiers arrived, Johan explained the situation.

"Hell, no!" Klas Berg cried, spit flying. Klas was a tall man who possessed an ox's strength; unfortunately, he also had an ox's stubbornness. His shadow, Arne, stood beside and a little behind him. Arne was a shifty character trusted by no one. "We are Swedish soldiers in Sweden! No damn way a couple of dirt farmers will tell me where I can or cannot go!"

"We will go around!" Johan said, standing his ground in front of the much larger man, "we will not bring disease to these good people!"

"Good people?" Klas sputtered, "get the hell out of my way, now!"

"Or what?" Nils asked. He and Matthias moved beside Johan and soon joined by Gunnar and Ulrika. The rest of the group stood off to the side, content to watch the situation unfold without taking part in it.

Klas breathed heavily through his nose, trying to stare them down, then realizing they were not afraid of him, threw a hand in the air and yelled, "fine!" He turned and shouldered his way through the soldiers behind him. Arne weaved his way through the soldiers, not having the bulk or the courage to shoulder any of them.

Johan exhaled and turned to the men and woman, who stood with him, "thank you, comrades."

* * *

The next morning, Johan found Klas and Arne's bedding empty. Outside the tent, Johan followed their tracks until he was sure of their direction. The two sets of footprints in fresh snow went straight back the way they had come the night before, toward Piteå. He stood staring at the tracks, deep in thought, when Matthias came up beside him.

"Klas and Arne?"

"Yeah." Johan sighed.

"Leave them; they will answer to the commanders," Matthias said.

"I worry about why they are so determined to get to Piteå and what they will do when they get there."

"Nothing good, I would wager."

"You don't think we should go back to Piteå?" Johan asked.

"And do what? Enter the village we were denied entry to?" Matthias said.

"Aah!" Johan growled, "those arseholes!"

"Bjorn and Stig are dead."

"Shit! What next?" Johan said, exasperated.

"Ulrika has the shits."

Johan's shoulders slumped.

"I'll gather wood for the pyre." Matthias clapped a hand on Johan's shoulder and then walked away.

Three days later, the group of fifteen approached the outskirts of Skellefteå. Ulrika died the night before, and neither Klas nor Arne returned. The good news, no one else displayed symptoms of the disease.

"What do you think, Johan?" Nils asked, "go in or bypass?"

"Why is it up to me?"

"Well —"

"Let's take a vote," Johan said.

"I need tobacco."

"Me too."

"We're out of coffee."

With the majority voting in favor of entering Skellefteå, the soldiers march forward.

"Look sharp, comrades. The locals will be looking for any sign of sickness amongst us."

They decided to look for a stable with a barn to use as their base. As expected, they found one at the edge of town, across the street from a small sawmill. Gunnar nudged Johan and pointed to a wagon full of bundles wrapped in stained sheets.

"The sickness is here," Johan said just as the barn's man-door opened and someone backed out. He was carrying a wrapped bundle between himself and another man.

"Hey!" The other hollered at them, "are you here to help?"

"No, we are on our way to Umeå; we are here for supplies," Johan answered.

"We need your help."

Before Johan could respond, Nils and Matthias rushed forward.

"Cover your faces!" The man yelled at the brothers.

The Trögers skidded to a stop, dug out their handkerchiefs, snapped them to remove any dried boogers, and tied them over their faces.

"I guess we are helping." Sighed Johan, "what can we do?"

"We need people to clean the patients, haul water, and find firewood, remove and burn the bodies."

Johan looked at the other soldiers, who all nodded back at him.

"We will help." Johan called to the man, then turned back to the soldiers, "let's pool our money for the coffee and tobacco. Gunnar, do you want to go buy them?"

"Yes!" He answered enthusiastically.

"Sven, Calle, can you take our bedrolls and set up camp in that sawmill?"

"Yeah, what if someone tries to stop us?" Calle asked.

"Convince them," Johan said. They dropped their packs, tied handkerchiefs over their noses and mouths, and walked to the stables.

"I am the parish priest, Arvid Jonsson, and this is our mayor, Gerhard Mattson."

Johan shook their hand and introduced the rest of the soldiers. Nils and Matthias, who had taken over the loading of the body, nodded to the two men when introduced.

"I will show you where to take the bodies," Gerhard told them.

With the Tröger's assuming the task of removing and burning the bodies, Arvid assigned duties to the soldiers. Johan and three others would cut and haul firewood, Sven and Calle would cook meals for the soldiers and make broth for the ill, the rest would clean the sick and anything else as required. Their discipline took over, and they soon developed efficient routines. Gunnar became the supply clerk, which included procuring handkerchiefs, blankets, cloth for washing, and food.

Inside the barn, the sick occupied almost every square foot of the floor. The lucky ones were three per stall while the rest were lying in rows in the large central bay. The sick moaned, cried, prayed, and defecated. The smell was oppressive. When they died, others would take their place. As the days passed, the soldiers experienced a variety of emotions. Most had differing levels of depression, anger, helplessness, and fear. On the eighth day, two of the soldiers became sick. Johan called a meeting that morning in the sawmill.

"We have a decision to make." He began, "stay and help or continue our march to Umeå."

"I will remind you that our orders were to return to headquarters at Umeå." Gunnar said, "there was no mention of prolonged stops along the way."

"If we stay, I fear we will all end up piled on the dead wagon." Another said.

Murmurs of agreement spread through the group, now numbering thirteen.

"Let's vote." Nils said, "all in favor of staying?"

Johan raised his hand, and after a brief hesitation, Nils and Matthias raised their hands.

"All in favor of continuing our march?"

Ten hands went up.

"What about Ulf and Peder?" Nils asked. They were the two soldiers who contracted the disease during the night.

"We will have to leave them with the pastor and report their condition when we get to Umeå," Johan said.

Breaking the news to the pastor and mayor went easier than they thought it would.

"Our thanks for all your help, Johan." Gerhard said, "we will take care of your men."

"Thank you, sir."

"Can I ask one more favor of you and your men before you depart?"

"Yes, what is it?" Johan asked.

"Could you cut and pile more firewood for the pyres?"

"Yes, of course."

Thirteen soldiers scoured the woods, cutting, hauling, and piling dry wood all day. It wasn't long before there was a large stockpile near the burning site. Exhausted, the soldiers returned to the sawmill, ate some stale bread and dried meat before crawling under their blankets and dropping into a dreamless sleep.

The next morning, Johan walked into the corral and made his way to the stall where Ulf and Peder lay. He was shocked at how quickly Peder had declined. He didn't wake up when Johan shook his shoulder.

"He was hallucinating during the night." Ulf said, "I couldn't make out all his words, but he seemed to be reliving battles. For almost an hour, he kept calling for his Mama."

Ulf looked pale and sweaty but nowhere near as bad as the others in the barn.

"We are leaving this morning for Umeå, Ulf," Johan said.

Ulf tried to rise, but Johan put his hand on his shoulder, gently pushing him back down.

"You need to stay here, Ulf, to recover."

"No one recovers here, Johan!" Ulf said bitterly, "you know that."

"I am sorry," Johan said, but Ulf had turned his face away from him. Sighing, Johan stood and walked out of the barn. He walked out of the door and leaned heavily on a hitching post with his head down.

"We are grateful, Johan." Gerhard said, "we all do our best, but we cannot save everyone."

He handed Johan a letter. "It is for your commanding officer." He said, "it is my testimony that the local authority requested your help."

Johan took the letter and expressed his gratitude. He had not thought to ask for anything like that. The mayor was more knowledgeable about such matters. Johan walked over to where the soldiers were waiting on the street. He stood in front of them.

"Peder is in a bad way, but Ulf looks strong." He said, "form up, men, let's walk out with pride."

No one spoke as they marched through the village in formation, with Johan in the lead. Everyone was aware of what the soldiers had done for them. People looked out windows as they passed, others walking on boardwalks stopped to watch them, some of the older men coming to attention and saluting, and each time, Johan would call, "on our right," or "on our left." The soldiers would turn their heads to face the old soldiers and return their salutes.

20

January 1809
Larsson Farm

The Larsson's barn soon became the local infirmary. It was not uncommon; there were many such scenarios throughout the countryside. Everyone did what they could for sick family and neighbors. At first, Lars tended the ill by himself in the barn, but as more of the infected arrived, Kajsa and Maria joined him. Anna cooked the meals and looked after Magdalena. Ollie was in charge of the animals and hauled water to the barn. Neighbors Israel and Harald would be summoned when necessary to move the bodies from the barn to the burn site in preparation for the priest's service and the cremation.

Two of the latest cremations included Emanuel and Kerstin. Erik was recovering but still weak. He helped as much as he could before exhaustion overtook him. He refused to wear a face covering.

"It may be because he doesn't care if he lives or dies now that his wife is gone." Kajsa opined one day.

"You may be right -" Lars began to reply before a coughing fit interrupted him. Kajsa looked at her husband with alarm. He was sweating, and the portion of his face above his handkerchief was pasty.

"How are you feeling, Lars?" She asked him when he stopped coughing.

"I am okay, just tired."

An hour later, Kajsa saw Lars rushing out of the barn. She followed him and watched as he ran into the outhouse, one hand clutching his behind. She waited for him to come out, and when he did, he looked frail.

"I will make a bed for you, Lars." She said when he came back to the barn. She held up a hand when he began to protest, "you are sick, Lars. Let me take care of you." He looked at her for a few seconds, then nodded. All he could think about was the humiliation of soiling himself in front of everyone in the barn; friends and neighbors he had worked beside and gone to church with will witness his indignity.

"Erik has recovered, as you will," Kajsa said.

Most of the afflicted were sleeping, so Maria and Erik took a break. They sat by the door drinking water while Kajsa knelt beside Lars, occasionally wiping his face with a cool, damp cloth.

"My parents died of this disease, did you know that, Maria?" Erik said.

"No, I did not know that. How old were you, uncle?"

"Eleven, or maybe twelve. I stayed with them after they died until the smell began." Erik said. "I was weak from lack of food, but I managed to carry my parents out to a nice area beneath a tree where they liked to sit some evenings. I buried my mother first and then started to dig my father's grave when a huge soldier came by and offered help. I turned him down. I needed to finish it myself."

"Why?"

"I don't know; I just knew I had to finish it."

Maria thought about that for a while and then said, "I think I understand."

"The soldier, his name was Johan."

"The same name as my Johan!" Maria said.

"Yes, but this Johan was a giant man! He gave me some of his lunch; it was the first food I had in days." Erik continued. "When he turned to leave, I asked him if I could walk with him for a while. Johan agreed, and we walked for miles. He was on his way to training, and I asked him if I could join the army. He told me the only way for me to join at such a young age would be as a drummer."

"I remember Grandpa saying you were a drummer in the war!"

"Yes, I went with Johan, and your grandpa and Manny, Jakob and Pehr, to Pomerania to fight the Prussians."

"Mama told us about Jakob and Pehr!" Maria said excitedly.

"Jakob died at a town called Malchin, and we thought Pehr died there too. But he was just wounded and taken prisoner. The Prussians left him at a farm; Pehr had lost his memory from his head wound."

"I would like to meet Pehr someday," Maria said.

"It will have to be soon; he must be 70 now." Erik mused.

"Then what happened, uncle?"

"In the winter of 1757, Manny, Johan, and I were taken prisoner by the Prussians at Demmin. They forced us to march in the bitter cold in our summer uniforms with little food. One morning, after the coldest night of the year, we found Johan had frozen to death. He had put his cloak around me during the night."

Erik was quiet for a few seconds, and Maria was about to speak when she saw tears rolling down the side of his face.

"I am tired, Maria; I think I will lay down for a while," Erik said after a few minutes.

"Okay. Erik?"

"Yeah?"

"Can you tell me more about the war when you wake up?"

"Yes. I will."

Maria watched Erik weave through the sleeping ill to his bed. He was always just Uncle Erik to her and her siblings. She never thought about what he did in his life before she knew him.

A knock on the door broke her out of her reverie.

"Maria, Harald is ill," Israel said when she cracked the door enough to see who was outside.

"Oh, no!" Maria gasped, "I am sorry, sir."

"Can I bring him in?"

"Of course, stay outside; I will come out to get him." Maria turned and caught her mother's eye. She waved her over.

"It's Harald." She said when Kajsa came to the door.

Kajsa nodded. She couldn't think of anything to say, her emotions frazzled.

"How are you, Israel?" Kajsa asked when she met him outside. Maria had gone to Harald, who lay in the wagon bed, where all the bodies had once lain.

"I am well, Kajsa."

"And Frida and Eva?"

"They are well too." Israel said, "thank you, Kajsa."

"I will look after your son."

Israel nodded and then watched as Kajsa and Maria helped Harald into the barn. They placed Harald beside Lars so Kajsa could spend more time with both of them.

"Will he be okay, Mama?" Maria asked when they moved back to the front of the barn.

"Harald always seemed to be sick when he was little." Kajsa said, "I fear he won't survive this illness."

The tears came quickly to Maria. She has been friends with Eva and Harald for most of her life. Maria thought of all the times she and Eva had chased Harald away when he tried to follow them. Eva!

"Did you ask about Eva?"

"Yes, Eva and her mother are both well," Kajsa said.

"Why did this sickness have to come here, Mama?"

"I don't know, Maria."

"Do you think I will get to be married and have children?"

"Of course, you will!"

"What if I get sick, or Johan gets sick, or if he dies in the fighting?" Maria cried, overcome with all the dangers threatening her future.

Kajsa couldn't think of anything to say; her faith tested with the deaths of her father and uncle and her husband fighting for his life on the barn's frozen floor. All she could do was hug her daughter.

That evening during a quiet period, Maria sat down near Erik and asked, "can you tell me more about the war?"

"Yeah, okay," Erik said, laying his head back on a rolled-up coat he used as a pillow. "Where was I?"

"Your large friend froze to death."

"Oh yeah. But Johan Berg was more than a friend. He and his wife, Sigrid, took me in and treated me like a son. Sigrid, by the way, married your uncle Manny after the war."

"Really?" Maria said, "how come I have never heard this before?"

"I guess it never came up. Anyway, for several weeks, I stumbled along in a daze." Erik said. "Manny looked after me, although I didn't know it at the time. Then one night, the Prussian camp came under attack."

"Who attacked you?" Maria asked.

"Not us. Austrian soldiers were attacking our captors, the Prussians," Erik said. "Austria was our ally during the war. But they could not tell us apart from the Prussians in the dark, so we had to be careful. We saw a Prussian on horseback get hit by a cannonball, and it took his head clean off!" It turns out the man was a Prussian prince! He still sat on the horse, hands holding the reins, and no head!" Erik chuckled, "I laugh now, but that was traumatic at the time. Anyway, Manny ran up and pulled the dead man off the horse, threw me over the saddle, mounted, and rode the horse away in a hail of musket balls. How we got away without being hit still amazes me. We made our way to the Austrian's main camp and surrendered to them."

"Surrendered?" Maria asked, "I thought they were your allies?"

"They were, but they did not know we were Swedes until they interrogated us. They took the Prince's horse, a magnificent animal by the way, and put us on a farmer's wagon pulled by a broken-down old nag. We finally made it back to Swedish lines. We made our way to Stralsund and stayed there for the rest of the winter. Many soldiers there suffered from the rödsot."

"You had rödsot there too?" Maria asked.

"Yeah, but I never got it until now," Erik said. "We lost more soldiers to sickness than from battle. It was terrible; we still wore our summer uniforms, and the food consisted of salted pork and pickled herring. I swore I would never eat those two foods ever again after the war."

"Hey!" Maria said. "I saw you eat pickled herrings!"

"Yes, but it was many years later." Erik sighed. "We next fought at a town called Malchin. That was where Pehr got shot in the head, and Jakob bayonetted. Jakob was trying to save Pehr when he was attacked and killed from behind. Jakob was our best fighter, no way he would have lost a fight if the attack had come from the front!"

"But Pehr is still alive!" Maria said. Her forehead wrinkled in consternation.

"Yes, he was only wounded, lots of blood, and knocked unconscious. We all thought he had died but, after they drove us back, the Prussians discovered him alive. They took Pehr prisoner, leaving him at a farmer's house where he stayed for the rest of the war. He said he lost his memory, and it came back when the war was ending."

"You don't believe that?" Maria asked, sensing Erik's skepticism.

"I would like to." Erik sighed. "I am tired, Maria."

"Okay. Can I get you anything?"

"Some water would be nice. Thank you, Maria."

21

Three days later, Johan rode into the Larsson yard on Tobias's horse. Tobias had loaned Johan his horse telling Johan he was doing him a favor. The horse did not get regular exercise while stabled in Umeå. The commander granted Johan leave after handing him a letter from Israel with the news that Harald was on his death bed.

He tied his horse at the hitching post in front of the house and knocked on the door.

"Aah!" Anna cried and then hugged him. "Maria is in the barn."

"Thank you, Anna." Johan turned to go then stopped, his back to Anna, "is Harald -"

"He died yesterday."

Johan dropped his head, and Anna had to fight the urge to hug him again. He nodded and went out the door.

"Cover your face!" Erik yelled when Johan walked into the barn. He quickly complied.

"Johan!" Maria whispered and then went to him.

"You know about Harald?" She said as they held each other.

"Yes, Anna told me."

"I am sorry, Johan." Maria said, "my father died two days ago."

"Oh, Maria." They continued to hold each other until Kajsa called for her.

"I have to go," Maria said.

"Okay, I need to go home for a few days." Johan said, "I will stop here on my way back."

Maria watched Johan walk out the door.

Maybe I need to stop loving people to stop the pain.

Too many people she loved have died.

"Maria!" Kajsa called, "I need you."

She went to help her mother with the latest crisis.

I am so tired!

Later that evening, Maria sat on the floor with her back to the wall near the barn door. Erik, sensing her despair, walked over and sat down beside her.

"This is like war, Maria." Erik said, waving a hand in front of him, "We fight against an enemy, and along the way, we lose friends and family. But we keep on fighting because there are so many others that depend on us."

Maria thought about that and looked over at Erik, "are we winning, uncle?"

"I honestly don't know, but I do know we will win as long as we keep on fighting."

"Thank you, uncle." Maria smiled at him. "that reminds me, what happened next, in Pomerania?"

Out of respect for Maria's loss, Erik had stopped telling his story after Lars died. But now, it may provide a welcome distraction. Erik took out his pipe, filled the bowl, and lit the tobacco. Maria loved the smell of the sweet smoke; it was the same brand of tobacco her father used to smoke.

"Let me see now. Oh yeah, we were near the village of Klempenow when next we fought the Prussians. We held the bridge when they attacked. They didn't have a chance; we shot them to pieces both times they tried to cross the bridge. I had sympathy for them, charging towards certain death as they did."

"They retreated and went upriver to cross at the next bridge, and we sent men to stop them but were too late. The Prussians crossed the river and advanced on us from our rear, and we had to retreat. A few days later, we received orders to take back the bridge from the Prussians. It was now our turn to charge into a hail of musket balls and cannon fire. I drummed the soldiers forward, increase the cadence to a charge. Our soldiers yelled their battle cries and charged onto the bridge. The Prussian muskets roared, and through the clouds of smoke, I saw our men begin to fall, friends of mine, but I kept on drumming."

Erik went quiet; his pipe forgotten while tears ran freely down his cheeks. Maria sat waiting for him to continue. Tears welled up at the corner of her eyes and spilled over.

He cleared his throat and continued, "Olof and Manny both went down, and then there was no one left standing. I walked onto the bridge, and I swore at the Prussians!" Erik laughed, shaking his head and wiping his eyes.

"What did you say, uncle?" Maria asked with a mischievous grin.

"Oh, those words are not for your ears." Erik said, returning the grin, "I saw some of the Prussians raise their guns, but the commanding officer held up his hand, and they lowered their muskets. I went to Manny first and helped him up. He was shot in the leg and had a broken wrist. I next helped Olof up. He had taken a musket ball to the shoulder."

"Grandpa never told us about that," Maria said.

"I got a medal for bravery that day, but it was Olof and Manny who deserved a medal that day, not me."

"Really, where is your medal?"

"In my soldier's trunk, at home. Kerstin used to take it out and clean-"

"I'm sorry, uncle."

129

Erik nodded, cleared his throat, and continued, "that was the end of the war for Manny and Olof. Their injuries made them unable to fight, so they were shipped home. I stayed in Pomerania for the remainder of the war but never again took part in another large battle, just a few small skirmishes here and there. Our biggest battle was with lice and disease."

A few weeks ago, the mention of lice would repulse Maria, but not after everything she had witnessed in this barn of late.

"As we were preparing to leave Pomerania, I was at our base in Stralsund when a prisoner arrived. He wore ragged clothing, but his walk looked familiar. I asked the guard, a friend of mine, who that prisoner was. He told me his name was Pehr. I had to make sure it was him. Now you have to remember, we all thought Pehr died; Olof and Manny had witnessed his death."

Maria nodded.

"So, I tricked the guard into letting me into the stockade, and I went to his cell. It was your uncle Pehr! He told me about how he woke up at a farm and that he had lost his memory. The musket ball had ricocheted off his skull, lots of blood but not fatal. Anyway, when the war was over, he said his memory returned, so he came to Stralsund, thinking he would rejoin the army and sail home. But the commander didn't believe him and put him under arrest. I heard they were going to execute him the next day for desertion."

Erik had cleaned his pipe bowl and was packing more tobacco in as Maria waited patiently.

"Then what?" She asked after he had lit the pipe and was leisurely puffing on it.

"What? Oh. So, I helped him escape by distracting the guard. That is the last I saw of Pehr for many years. No one knew where he was. It turns out he became a shoemaker in Prussia, even owned a store."

"But I thought Pehr lived in Norway?"

"Yes, that was later, after the troubles on the Viking Trail. But that is another story."

After a lengthy silence, Maria asked, "well?"

"Well, what?"

'Are you going to tell me the story?"

"No."

Another silence.

"Why not?"

"Only Pehr knows the whole story."

"Hmph, we can't even visit him with the wars and this disease!"

"Things will get back to normal; I promise you that, Maria."

"Can you promise I will not get sick and die, and Johan will survive the war?"

Erik was taken aback by the question. He did not realize the extent of Maria's anxiety; he had no words for her.

22

Johan rode into his family's farmyard. Dagmar, Tobias's horse, nickered, and Agnes returned the greeting. Johan unsaddled Dagmar and rubbed her down with the saddle blanket before releasing her into the corral. Dagmar wandered in, dropped to the ground, and rolled in the dirt while Agnes watched from a distance. Agnes wandered over in a roundabout route, then stopped and stared at Dagmar. Dagmar got up and slowly wandered over to Agnes. The two horses touched noses and blew into each other's nostrils. They then chased each other around the pen.

Israel had come out of the barn and walked over beside Johan.

"Look at Agnes, Papa; she is acting like a foal!"

"Huh, where did the horse come from?"

"Tobias loaned her to me to come home."

"You heard about Harald then."

"Yes." The two men stood silently, both resting their forearms on the top rail of the corral, watching the two horses frolic around the pen.

"What kind of horse is that?" Israel asked.

"Tobias said she's one of his father's crossbreeds, Icelandic and Sámi."

"She looks solid, a little small, though."

"Yes, I would like to get one like her someday."

They stood for a while admiring the horse, then Israel said, "Go inside and see your mother, Johan."

An hour later, Johan went back out to the barn with two enamel cups. He dug into his saddlebags, took out a flask, and walked over to his father, handing him one of the cups. Johan pulled the cork out of the flask with his teeth and filled his father's cup half full of brännvin and then did the same with his cup. Israel looked at Johan for a while and then nodded. He sat on a milking stool while Johan upended a pail to sit on.

"This is good!" Israel said, after sipping the drink, "what is it."

"Brännvin."

"Hmph. Can I make it?"

"I'm not sure; I can ask when I get back to Umeå." Johan took a deep breath and then said, "Mama wants me to come home and live here after the war, with Maria."

"Yeah, she mentioned that. She's worried I can't handle the farm alone now that Harald is gone."

"Well, you're not young anymore."

"Young enough to take you over my knee!" Israel said, "pass me the flask."

"Do you feel the same way? About me moving back here, with a wife?"

"Well, I can still take care of the farm and, if I need help, your brothers are nearby. And you will be close. I hadn't considered it, but I suppose you will get Harald's five acres to add to your five."

"Okay." Johan said, "I should fall some trees for a house now, so the wood will be well seasoned when the war is over."

"That is a good idea, son." Israel's mood improved with that situation settled.

By sundown, they had their arms around each other's shoulders and were singing bawdy tavern songs that they had taught each other. Of course, Israel knew more songs and did most of the teaching. Once the brännvin had run out, Israel produced a jug of his homebrew. Later that evening, after Frida had given up on calling them in for supper, she sent Eva out with two food plates for them. Eva lingered in the barn, amused at how they were acting, although she couldn't understand half the words they were slurring. When their language got a little too salty, Eva went back to the house. Walking across the yard, she noticed the wind had picked up considerably, and snow began to fall.

Several hours later, they ran out of homebrew.

"I have some more in the kitchen." Israel slurred. They were quite drunk at this point. He pushed on the door and fell back into the barn, Johan catching him, and then both fell.

"Door got stuck," Israel mumbled.

Johan got up and pulled Israel up, almost going down again before he braced himself.

"Let me try," Johan said and then gave the door a push. It didn't move.

"Try the big doors," Israel said, he had retaken his seat.

The large double doors did not move. Johan threw his shoulder into the doors and immediately regretted it.

Did someone lock us inside?

"Go up to the loft door and see what's blocking the doors," Israel said. He was swaying on his stool.

"Okay." Johan, in his present condition, should have been concerned with climbing ladders but instead felt invincible. He climbed the ladder and walked across the loft to the door they used to lift hay. Snow blasted Johan when he opened the door. A strong wind blew the snow sideways in his direction. He shielded his face and peered down at the door, and was shocked to see snow piled to the tops of the doors.

"We're snowed in!" Johan yelled when he shut the loft door. No answer. Johan went to the loft's edge, lowered himself to his belly, and looked under the loft edge. His father had fallen over and was snoring contentedly.

What do I do?

We can't stay out here all night and freeze to death.

Mama and Eva can't dig us out.

Why did I drink so much?

There was a large scoop shovel down by their milk cow's stall. Johan would have to go down, get the shovel, climb back up, jump down from the loft door, and then dig a path to the man-door. The yard wasn't as deep as most of the snow blew across to the barn.

I am so tired!

Dammit!

Johan climbed down the ladder, slipping on the third rung from the bottom and dropping the rest of the way, catching a rung under his jaw. His teeth clacked painfully. Cursing, he went to get the shovel and climbed back up the ladder, carefully. He went to the loft door, opened it, and, without hesitation, jumped out. He landed in the snow, sinking to his waist. After struggling mightily, he finally worked his way out of the deep snow.

He was on his hands and knees, trying to catch his breath when he heard someone yelling at him. It was Eva, standing on the porch. He waved to her and then began shoveling a path to the door. He stooped twice, once to catch his breath and once to vomit.

"Watch your step." He said to Eva when she appeared behind him.

"Why?" She said, "eew!"

Johan handed her the shovel and sat against the edge of the tunnel he had made. They finally cleared a path to the door and managed to pull it open. Israel wouldn't come fully awake, so they each draped an arm over a shoulder and carried him to the house. The cold air hitting the sweat on Johan's back chilled him to the core.

By the time the storm had subsided, Johan was overdue at the base. He road Dagmar straight to Umeå without stopping at the Larssons.

23

In early March, Johan was back in Tornio. With him was his friend and Maria's cousin, Jon Emanuelsson. They were part of a force with soldiers from several regiments sent to relieve some of the men stationed there. The force protecting the northern gateway into Sweden numbered seven thousand.

Tobias and the Trögers were south of Umeå with colonel Sandels's battalion. Before Tobias left, Johan had expressed his gratitude to Tobias for his horse's loan a few months earlier. Due to the weather, Johan did not face disciplinary action for technically being AWOL when he returned a day late.

"It is not much better here since we left in December," Johan observed. They had just arrived and were looking for their barracks. Some new, clapboard buildings had been built since they were here last.

"No, but it's just as cold," Jon said. "And it won't be the same without the Trögers."

"Yeah, and no Ulrika Dahl, either."

"Oh yeah!" Jon mused. "Tell me, Johan, did you ever have relations with him, I mean her?"

"Ugh! She was a handsome woman and all, but I can't get over the fact that we thought she was a man for months. I even washed in front of her!"

"Did she look?"

"I don't know!" Johan said.

"Hey, let's go find a good barracks before all the best ones are full!"

"Good idea, Jon!"

And they ran, laughing like children. Rounding a corner of the storehouse, Jon ran into an officer, knocking him down and landing on top.

"What the hell?!" The major bellowed.

"Sorry, sir!" Jon said, still laying on top of the major.

"Get the hell off of me!"

"Oh. Right!" Jon pushed himself off of the major. In his haste, he did not notice his right hand sinking into fresh horse droppings.

"Help me up!" The Major demanded, holding out his hand.

Jon grasped the proffered hand and hauled back on it, pulling him halfway up before the Major's hand slipped through Jon's manure slippery hand. The Major fell backward into the aforementioned manure mound.

"Fek!" The Major bellowed. "Get out of my sight!"

Relieved to be given an escape, Jon bolted around the building.

"Here, sir," Johan said, holding out his hand. "It is clean." He clarified, seeing the look of suspicion on the Major's face.

"Do you know that man?"

"Never saw him before," Johan said with a straight face.

"I see. What is your name, soldier?"

"Sparrman, sir, Johan Sparrman."

"Well, Johan Sparrman, I am Major Öden Love. Welcome to hell."

"Aah, thank you, sir." Johan said, "but I have been here before, after the retreat."

"Is that so? Both you and Sven?" Öden asked, jerking his thumb toward the direction in which Jon had disappeared.

"You mean Jon? Shit. Sorry, sir."

"Hah!" Öden laughed. "Go find a clean pallet; I recommend the third bunkhouse on the right.

"Thank you, sir!"

It wasn't until after the evening meal before Johan realized the third bunkhouse, where he laid claim to a bunk near the door, was situated next to the latrines. The bunkhouses were stick and frame buildings with rough-sawn board siding. The boards had shrunk after drying, leaving gaps as large as a quarter inch in some places.

Johan was sitting on his bunk, talking to Jon, who had the bunk opposite his. The ripe aroma from the latrines seeped into the bunkhouse through the walls.

"He did this on purpose? Told you to bunk here?" Jon asked. He had been slinking around camp, avoiding the major since the incident.

"Yeah, but I think he did it as a joke," Johan said. "He seems to have a sense of humor about him."

The door slammed open with a bang, and in strode the major. The soldiers in the barracks jumped to attention.

"Jon, with shit on his hands!" He yelled. "Step forward!"

Jon was standing behind where Öden stood, having just avoided the door crashing inward. He stepped forward, inches from the Major.

"Yes, sir!" Yelled Jon, causing Öden to wince and to wipe spittle off the side of his face.

"Fortuitous that you quartered so close to the latrines," Öden said, turning to stand nose to nose with Jon. "You will be in charge of cleaning the latrines. You will clean them in the morning before reveille, after all the meals, and after lights out!"

Turning to leave, he nodded to Johan. "Smells here. Why would you choose such a smelly location?"

"Must have been divine guidance, sir."

"Hah!" The Major bent over laughing. He laughed so hard a small fart escaped him, which made him laugh harder. He was still chuckling as he walked out of the bunkhouse.

"You two seem to be good friends!" Grumbled Jon, waving the fart scent away from his face.

"The trick is not to knock him on his ass and drop him in manure."

"Ha, ha."

* * *

"Johan!" Jon cried as he banged on the latrine door. "The Russians are coming!"

"Okay, Jon." Johan chuckled. It was good to chuckle about something after the night he had. Something from the evening meal had not agreed with him, to say the least. He did not quite make it to the outdoor toilet in the middle of the night when the shits started. He had to drop his pants on the path to the latrine and squat before a hot stream of diarrhea spewed out. His immediate fear was and still is that he got infected with dysentery. Since that first bout, he had spent most of the night sitting in the outhouse, only venturing out to look for water or when another soldier needed to use the facilities. After smelling diarrhea, most soldiers would give him a disgusted look as they walked by him, but some looked at him with sympathy. All gave him a wide berth. Now, early in the morning, he felt like a red-hot poker had prodded his arse.

"Come on! Grab what you can carry; we are moving out!" Jon called. Johan could hear his friend's receding footsteps and realized this was no joke.

"Shit," Johan muttered. At least his stomach felt empty now. His ribs hurt like hell, and he felt weak, but he thought the worst has passed.

Walking gingerly and slightly hunched out of the latrine, Johan witnessed what looked like coordinated confusion. Soldiers ran in every direction while officers bellowed orders from horseback. The panic was palpable. He was almost to his barracks when Major Öden Love reined his horse into a skidding halt.

"You don't look well, Sparrman!"

"It is nothing, sir. Something I ate last night." Johan answered after saluting.

"Are you certain it's not the rödsot?"

"Yes, I will be okay."

"Maybe you should stay here with the sick," Öden said.

"I am okay, sir. Wait. What do you mean, stay here?"

The Major ignored the question and said, "the Russians have crossed the Kemi River in force; they are coming."

"I am ready to fight, sir," Johan said, straightening up even though his abdomen was still a little cramped.

"No, son. We are in an indefensible position here with the gulf and river frozen over. We will retire to Kalix and mount our defense there."

"Yes, sir." Johan saluted again.

Öden returned the salute, wheeled his horse around, and galloped off. Johan rushed into his barracks, gathered his backpack, bedroll, musket, sword, and canteen, and ran out to join his unit.

Johan stepped into the column beside Jon.

"Is it the rödsot, Johan" Jon edged away from Johan.

"No, it was the pork we had last night."

"I had the pork, and I'm okay."

"I'm good, Jon." Johan said, "if it were rödsot, I would be in no condition to be marching."

"That is true," Jon said, moving back in line with Johan.

They were marching westward through Tornio and were passing the infirmary. A few haggard-looking men were trying to walk out of the barracks. The only thing covering them were soiled threadbare woolen blankets.

"What are they doing?" Jon asked.

"They are to be left behind," Johan said, remembering what Öden had said earlier.

"No! You remember what the Russians did to healthy prisoners?"

"Yes, I remember," Johan said dejectedly.

They marched past the sick soldiers who held out their hands, some pleading, "don't leave us." Johan and Jon, and everyone else in the column, had friends in the sick barracks. Most of the marching men had tears streaming down their faces. None will ever forget those soldiers left behind.

That night, the temperature dropped to -37°C. Rather than camp on the trail, they stopped a few times to eat and warm themselves before continuing. The soldiers could not get their fingers to work at one stop, so they huddled together to rest without a fire to warm them.

No one talked as they marched. Everyone concentrated on putting one foot in front of the other as a strong wind blew in from the gulf. Snow hit their faces like pellets, and the temperature dropped several more degrees. Many soldiers suffered severe frostbite on their faces, ears, fingers, and toes. It took two days to march the thirty-two miles to Kalix.

24

Gösta Mårtensson stared resolutely at the snowpack covering the Bay of Bothnia. He stood with thirty-five hundred fellow Russian Imperial Army soldiers on the western coast of Finland. They had been waiting in the bitter cold for Field Marshal Barclay de Tolly to lead them out onto the ice.

Gösta could care less who would be victorious. He had another mission in mind; to exact revenge on the people that he blamed for his exile from Sweden. He fled Sweden at seventeen after he had raped the local pastor's wife, Camilla, beaten the pastor, and stolen their horse and buggy.

It was her own damn fault, leading me on as she did.

He blamed the pastor for interrupting his relations with Camilla, which, until then, was consensual, thoroughly enjoyable, and quite educational. That had changed after the pastor arrived home unexpectedly, discovering the two of them in the throes of passion and then pulling Gösta off his wife. That resulted in Gösta severely beating the pastor and then forcefully satisfying his lust on the suddenly non-consenting Camilla before fleeing the parsonage with the pastor's horse and buggy.

They will pay for what my life has become!

In the twenty-seven years since fleeing his homeland, Gösta had wandered Finland. He always seemed to be one step ahead of local authorities or angry husbands, running from his latest misadventure. Most were episodes of adultery with someone's wife, some willing, some not. He preferred the unwilling. Other misdeeds included theft, muggings, and assaults. After several years, he ran out of towns where he was welcome and had migrated southeast to St. Petersburg, Russia, where he found himself in the army. He did not remember the circumstances of his enlistment other than it was not voluntary. It was at the end of an extended drinking spree.

The Field Marshall finally appeared on horseback, trotted to the column's vanguard, and unceremoniously gave the order to advance. Barclay had sent the Russian First battalion to mark the best route through the fractured ice the day before. Ice ridges resembling a mountain range had formed when sea ice expanded, pushed sheets skyward, and then froze in place. Gösta and his comrades marched onto the bay and began their journey. A journey estimated to be about seventy miles through, around, and over the ice fractures and ridges. Vasily, the soldier to Gösta's right, glanced over at him and was about to make conversation with him when he saw the menacing scowl on his face. He slowly edged away from Gösta. Vasily decided he should find another place in the column, as far as he could from this fearsome-looking man.

After a few yards, the troops marched past the mounted officers. The mounts will follow on snow that was packed by thirty-five hundred pairs of boots. Gösta found himself weaving between blocks of ice and, at times, crawling over them. The regimented formation broke down, much to the relief of Vasily. Each soldier had to make their way through the icy obstacle course of the gulf's shoreline. Vasily took this opportunity to put as much distance as he could between himself and Gösta. The move would turn out to be a fatal decision on his part.

Vasily was a hundred yards from shore when he stepped on a patch of snow. The patch looked like all the rest of the snow, but underneath, the ice had fractured. Before he could react, Vasily fell through the fracture and plunged into the frigid waters of the bay. He instinctively sucked in his breath before he was submerged and dragged under the ice by the undertow. The thousands of boots moving in one direction on top of the ice caused waves to form underneath.

The panic didn't set in immediately. The shock of the cold water and Vasily's anger at his carelessness dominated his senses. It was when he began searching above him for an opening in the ice when the panic crept in. He was a fit man with large lung capacity, but he knew he had to quickly find a way through the ice. Frustrated, he began pounding the ice with a fist, which amounted to a useless bumping. The ice above him was translucent, and he could see a shape moving above him. In desperation, Vasily opened his mouth and yelled, "HELP!" Ice cold water filled his mouth, and he did not have the breath to push it out. Succumbing to his fate, Vasily calmly inhaled the water, which quickly filled his lungs. He slowly drifted down, curious to see what was on the bottom. Before he could find out, his mind went blank.

* * *

After four hours of dragging wagons and canons around and over the ice field, it became apparent they could not continue their journey with their wagons. Barclay stood watching the men struggle with a wagon loaded with supplies. The pillars of ice seemingly impassible.

"Leave them!" He yelled. "Take two day's supplies out and leave the wagons where they stand!"

Thus, it was that they left the wagons. Some soldiers took the horses and canons on lengthy detours around the worst of the obstacles. Barclay would not leave his artillery behind! Officers and soldiers alike crawled over the boulders and squeezed through gaps for two more hours before emerging onto the barren, ice-covered sea.

Their relief was short-lived, however, when the wind rose. Gradually at first, then growing in intensity to almost hurricane level. Barclay, and not for the first time, considered turning back. But that would make him appear a quitter and a failure, here and in Russia. So, he bent forward and stumbled on. The wind buffeted his face with snow and ice crystals and took his breath away. Tears froze on his cheeks, and ice had crusted on his mutton chops. He could no longer feel the tips of his nose and ears. Barclay was no stranger to bitter cold, but he never had in his life experienced such cold as this where it seemed to seep into the marrow of his bones. The constant shivering was draining his energy. He turned his back to the wind and saw his fellow officers stumbling along like drunken men.

This is crazy, but we have to keep going, even if it kills us all!

In February of 1807, Barclay commanded troops covering the Russian army's retreat from Napoleon's Grand Army in East Prussia at the Battle of Eylau. At the town of Gofa, his troops, against all odds, constricted the entire Napoleonic army. He did not back down then, and he will not back down now.

His officers followed his example and turned their backs to the wind. Barclay watched them and thought with a chuckle, *my officers have turned their backs on me! That is a story I will enjoy telling over vodka someday!* Just then, one of his generals tripped on a clump of ice, stumbled, and the wind first stood him upright and then blew him face-first onto a clear patch of ice. Barclay rushed over and knelt beside the man.

"Yakov, are you okay?"

"I think so. Fortunately, my face broke the fall!" Yakov yelled over the howling wind, grimacing at the effort.

"Hah!" Barclay guffawed. Then, more seriously, "is it broken?"

"Yeah, I think it is."

Barclay knelt in front of Yakov, grasped both of his jaws in his hands, and placed his thumbs on either side of Yakov's bloody and crooked nose.

"Yup, it's broken." And he quickly pushed hard, popping the nose back into place or close to it.

"Damn it!" Yakov howled, then contritely, "sir."

"It is alright, comrade," Barclay said, holding his hand out to him. "Let's go."

The blowing snow obliterated Barclay's field of vision but what he could see was not comforting. All order had broken down; troops were in disarray, stumbling along following the tracks of those before them. Although he worried about soldiers losing their way in the blowing snow, Barclay accepted this under the current conditions.

Four hours later, exhaustion was taking its toll. The wind seemed to have abated, and there was less blowing snow. Barclay saw soldiers stumble and fall, helped up by their comrades, and then shuffle forward with heads down. He called a halt when they reached a shelf of ice pushed up and over the surface ice, which offered relief from the wind. The cooks built several fires and prepared food. Many soldiers curled up to sleep close to the cooking fires, too exhausted to wait for their suppers.

After the meal, they set up Barclay's tent beside the ice ridge, and here he gathered his officers.

"What happened to you, Yakov?" Major Dmitry Ilyin asked when he saw Yakov's black eyes and blood-encrusted nose.

"The Field Marshall; he helped me after I fell."

"Well then, I better not fall in front of him!" Dmitry said.

Despite the circumstances and the borderline insult, Barclay burst out laughing, soon joined by the others.

"How many missing?" Barclay asked after they recovered.

The officers reported their numbers; in total, fifteen soldiers were missing.

"I heard reports of men walking along and disappearing through the ice." One officer said. "The soldier behind would find the missing man's tracks leading to a hole in the ice. A hole previously covered by a thin layer of crusted snow."

The officers dutifully shook their heads.

"The temperature's dropping," Barclay said. "I fear we will lose many more men if we overnight here."

"You want to keep going through the night?" Alexander Nikishin, another Major, asked.

"Yes, we will leave at midnight. That will give the men another five hour's rest."

The men considered this, each in their own way for a long minute before slowly nodding.

"It is wise, your plan," Yakov said. The others voiced their agreement.

"Relay the order and get some rest; we leave at midnight," Barclay said, dismissing his officers.

25

Gösta leaned forward into gale-force winds. He had the look of someone pulling a plow through heavy clay. Snow and ice pellets peppered his face as he followed the footprints of those in front of him before they disappeared with the drifting snow. The officers had ordered the march to resume at midnight after six hours of rest. Gösta wasn't sure if the rest had been a good thing or bad. All he did for the six hours was waste energy shivering. Getting up to march was extremely difficult; the only saving grace was the cup of vodka dispensed by the cooks. But the warmth it provided was short-lived.

After several hours, the wind abated somewhat. Gösta was stumbling along mindlessly like all the rest when he nearly tripped over a soldier lying on the ice, curled up in a fetal position. Cursing, He stepped around the man and continued forward. The soldier behind him hollered, "Hey! Help me with this man!"

"Leave him," Gösta shouted without turning around.

The soldier bent and tried to revive the fallen soldier without much luck. Another soldier arrived, and, between them, they got the man to his feet. He couldn't walk without support, so the two soldiers had to help him, which further drained their energy reserves. Gösta glanced back and shook his head, "idiots," he mumbled.

The army stopped several times throughout the night for short rests, each more difficult than the last to get back up and continue walking. At one stop, Gösta spotted the two men who had stopped to help the fallen soldier.

"Where's your friend?" He asked them when they approached.

They glared at him and walked past without comment.

"You left him on the ice to die, didn't you!" It was a statement rather than a question.

One of the soldiers turned back but, after seeing Gösta clearly for the first time, decided against confronting him. Gösta grinned at their receding backs, shook his head, and went looking for food.

The wind died down, and the marching became easier. Exhaustion seeped into the depths of their bodies; their limbs felt like they were weighted down. The soldiers concentrated on placing one foot in front of the other. Gösta noticed with alarm that the snow seemed to be getting deeper. For most of their journey so far, the ice was either windswept or covered with hard-packed snow. Now, he noticed his shoes sinking into the snow cover.

By late afternoon, the snow had become knee-deep. Progress slowed, and Gösta soon caught up with the soldiers in front of him. Looking behind, he was not surprised to see hundreds of soldiers packed together.

I hope the ice holds up under all the weight!

And just as he thought that an officer bellowed, "spread out!"

"Look!" A soldier yelled, pointing westward.

Everyone within earshot squinted into the early evening gloom.

"There!" Someone yelled. "I see it; a fire!"

In the distance, a speck of light winked at them through the falling snow. With renewed energy, the soldiers pushed through the deep snow. Those breaking trail in front moved to the rear when they tired, and other soldiers moved forward to take their place. Finally, men of the first battalion emerged from the curtain of falling snow. They led the way to a Swedish island post that they had captured earlier that day. They were now only twelve miles off the Swedish coast. Dozens of able-bodied soldiers began dismantling the wood from two merchant ships frozen in the ice. They burned the wood to warm and cook for the thirty-five hundred soldiers, less, of course, the fifteen missing soldiers. The lights of a hundred campfires on the bay, visible from Umeå, panicked the town's residents. Shouts of "the Russians are coming!" echoed throughout the streets.

The next morning, Gösta was near the vanguard of Barclay's forces when they marched toward Umeå. As always, before an impending battle, he felt the bloodlust building. He was not happy to see a Swedish envoy approaching them under a flag of truce. Gösta watched as the envoy handed Barclay a letter. It was a request from the Swedish commander for a parley, which Barclay indicated agreement.

The Swedes, caught by surprise and with only 1,000 men, surrendered the town and its supplies. They retreated south as the Russians entered Umeå from the east. The Russians took possession of the Swedish barracks and set up a command post in the officer's quarters. As agreed in the parley, Barclay strictly forbade any looting or abuse of the citizenry. Upon hearing the conditions of the surrender, Gösta flew into a rage. Captain Popov told him to calm down on the threat of arrest. Gösta bided his time in a sour mood, and when supper was over, he slipped out of the barracks and crept towards the town center.

He walked along a residential street, peering in windows as he passed each house. Residents scurried away or into their homes when they saw the Russian soldier with his musket and bayonet hanging on his shoulder. Gösta stopped when he spotted what he was looking for, a pretty woman with a busty figure. She was setting the table as a man sat smiling at her. Gösta pounded on the door with the heel of a hand and shouted, "Open the door!" He could hear frantic whispering from inside, so he pounded on the door again. A scraping noise, maybe a beam lifting, and then the door slowly opened. Gösta kicked the door hard, knocking the man backward, and then followed the man as he stumbled back. Gösta slipped his musket off his shoulder and drove the butt into the man's forehead. The man's eyes rolled back in his head, and he dropped unconscious to the floor. Gösta never broke step as he continued forward and grabbed the woman and placed a hand over her mouth to suppress her scream. She grabbed both his wrists and bit down on his hand. Gösta jerked his hand back and punched her hard with his other hand, knocking her out cold.

SPARRMAN • A SOLDIER'S TALE

"Well, shit!" Gösta muttered, looking down at the unconscious woman. He would have preferred a fight when he raped her. Sighing, he went back to the front door, kicked it shut, and slid the beam back in its brackets. He took an apron from a wall hook and tore it into strips. Gösta used the strips to tie the man's wrists and ankles. He also used strips of cloth to gag both of them. He then lifted the woman and carried her to the bedroom.

After satisfying his lust, Gösta came back into the dining room and sat at the table. He was picking at the food laid out when he heard a muffled noise and looked at the man lying on the floor, staring back at him.

"Your wife is a good cook!" Gösta said, his mouth covered in grease. "And she is good in bed, too! I think I will have another go at her once this food settles."

A loud burp escaped him, and he tossed a turnip at the man, hitting him in the face. Gösta's laughter died when the woman came screaming out of the bedroom, holding a heavy candlestick high over her head. Gösta quickly disarmed her and threw her face down on the floor near her husband. She had untied her gag, so he stuffed a table napkin in her mouth and flipped her onto her stomach. He grasped both her wrists in one hand and pulled her dress up. Gösta fumbled with his trousers, freed himself, but was interrupted by a pounding on the door.

"What is going on in there?" A voice demanded in Swedish.

"Nothing; go away!"

The pounding returned, and Gösta stood up, buttoned his breeches, and opened the door. Two Swedish policemen pushed their way into the house and took in the scene.

"Take his weapons, Arvid," Oskar said.

"Don't, Arvid, unless you want to die," Gösta said calmly, repeating the man's name. The policemen hesitated, surprised that this Russian soldier was speaking Swedish so fluently.

The two men recovered and then started to raise their muskets when Gösta tackled both of them. All three went down in a heap, fists punching, teeth biting, and fingers gouging. The woman slowly got up, pulled the napkin out of her mouth, and waddled over to pick up one of the muskets from the floor. She raised the musket's stock and looked for an opening as the men fought and rolled on the floor. She saw her chance, Gösta's face in a grimace as Arvid straddled him and had both hands around his neck. Gösta saw the musket stock begin to descend toward his face, and he quickly shoved Arvid's head in front of him. The musket connected with the base of Arvid's skull, knocking him out. Gösta pushed Arvid off and then kicked Lena's legs out from under her. As she went down, Gösta rolled over and was about to rise when Oskar cocked his musket and aimed it at Gösta.

"Do not move!"

Gösta sat back down on the floor and sighed.

"What is your name?" Oskar asked the woman who had slowly gotten to her feet.

"Lena."

"Lena, do you have some rope?"

"What," Lena said. She had gone to her husband and was untying his bindings.

"Ah, for fek sakes; he wants rope to tie my wrists, you pig!" Gösta said through gritted teeth.

The husband, Daniel, stood, swayed, then took a step toward Gösta but stopped when Oskar held his hand out. He spat in Gösta's face and then made his way slowly toward the back of the house. Lena moved to support Daniel when he continued to sway on his feet. Oskar averted his eyes when he saw the torn dress exposed the woman's upper legs from behind. When they returned, she had wrapped a blanket around her waist. Daniel held out a coil of rough hemp rope to Oskar.

"Can you tie his wrists?"

Oskar had considered handing the musket to him so he could securely tie the rope himself but quickly dismissed the idea, rightly assuming Daniel would shoot Gösta. Lena mumbled something which Oskar didn't hear clearly.

"What did you say?" He asked.

"She wants you to bring me back tomorrow, to service her again," Gösta said, then grunted when Daniel jerked the roped tight on his wrists.

"You disgust me," Oskar said. "I hope they stand you up against a wall and shoot you. I will volunteer for that assignment!"

"Then I will be safe; I doubt you could even hit the wall!"

Oskar went toward him, thought better of it, and circled behind Gösta. He inspected the bindings, impressed by the quality of the knots Daniel had used. Grabbing Gösta's armpit, Oskar planted his feet and heaved him to his feet. Gösta spun around and slammed his forehead down on Oskar's nose. Blood gushed as Oskar dropped to the floor. Gösta grinned, and then a fist slammed into his face. He fell flat on his back, arms and legs splayed.

Daniel stood over him, flexing his hand when Lena handed him one of the muskets. He took it and aimed it at Gösta's face. After a few seconds, Daniel reversed the musket and drove the stock down on Gösta's crotch with all his might. Gösta bolted upright and screamed. His hands flew to his crushed testes, and then he spewed vomit. Lena had started laughing but abruptly stopped when she saw the contents of the vomit.

"Are those my cloudberries you are puking out?" Lena yelled. "Do you know how hard it is to find those?" She grabbed a musket and held the bayonet inches from Gösta's face.

Three more policemen charged into the house; they grabbed the muskets from Daniel and Lena's hands. The sergeant stood looking at all the blood and asked, "what evil has visited upon this house?"

Lena pointed at Gösta.

* * *

Gösta lay on his cot in utter agony. One eye had swelled shut, several teeth were missing, his nose broken once more, and he was sure he had a few cracked ribs. Those injuries paled in comparison to the agony of his crushed testes. Once the policemen had Gösta in the jail, they locked the jail's door. Two policemen held Gösta while Arvid and Oskar took turns punching him. The sergeant had stood guard by the door.

Oh, they will pay for this!

The pain in his crotch was worse than anything he had ever experienced. He looked at the policemen sitting at their desks, jeering and laughing at him. Arvid and Oskar went home to recover from their injuries; aside from being cracked on the head with musket stocks, they may have broken their hands punching Gösta's hard skull.

A pounding on the jail's door startled them.

"Where is my soldier?" Someone bellowed as the pounding continued on the jail's door. The sergeant jumped up and ran to the door.

"Who is it?"

"Field Marshal Barclay de Tolly! Open this door, or I will get one of my cannons!

"Now you're in for it!" Gösta mumbled through his swelled lips.

The sergeant gestured to one of the policemen to open the door. When he did so, Barclay pushed his way past the policeman, followed by two Russian cossacks.

When Barclay saw Gösta's condition, he stood nose to nose with the sergeant and yelled, "what the hell did you do to my soldier?"

Barclay pushed the sergeant aside when he didn't answer and strode to the cell. Gösta sat up and hissed at the pain the movement caused. He stood unsteadily and stumbled to the cell bars.

"What did you do?" Barclay breathed.

"These men." Gösta said, indicating the Swedish policemen, "they don't speak Russian."

"I don't give a fek what they understand or not! Tell me what you did!" Barclay's eyes were bulging, a vein in his forehead was throbbing, and Gösta had to fight the urge to wipe the spittle off his face. Despite Gösta's lack of fear for any man, he, at this moment, felt a shiver of fear begin where his testes throbbed and slowly rose to the pit of his stomach.

"I, ahh."

"Spit it out, man!" Yelled Barclay.

"I was just having some fun with a woman, and then everyone attacked me."

"You disgust me!" Barclay said, "she is Swedish."

"Yeah, yes."

"I have a fitting punishment for you, Gösta."

"Yes, sir."

"Open this door!" Barclay yelled at the policemen. They stared back at him, not understanding the Russian words. Barclay strode angrily over to one of the desks and grabbed the cell key. The policeman sitting behind the desk flinched and leaned back as far as he could.

Barclay opened the cell door and then stormed out of the jail, followed by the two cossacks and a limping Gösta, one hand holding his injured ribs. He stopped at the door, turned to the policemen, and said, "I will be back, and when I -"

"Gösta!" Barclay yelled from the street. He was sitting on a horse in front of a dozen Russian cossacks. There was no horse for Gösta. Barclay and the cossacks turned and galloped away. Gösta slowly limped down the street, sucking in his breath with each footfall. The first piece of frozen horse dung hit him in the back. Gösta hunched his shoulders to protect his head as more dung flew at him from residents on both sides of the street. He arrived at the barracks an hour later, bruised and bloodied and smelling of horse shit.

26

As expected, the residents of Kalix were not happy to see the Swedish soldiers arrive. They carried dysentery with them, would drain their food stores, and may lead the Russians to their village. To add insult to injury, the Swedes transformed their church into a stable for the horses.

The Västerbotten regiment, including Johan and Jon, were ordered to build bulwarks on the road leading into the village from the north. Dense bush of spruce, pine, and poplar lined the road, simplifying their task. Other regiments were fortifying the Kalix River at the southern end of the village. Once they finished, artillery pieces moved in, and most of the men went back into town to await the call to battle. Johan and Jon, and eighteen others took the first watch. Dry wood was gathered for a bonfire to be lit as a signal.

"How are you feeling, Johan?" Jon asked.

Johan had struggled the first day of the march. Jon and another soldier helped him walk until Major Öden Love rode by and ordered Johan onto a wagon.

"I am well, Jon. I feel strong again."

"It is good. I worried you had the rödsot!"

"Yeah. I would be frozen on the side of the trail right now if it was rödsot."

"The major wouldn't allow that. There have been whispers of your friendship with the major."

"I wouldn't call it a friendship. And why would other soldiers be corned about that?"

"Suspicious, I guess."

"How do you feel about it, Jon?"

"If it keeps me away from latrine duty, I condone your friendship."

"Condone?" Johan asked with a confused look on his face.

"Agree to allow you to be his friend."

"Why, thank you, sir!" Johan said, bowing low at the waist and then dropping to his knees and clasping his hands. "Would you also condone me to marry your cousin, Maria, pleeease?"

"I condone it." Jon said somberly, "now rise, lowly peasant."

"Fek." Johan cursed and grinned as Jon laughed.

The next day, the Russians arrived. They stopped a few hundred feet away, and their column stretched beyond sight.

"What are they doing?" Jon asked. They were back on watch after a sixteen-hour break.

"I don't know, but I am glad they are waiting!" Johan said. "There are so many!" With only twenty men at the barricade, they would be quickly overrun. They had lit the bonfire and added some green willows to make the smoke that would signal the enemy's arrival.

"What is taking them so long?" Jon complained, looking back nervously towards the village.

"There, they are coming," Johan said as several horsemen trotted into view around a corner of the road into the village.

"Finally!" Jon said, and then, "where the hell are the troops?'

A lieutenant-colonel, Major Öden Love, three captains, and two sergeants rode up to the bulwarks. Öden ordered an opening be made wide enough for a horse to pass through, and a sergeant unfurled a white flag and handed it to the lieutenant-colonel. A groan escaped one of the soldiers, eliciting a glare from Öden. The lieutenant-colonel and Öden rode through the opening and towards the Russians. Johan watched as two Russians rode out to meet them.

"What is going on?" A soldier asked no one in particular but was looking toward the officers. They ignored him.

"Johan, ask the major when he comes back."

Everyone looked at Johan, including the captains, who had puzzled looks on their faces. Johan nodded at the soldier and looked back at the parlay. What he saw made him gasp. The lieutenant-colonel and Öden removed their swords and handed them to the Russians. They saluted each other and then rode back to their respective lines. When the lieutenant-colonel and Öden rode through the gap in the barricade, Öden ordered it taken down.

"Are we surrendering, sir?" Johan asked.

"Yes. The main force of the Russians went around us. We are surrounded."

"We can fight, sir!" Another soldier said.

"Russian forces crossed the Kvarken and have taken Umeå. Our troops there are retreating south. We have lost Finland."

The statement brought gasps from all the men.

"My wife and children!" A soldier said, panic on his face.

"Our citizens will be treated with respect, soldier."

The soldiers began talking amongst themselves as the officers rode towards Kalix. Öden held back and told the men, "head back to Kalix. We will march to Umeå. Leave the canons."

The order elicited a chorus of opposition from the gathered soldiers.

"Sparrman, control your men!" Öden ordered.

"I'm not an officer, sir."

"What? Oh." Öden said, then he yelled, "Jon with shit on your hands, get that barricade down! Now!"

"Do you think the Russians will make it to Överboda, Johan?" Jon asked after Öden rode away.

"I hope not. Come on, Jon, with shit on your hands, let's get this barricade down and get going."

"Fek!" Jon cursed, "do you think he will ever forget that?"

"I don't know, Jon."

They walked back toward Kalix with the Russians following them. The hairs on Johan's neck stood up as he waited for a musket ball to slam into his back. By the actions of his comrades, they were experiencing the same sensation. It was all they could do not to break into a run. Taking matters into his own hands, Johan called, "double time, men!" They broke into an orderly trot, relief on their faces as they put space between themselves and the Russians.

The Swedish northern army gathered their personal effects and was allowed to leave Kalix. Russian troops lined the road and watched the Swedes depart. There was no cheering or gloating. The Swedes marched with heads held high, while the Russians stood at attention, some respectfully holding salutes as their enemies marched past.

It took the Swedes two weeks to march from Kalix to Umeå. Two cold, hungry weeks. They had no muskets; the Russians had taken those. The only food they managed to procure were from the villages along their way. The smaller towns did not have the resources for such a large army. They heard the rumors at each stop; Umeå had fallen to the Russians. If that were true, northern Sweden was lost.

In Skellefteå, the mayor told them that the Swedish army left without firing a shot when the Russians entered Umeå. They were surprised to hear that the Russians only stayed a few days and then marched back across the frozen Kvarken to Finland. They took Swedish supplies and artillery with them.

Dysentery was still rampant within the army and was spreading to the populace at an alarming rate. Many doors remained barred to the returning soldiers. When they arrived at the Umeå barracks, they were appalled at the mess. The Russians had left garbage everywhere, did malicious damage to the furniture, broke windows, and left piles of feces in some areas.

"At least they didn't burn it down," Jon said.

"We may have to burn it after what they did!" Johan muttered.

It took two weeks to clean the mess and make repairs to their barracks. They were ordered back north after being rearmed with used muskets. The Russians had moved back to Tornio and joined by Barclay's forces. The Swedish soldiers left at the Tornio infirmary were never heard from again.

27

May 1809
Skellefteå

On the 8th, Russian forces advanced south from Tornio and captured the village of Piteå. Two days later, six thousand Russians march further south to Kåge, eight miles from Skellefteå.

All that stood in their way was the Swedish northern vanguard consisting of eight hundred soldiers of the Västerbotten regiment, Finnish Vasa regiment, and Karelian Dragoons. Johan Sparrman, Gunnar Johansson, and Jon Emanuelsson were among these soldiers, quartered near a church in Skellefteå. On the morning of the 15th, two thousand, five hundred Russian soldiers attacked from the north. An additional two thousand, five hundred Russians traveled on the frozen bay and advanced from the east.

Johan, Gunnar, and Jon were at the Skellefteå River when the Russians arrived. They had tried to demolish the bridge but only weakened it to the point cavalry and artillery could not cross. Russians poured across the frozen river and attacked the smaller Swedish contingent. Vastly outnumbered, the Swedes had to retreat from the overwhelming onslaught. They fell back to the church where the bulk of the Swedes and Finns were preparing to retreat south.

About five miles southeast of Skellefteå, they were met by the Russian forces advancing from the east, effectively cutting off their retreat. The Swedes surrendered after a quarter of their men were killed or wounded in the ensuing battle. The rearguard, which included Johan, Gunnar, Jon, and forty-seven other Västerbottens, was behind a shallow creek bank. They had engaged in delaying action on the Russian's right flank. Sergeant Augustus (Gus) Andersson lifted his spyglass and scoped toward the main Swedish army to see how they were faring.

"Shit!" He yelled. Then, when he saw some of his men staring at him said, "we have surrendered."

"No! I will not surrender again!" Gunnar cried. He backed away from the sergeant, a terrified look on his face. Johan and Jon, remembering the condition Gunnar was in after the prisoner exchange not that many months ago, moved beside him. Gunnar had lost most of his teeth during his captivity and still suffered various stomach ailments from the ordeal. A few other soldiers who had witnessed the prisoners' return that day also moved to his side.

"We would rather fight to the death than surrender to the Russians, sir," Johan said.

The sergeant, stunned at this display of subordination, was about to berate them when more soldiers moved to Gunnar's side. Soon, the sergeant stood alone.

"All right." The sergeant sighed, "let's get to Umeå and warn them."

The creek banks lined with poplar trees and snowdrifts hid them. When sergeant Andersson led them northward, Gunnar said, "we are going the wrong way, sir!"

"No, we need to get behind them and then cut west." Gus said, "they will be looking for us toward the south."

They ran hunched over down the center of the creek. They reached a fork in the creek, one arm continuing north and the other southwest; they took the latter. When the creek petered out, they marched due south until darkness forced them to stop near the settlement at Hjoggböle. The men appropriated a barn to sleep in and confiscated a pig to butcher against the farmer and his wife's protestations. Gunnar, and a few others with missing teeth, had to cut their meat into small pieces and then gum them before swallowing.

They were on the move before sunrise moving fast and light, anxious to beat the Russians to Umeå. Four days later, they arrived at the regimental headquarters in Umeå with the Russian army a day's march behind them. Soldiers ran in every direction carrying equipment, loading wagons, and driving horses pulling artillery pieces through the street.

Sergeant Andersson stopped a sergeant and asked what was happening.

"We are evacuating to Hörnefors!"

"Hörnefors?" Gus was shocked. They were abandoning Umeå to the Russians again! "I need to report to the commander."

"They are already gone. Your report will have to wait."

Gus went back to where his men stood waiting and relayed the information.

"We all have families in the countryside! What will happen to them?" Johan asked when Gus informed his men of the situation. Everyone began talking at once, asking the same question Johan asked.

"I cannot grant anyone leave." Sergeant Andersson said, "we need to join the evacuation and await further orders! Take an hour to find some food and to write your letters. We will meet back here at-" he looked at his pocket watch, "three o'clock." The men walked away, grumbling.

* * *

July 5
Hörnefors

Johan and Gunnar patrolled the mansion grounds while Colonel Sandels and his officers were inside celebrating King Karl XIII's coronation. After arriving in Hörnefors, they had set up fortifications in preparation for the Russian advance and waited.

The Russians had regrouped in Umeå; they had taken over the Swedish army's headquarters and collected the spoils of war. Most of the seizures were the armaments left behind by the retreating Swedes, but they also taxed the local citizenry. Farms were required to contribute barley, brännvin, cattle, and butter to the Russians, the Håkansson farm included. Because the Larsson farm housed dysentery victims, the Russians gave it a wide berth, thus saving the Larssons from taxation.

"It must be nice to be in a grand mansion eating fine food and drinking fancy wines!" Jon said.

They could see the officers through the windows, talking and laughing as servants topped up their champagne flutes.

"What do you think of our new king?" Johan asked.

"I have no idea."

"Yeah, me neither. But it seems wrong to celebrate a coup against King Gustav."

"I know. Look at them," Jon said, "traitors if you ask me."

"Hey, where's Gunnar?" Johan asked.

"With the rearguard -" Before he could finish, cannon fire erupted from the northeast.

"Let's go!" Johan said.

"We can't leave our post, Johan!" Jon said, "especially when we are guarding all these officers."

"Shit!" Johan cried. "We need to help Gunnar!"

They could hear the intensity of the battle increase, now including musket fire.

"Look." Jon pointed to the officers pouring out of the mansion. Stable hands ran out of the stables with their horses. Sergeant Andersson approached Johan and Jon as the officers mounted their horses and galloping across the Hörneån bridge.

"Let's go!" The sergeant yelled.

"What about the rearguard, shouldn't we go help them?" Johan asked.

"They'll do their jobs, and we'll do ours, now get moving, soldier!"

After a brief hesitation, Johan followed Jon and the sergeant across the bridge.

* * *

Gunnar was talking with a fellow soldier when the man flew backward. Blood misted Gunnar's face a split second before he heard the cannonade. He turned in that direction and was shocked to see thousands of Russian soldiers advancing on their position. Gunnar and three hundred men were the Swedish rearguard, the army's first line of defense.

Recovering from the initial shock of his comrade's sudden death, Gunnar aimed and fired his musket. Satisfied when he saw a Russian soldier fall, he reloaded and fired, and repeated the action, over and over.

"Fall back!" Lieutenant colonel Duncker ordered. Gunnar knew from experience that they would retreat until they found good cover and then make another stand. They did so several times, each time with fewer men. With only one hundred soldiers remaining, they made their last stand at the Hörnefors bridge. Gunnar found a spot behind the fortifications placed there days earlier and began shooting. He sat down with his back against the log bulwark while he reloaded.

What is that?

Gunnar had looked to the northwest and saw movement.

"Sir?" He had moved beside the lieutenant colonel.

"What!"

Gunnar pointed at the movement. Duncker followed the direction of Gunnar's finger and lifted his spyglass to his eye.

"Fek!"

"What is it, sir?" A captain asked.

"Russian forces, thousands of them. We are surrounded."

"Are we surrendering, sir?" A soldier asked.

"No!" Duncker said.

"No!" Gunnar blurted at the same time.

Duncker looked at Gunnar, nodded and clapped him on the shoulder, and said, "good man."

Duncker ordered a portion of the bulwarks moved to protect their left flank. Half of the rearguard took up positions there. The one hundred defenders now prepared to meet more than five thousand enemy attackers on two fronts. Their weak points were behind them if the attackers circled their position.

"Here they come. Make every shot count, men!" Duncker yelled.

Cannon fire decimated them. After twenty minutes, only forty soldiers remained, and they had run out of ammunition. Gunnar attached his bayonet, and the others followed suit. Duncker unsheathed his sword and dagger, holding one in each hand.

"It has been an honor, gentlemen." Duncker said, "keep down until they are upon us."

The silence outside their bunker was deafening; the shooting had stopped entirely. They all sat with their backs against the logs. Several soldiers packed and lit pipes; others whispered prayers.

"Harvest should be good this year." One of the men said.

"Really?" Duncker asked, "how can you tell?"

"I got a letter from my wife." The soldier said, puffing on his pipe, "she wrote that she needed help with the harvest, so my brother moved in to help."

"Huh." Duncker grunted, "you know the harvest is at least a month away."

"She said it started early."

"Well, I'm glad for you, son," Duncker said after a brief hesitation.

"Sir?"

"Yeah?"

"Will I see my wife again?"

"Not in this lifetime."

"Here they come." Someone said.

Gunnar rose to one knee and held his bayonet forward. Duncker stood in the middle with his sword held high, yelling encouragement to his men. A hail of musket fire hit them from both directions. A ball hit Ducker, turning him, but he remained upright. Then the Russians were upon them. Duncker swung his sword at a Russian, fatally wounding the man. Gunnar moved his bayonet to the right when a Russian charged over the bulwark. He caught the man in the midsection; the man's momentum pulled Gunnar's musket out of his hands, so he pulled his dagger out and knocked another enemy's bayonet aside. Russians were pouring over the banks as Gunnar plunged his blade into one of them. Gunnar quickly pulled his dagger free and faced the next attacker. People were grunting and screaming all around him as he stabbed another Russian.

Gunnar found himself back-to-back with Duncker, both fighting off attackers. Gunnar felt something sharp poke his back; turning, he saw the tip of a bayonet sticking out of Duncker's back. The point disappeared, and Duncker dropped to his knees. Gunnar yelled and attacked the Russian, plunging his dagger into the man's chest. He turned to his commander when a bayonet plunged into his back, followed by another to his side. Duncker laid down and clutched his wound when Gunnar fell to his knees and let his body fall on top of Duncker.

After the battle, Russian lieutenant colonel Karpenkov surveyed the carnage.

What a waste of brave men!

He stopped in front of the wounded Duncker and yelled, "medics!" He pulled Gunnar's body off the Swedish lieutenant colonel. Duncker tried to speak, so Karpenkov knelt beside him and put his ear close to Duncker's mouth.

"That man, his name is Gunnar Johansson, take care of him first."

"He's dead."

"Aah."

"We will treat his body with respect, as well as the rest of your men."

"Thank you."

"Medics, get the hell over here. Now!" Karpenkov yelled.

Duncker would succumb to his wounds the next day in the Russian encampment. He would be buried in Umeå, beside the Russian colonel, Aerekof, who had also died in the battle. The rest of the Swedish rearguard had fought to the last man.

* * *

A few miles away, Johan and Jon stood looking in the direction of the rearguard's position. The guns had gone silent. They waited for Gunnar and the rearguard to appear, but they never did.

"Gunnar would not surrender," Jon said.

"No, he would not." Johan agreed.

The Swedish defenses were on the west side of the Öre River bridge. They felt the vibrations in the ground first. Next, a huge dust cloud appeared in the distance, and then the Russians appeared, thousands of Russians.

"Holy shit!" Jon said.

"You will not die this day, comrade."

"Nor will you, my friend."

Their position was good; the Russians would be constricted by the bridge, allowing the Swedes to concentrate their cannon fire. The battle raged until darkness fell; either side accomplished little. The next morning at sunrise, the Swedes found themselves alone.

Johan and Jon were within earshot of colonel Sandels and several officers.

"Should I prepare the advance, sir?" One of the officers asked.

"No, it may be a trap," Sandels replied.

"We can scout ahead, sir, and report the Russian's position," Johan said.

Sandels ignored him and turned to his officers, "send out scouts."

"Yes, sir." One of the officers said and then gestured to Johan and Jon to follow him.

"Don't ever speak to the colonel unless he addresses you!" He said, inches from Johan's face, "you two will be in front of the scouts. Now get out of here!"

Johan and Jon ran across the bridge and then slowed. They watched the bushes on either side of the road for a possible ambush.

"This is nerve-wracking," Jon said.

"Don't worry, if they are waiting in ambush, they will let us pass and wait for the main army."

"You think so?"

"Yeah, why would they give their positions away for two soldiers even if they are the two best soldiers?"

"You could be right," Jon said, visibly relaxing.

They were surprised to see all the mounds when they approached the Hörnefors bridge. The Russians had lined up the bodies in neat rows and covered with a layer of dirt, and in some cases, sod.

"Look, there's a cross." Jon pointed toward a wooden cross at one end of a sod covered mound.

"What does it say?" There was Cyrillic lettering marked on the cross.

"How should I know?" Johan said.

"Must be significant; let's take a look."

Johan hesitated, not wanting to disturb a grave, even a temporary one. "Go ahead."

Jon bent down and lifted a piece of sod near the cross. He took his handkerchief out and brushed the dirt off the face.

"It's Gunnar!"

"Aah."

They stood over their friend, both silent for several minutes. Jon placed his handkerchief over Gunnar's face and replaced the sod.

"They showed our dead respect this time," Johan observed.

"Yeah, and they singled out Gunnar."

Johan sat down beside Gunnar's mound and lit his pipe; Jon followed suit.

"Do you remember that time Tobias gave him that piece of reindeer jerky?"

"Yeah," Jon laughed, "he couldn't rip a piece off with no teeth, so he had to use his knife, and then he sucked that piece all day!"

"Hah, I saw him spit it out before supper."

They reminisced about their friend until their pipes burned down, and then they continued searching for the Russians. It was not difficult; thousands of men and artillery left an easy trail to follow. They caught up with them three miles north of Hörnefors.

"Looks like they are heading back to Umeå," Johan said.

"Let's get back and give our report."

"Fek," Johan said. He did not know why he said that, but it sounded right.

28

O llie steered Sofia to the hitching post in front of the church rectory. It is not his first time here in recent weeks. He has come to ask the pastor to perform the service for several dysentery victims. He walked up to the door and knocked. Ollie liked pastor Nyselius; he's young and talks to him as he would a man.

Samuel Nyselius opened the door and smiled at Ollie.

"Välkommen, Ollie!" He said, "it is good to see you, but I fear your visit is not good news."

"Hi, Sam," Ollie said. The pastor insisted his parishioners call him Sam. Not many did, but Ollie liked to; it made him feel grown-up. "No, it is not good. Three more have died."

"The bodies are by the pyres?"

"Yes."

"My housekeeper, Camilla, wants to come and help your mother and sisters. Is it okay if she goes with you? I am traveling on horseback."

"Aah, okay," Ollie said. He did not look forward to a long ride with the woman. Camilla Silfversköld had taught the parish children Sunday school, including Ollie. She had been a stern taskmaster and seemed to have singled Ollie out, often rapping his knuckles with a diamond willow cane when he made a mistake. Ollie was not ashamed to admit to himself that the woman terrified him. Camilla, at one time, was the wife of a previous pastor, Jarl Silfversköld. After Jarl's death, the new pastor allowed Camilla to stay in the rectory, first as a schoolmistress and later as a housekeeper.

The pastor walked back into the rectory, leaving the door open. Ollie strolled over to the well and turned the crank, bringing a pail of water to the surface. He unhooked the pail and carried it over to Sofia. After she had her fill, Ollie took the pail back and hooked it back to the rope, and lowered it down the well. Hearing the pastor and the schoolmistress coming out of the rectory, Ollie walked back to the wagon.

While the pastor loaded her suitcase in the back of the wagon, Ollie offered his hand to Camilla, but she brushed it away.

"I'm quite capable of getting on myself, young man!"

It's going to be a long ride!

Camilla had to bounce on her feet a few times before making it up onto the bench. Ollie resisted the urge to boost her up by her rump, but he did stand behind her, ready to catch her if she fell backward. Ollie climbed up onto the bench and said to the pastor, "adjö, Sam!"

"Oh, I almost forgot!" Samuel said, "I'll be right back!" He ran back into the parsonage while Ollie sat in a very uncomfortable silence beside Camilla on the wagon's bench.

"A letter came for Maria." As he handed the letter to Ollie, Samuel said, "it was delivered here; I suspect because of fear for the rödsot."

"Thank you, Sam."

"Have an enjoyable trip, Ollie! I will be there in a few hours." The pastor said with a wink.

He's really enjoying this!

"Sit up straight!" Camilla ordered.

Ollie quickly straightened up, pulling his hand back without thinking. Camilla noticed this and suppressed a smile.

"Don't worry, young man." She said, patting his knee, "I am your guest; I won't be rapping your knuckles."

"Well, that's a relief!"

They rode a few miles in silence. Camilla seemed to be enjoying the scenery. The mid-July heat was pleasant, not too hot, just right. The sky was clear, the air fresh, and birds sang in trees. It was easy to forget, at least for a little while, that the country was at war and an epidemic was raging.

"Have you been studying the scriptures?"

Ollie jumped and then replied, "O God, I open my ears to hear your Word!" He tilted his head and cupped his ear. "Nope, nothing."

Camilla gaped at Ollie and then burst out laughing. Ollie looked back and joined in the laughter.

"Oh, I cannot remember the last time I laughed like that!" Camilla said after they recovered.

"Why not?"

"I have not had much joy in my life since my husband died. Nor for many years prior, truth be told."

"I'm sorry."

"Why would you be sorry? It is not your fault."

"Aah-"

"I'm just teasing you, Gösta," Camilla said, patting his knee again.

"I'm Ollie."

"What?"

"You called me Gösta."

"I did?" Camilla said, "I-" She went quiet and stared at the trees passing by on her side of the road.

"Välkommen, Camilla!" Kajsa called when Ollie drove the wagon into the yard. Kajsa and Maria were taking a break, sitting outside on a bench under a large birch tree and drinking cider.

"Hello, Kajsa, Maria." Maria visibly shrank back at the mention of her name. After several years, the sight of the schoolmistress continues to instill fear in her former students.

"Camil-, Mrs. Silfversköld has come to help," Ollie said.

"Thank you, Camilla; we can use all the help we can get," Kajsa said. The exhaustion was apparent on her and her daughter's faces and in their postures. "You will stay in the house. Maria, show Camilla to my room."

Maria's eyes went big before she recovered and said, "of course, come with me, Mrs. Silfversköld."

"Oh, Maria, you can call me Camilla." She said, waving the fearsome walking stick toward her.

"No, I don't think I can. Here, let me take your bag."

"Is she going to be any help, Mama?" Ollie asked as they watched her shuffle toward the house.

"Yes, of course. Camilla will provide comfort to the sick." Kajsa said, "is pastor Nyselius coming?"

"Yes, he said he would be here in a few hours."

"There is porridge on the table, have some and then go get Israel."

"Anna, we have a visitor!" Maria called as she walked into the house with Camilla.

Anna ran into the front room, skidded to a stop, and uttered, "eep!" She looked ready to bolt and glared at Maria, who stood beside and a little behind Camilla, grinning.

"Aah."

"I think I shall call you 'Aah' from now on!" Maria said gleefully, "please show Mrs. Silfversköld to Mama's room, Aah."

Anna stared at Maria, the look promising reprisal, and then said to Camilla, "come this way, Mrs. Silfversköld."

"Oh, Anna, you can call me Camilla."

"No, I don't think I can."

Maria quickly left before Anna came back. She giggled on her way out the door but then stopped when she looked toward the barn. She sighed and walked there with a heavy heart. The care of the sick and watching them die were taking a heavy toll on her.

"Maria!" Ollie called, waving the letter over his head, "this is for you."

Maria ran to take the letter from Ollie; her mood instantly lifted. She sat on the bench outside of the barn where she and her mother would take their breaks. She is pleased to see this letter is more substantial than the scribbled note Johan sent with the Sámi. He begins the letter by explaining why he did not stop to see her on his way back to Umeå after the snowstorm. Here, he tells her of the ten acres his father will give him when they marry and his plan to farm instead of soldiering after the war. He relates his experiences at Tornio and she laughs at the part about Jon knocking down a major into horse manure. Johan writes about his march south to Umeå and that he had no chance to visit as they had to retreat from the town. Scattered between all this were several terms of endearment and his wish to hold her once again. He was shy with that part, and she will have to tutor him in his letter writing skills, but she did walk into the barn holding the letter to her chest and with lifted spirits.

29

August 16
Umeå countryside

J on could not believe his ears. "You are going to make your roof tiles out
of clay?"

"Yes, there is a lot of good clay near a creek not too far from my land,"
Johan said.

The two were scouting about five miles north of the Öre River. The
Swedish northern army had camped on the south side of the river
approximately twenty-five miles southwest from Umeå. They were expecting
the Russians to advance on them from the town. Johan and Jon had come to
a large valley and had dismounted to let their mounts graze.

"But why clay, I have never seen such a thing? And wouldn't it be too
heavy?"

"Haven't you looked up at some of the roofs in Umeå?"

Jon thought for a while, then said, "no, now that I think about it, I haven't. But how would you even make these tiles?"

"I will lay poles on the ground and shape the clay over them, and shape the edges to fit together."

"Huh?"

"It would be easier to show you. I will come and get you when I am building my house, and while you are there, you can help!"

"Hah! And what will you build the walls with, straw?"

"Aah, I haven't thought about it, maybe logs."

"No, it can't be something as plain as logs, not with a clay roof!"

"You could be right, maybe fieldstone?"

"No, Johan, the stone would be too cold in the winter, cool in the summer, though," Jon said. He saw movement in his periphery vision and looked to his right, "Oh, oh!"

"What?" Johan asked, following Jon's line of sight, "Oh, shit!"

Three hundred yards away, four thousand Russian soldiers watched them from the other end of the valley.

"Well, fek!" Johan said, seeing their horses had wandered a few dozen yards away. "We could make a run for the horses, but they would probably shy away from us."

"The Russians on horseback will run us down before we get to our horses, or if we try to run back the way we came."

"Well, then it's surrender or fight," Johan said and took his bayonet out of his pack and attached it to his musket.

"Looks like you made up your mind!" Jon said, "you will die this day, comrade."

"As you will, my friend, but, like Gunnar, we will go down fighting!"

"For Gunnar, then."

They bent forward and marched toward the Russians with muskets held in front of them when they saw a rider galloping toward who they assumed was the Russian commander. The commander, general Kamensky, grinned and shook his head in amazement at the sight of these two lone Swedish soldiers marching toward them. As Johan and Jon continued their march, Kamensky appeared to be conferring with the rider. Suddenly, he yelled an order, and the Russians turned and retreated the way they had come. The commander took one last look at Johan and Jon, doffed his hat, wheeled his horse around, and galloped away.

Johan and Jon began cheering and shaking their muskets in the air as they watched the Russians disappear into the woods at the end of the valley. After a few seconds, they stopped cheering and stood quietly.

"What do you make of that?" Johan asked. His voice was shaky, but he was relieved that the debilitating shaking he had experienced after battles had not taken hold of him.

"Isn't it obvious!" Jon turned to Johan, thumped his chest, and said, "they saw two of Sweden's best warriors and ran away like the cowering dogs they are!"

"Look! They're coming back!" Johan cried.

He burst out laughing when Jon spun to his right, eyes bulging and musket at the ready.

"Fek!" Jon yelled, dropped his musket, and tackled Johan. Johan grappled good-naturedly with Jon, laughing hysterically. They soon exhausted themselves, released each other, and lay on their backs gasping for air.

"What do we do now?" Jon asked when he caught his breath.

"Someone needs to go back and report to the commander, and someone needs to follow the Russians, to see what they're up to."

"What do you want to do?"

"I don't know, what do you want to do?"

Of course, they both wanted to be the one to follow the Russians.

"I'll go back," Jon said.

"Okay."

"What the fek! You are supposed to say, 'no, I'll go'!"

"Yeah, I'm not going to say that."

"Fek," Jon said. He got up and walked toward his horse.

"Bring mine too, comrade!"

Jon was about to curse but just grinned and shook his head. He caught both horses and called, "hey Johan, there's some good roof clay here!"

"Where?" Johan called back and trotted over to where Jon stood.

"My mistake, it's just horse shit! Hey, maybe you could make your roof out of horseshit!"

"You will see, Jon, my house will be the finest in all of Sweden!" Johan said, ignoring Jon's laughter. "Adjö, my friend!" He called as he galloped north.

Johan followed the Russians to the outskirts of Umeå. He kept out of sight most of the way until some of the soldiers in the rear spotted him. They chose to ignore him, so Johan followed at a distance in plain view the rest of the way. He waited an hour outside of the town until he saw what he was hoping to see, a civilian wagon coming from the town.

"Hello friend, what news have you?" He asked the man when the wagon came abreast of him on the road. A woman sat beside him, and two dirty little faces peaked out between them. The man appeared to be in a sour mood.

"Paying my 'tax' to the Russians!"

"I am sorry to hear that," Johan said. He knew most civilians blamed the occupation on the Swedish army's inability to protect the homeland. "Did you notice any strange movements by the Russian army?"

"They appear to be preparing for an attack from the north. I heard some cannon fire from that direction."

"Huh." Johan was not aware of any Swedish forces north of Umeå. "Thank you, safe travels."

The man nodded curtly, flicked his reins, and rode past Johan without responding. The two children scrambled to the back of the wagon and waved at Johan; he grinned and then galloped past the wagon on his way back to make his report. He heard the man mutter something as he rode past but couldn't make out the words. Just as well; it wouldn't be anything complimentary.

30

Anna had made tea and was setting out cups, saucers, and cookies. But there were no cookies! "Who ate all the ginger snaps," she cried.

"Oh, sorry, Anna." Camilla said, "I was feeling a bit peckish and nibbled on some."

Peckish, fekish, you did more than nibble, you wrinkled old bat!

Anna glared at Camilla when she was sure the old lady wasn't looking.

"You can make some more, Anna," Kajsa said.

Maria was grinning, knowing that Anna failed whenever she attempted to bake cookies.

"Yes, I can help you!" Camilla said, "I noticed the cookies were missing a little something."

What!

Now it was Maria's turn to scowl at Camilla; she had baked the last batch of cookies. Kajsa couldn't help but smile at her daughters; she could read their thoughts so easily. The past few days inside the house had been awkward: Maria and Anna had kept their distance from their houseguest. Ollie, strange as it seemed, enjoyed her company. Although Ollie usually only came into the house for a quick meal and late at night to drop into his bed. He had taken on most of the running of the farm since his father's illness and death. Helping with the sick in the barn added to Ollie's workload. Kajsa was proud of her son; how would they have managed without him?

"Okay, Anna." Camilla said after Kajsa and Maria left for the barn, "let's make those cookies!"

"Aah. I'm busy." Anna said, looking around frantically for something else to do.

"Nonsense!" Camilla said, "there's nothing more important than ginger snaps!"

Huh, maybe she's not a witch after all!

Anna shrugged and began taking the ingredients from the cupboards and setting them on the table. Camilla looked over the assembled items and said, "aah, I see what you are missing!"

Anna, who had been watching Camilla's profile, looked down at the table.

"Nothing is missing."

"Yes, there is no orange flavoring."

"What is that?"

"Orange flavoring? It is not a surprise you don't know it; orange flavoring is hard to come by, and only the finer houses would have some."

Why you old …,

"Wait," Camilla said and shuffled to the room she shared with Kajsa. Anna peeked around the kitchen wall into the bedroom, watching as Camilla rooted through her suitcase. She jerked her head back when Camilla found what she was looking for and turned to come back to the kitchen.

"I found it!" She said, holding up a glass jar, "I was worried that I left it behind; it is one of my most prized possessions. I have it shipped at great cost from Italy."

"Italy!" Anna said with large eyes, "have you been to Italy?"

"Heavens no, but I would have liked to."

"My grandfather went to Prussia, but that was for a war." Then, Anna said, "hey, do you use church money to buy this – orange stuff?"

"Hmm, yes, I suppose I do."

"Then it is holy orange?"

Camilla laughed, startling Anna, then, seeing the look on Anna's face, said, with a wink, "yes, these cookies will be holy cookies, but it will be our secret!"

Anna grinned and said, "okay."

An hour later, they sat at the kitchen table looking at the cookies cool on the open window sill. Anna breathed deeply of the aroma wafting into the kitchen.

"Can you smell the orange?"

"I think so. I have never smelled an orange before." Anna said, "are they ready to eat yet?"

Camilla got up and put her finger on one, "yes, I think they are. Can you make some tea, Anna?"

She carried the pan to the kitchen table while Anna jumped up to make the tea. Anna came back to the table and reached for a cookie. Camilla pulled the pan away and said, "not until the tea's ready." That earned a frown from Anna, but the animosity she usually had when she was around Camilla had disappeared.

Anna poured the tea and waited as Camilla stirred in sugar and cream.

"Okay," Camilla said.

Anna grabbed a cookie and was about to take a bite when Camilla cried, "wait!"

Anna, her mouth open, a ginger snap inches away, looked at Camilla.

Are you kidding?

She lowered the cookie and said, "what?"

"You must first place the cookie in the palm of your hand and make a wish."

Anna looked at Camilla, wondering if she was playing a trick on her. Sighing, she put the cookie in the palm of her hand.

"Now, make a wish."

Anna raised an eyebrow. Camilla nodded.

Fine, I wish you never - no, she's okay.

I wish I can eat this cookie now!

"Okay, I made my wish."

"Now, tap the middle of your cookie with a finger. If it breaks into three pieces, your wish will come true!"

Anna shrugged and tapped her cookie, breaking it into two pieces.

"Shit!" Anna cried, then, "I mean darn."

"It's okay, Anna, it will be another of our secrets. You can try again."

"Can I eat this one first?"

"Yes, of course, you can."

Anna took a tentative bite, not sure how the orange flavoring would taste.

"Oh my God, these are good!" She cried.

"You shouldn't take the Lord's name in vain."

"Sorry. Another secret?"

"Okay, Anna, another secret."

"I want to try again!"

"Well, they are your cookies."

Anna placed another cookie in her palm, thought of a new wish, nodded, then tapped the cookie.

"I did it!" She cried, looking at the cookie broken into three pieces.

"What did you wish for?"

"I, aah-"

"It's okay to tell others your wish."

"I, aah, I wish no one else would get sick and die and that you could stay with us forever," Anna said, her face blushing.

"Two wishes! I am not sure you can do that with one cookie. You better try another one." She said with a wink. "Oh, and I am a hundred years old, so staying here forever may only be a few days!" Camilla said, attempting humor to cover the surge of joy she felt in her chest.

When was the last time I felt joy?

"Mmmm!" Anna groaned with her eyes closed as she ate the cookie pieces. She already had another cookie in the palm of her hand, ready for her next wish.

Kajsa and Maria had a little more time on their hands. They were down to four people with dysentery to look after. At one point, they had twelve.

"Do you think it's ending, this disease?" Maria asked.

"I hope so, but we may get more once the war's over and all the soldiers come home."

"Why?"

"I think fighting wars is the cause of this disease."

"You mean Johan may bring more disease to us?" Maria asked.

"He may, I suppose, the same as Toby did."

"Do you hate Toby, Mama? For passing the disease to Papa, Grandpa, and Manny?"

"I felt bitterness before, but I realize now that it isn't his fault. He was fighting to protect us from enemies when he caught this disease."

"So, do we just welcome all the soldiers back and hope we don't get sick?"

Kajsa thought for a few minutes, then said, "maybe we should tell Johan and any other soldier to wait a few weeks before coming to visit. To make sure they don't have the disease."

"Okay."

After supper that night, Anna placed a dish with the ginger snaps on the table.

"Taste these snaps, Mama; they are so good!"

Kajsa looked down at the cookies. All were in pieces.

"What happened to them?"

"I wish I knew!" Anna said, winking at Camilla.

Kajsa looked at the two co-conspirators, wondering what they had gotten up to, and then picked up a piece of cookie and bit into it.

"Mmmm, these are good!"

31

The sun was low in the sky when Gösta pushed the wheelbarrow full of manure and straw out of the stables. Since the incident with the Swedish couple, he had the lowest of menial jobs within the army. Worse, he had not been allowed to participate in any battles. The march back across the bay had been the most painful journey of his life. Every footstep shot excruciating pain through his ribs. By the time they set foot on Finnish soil, he was on the verge of madness. Still not fully healed, the order came to march north to Tornio. That brought him closer to madness. Then, they marched south to Umeå. That may have pushed him over the edge.

Gösta stood aside as several officers rode into the stable. Captain Popov, who once was the closest Gösta had come to having a friend in the Russian army, briefly looked at him with contempt before riding past.

Fek them all!

He had already decided to sneak away from the army whenever they leave Umeå. He had an old score to settle with the pastor and maybe with his wife, Camilla.

What was his name?

Gösta waited until the officers left the stables before he went back inside. He rolled the wheelbarrow up to the next pile of manure and began shoveling.

"They came by ship?" A man said a few stalls away.

"Yes, thousands of them. They landed north of here."

"Shit!" The man cursed, "so, we are surrounded?"

"Sounds like it."

Suddenly, cannon fire erupted nearby. Gösta ran outside, followed by the two stablemen who had been talking. They could see clouds of smoke rising above the river. Horses pulling cannons raced toward the bridge, and soon, Gösta could hear those cannons returning firing toward the Swedish gunships.

That's it, tonight after dark, I will leave and be rid of these Russian bastards!

Gösta walked back into the stable and walked along the stalls looking at each horse.

I think I will take this horse!

The horse was a fine Russian Don, and it was Captain Popov's personal mount. Gösta recognized it from when Popov rode by him earlier.

That will teach the pompous bastard!

"Hey, what are you doing there? You got shit to shovel!" One of the stable hands had turned back and saw Gösta.

Gösta made an obscene gesture involving his crotch toward the man and then walked toward him. The man tapped his friend on the shoulder and nodded toward Gösta. They both walked toward Gösta.

This is going to be fun!

Gösta stopped beside a workbench and waited for them. He did not want anyone outside seeing what was about to happen. He had waited far too long to vent some of his anger. These men coming toward him had massive forearms and broad shoulders from years of blacksmithing and shoeing horses. But they did not have the look of fist fighters about them.

Gösta waited until they were two steps away before he grabbed a twenty-inch set of tongs from the workbench and swung the heavy iron tool in an arc catching one of the men on the side of his head. The man collapsed into his friend, throwing him off balance. Gösta swung the tongs once more, but the second man brought his arm up to protect his head. Gösta felt and heard the bone break and then swung again. The man bellowed in agony, ducked under Gösta's weapon, and then dove into Gösta's midsection.

They went down with Gösta underneath, and the man used his uninjured arm to push himself up. Gösta knew he had to do something before the man could use his good hand. From years of tavern fighting, Gösta knew he had to exploit any weakness. He punched at the man's broken forearm repeatedly until the man fell back to protect his injury.

Gösta quickly rolled over, jumped up, and kicked the man's head. The man's head snapped back, his eyes rolled up, and he fell over onto his side. Gösta bent over with hands on his knees and gasped for breath.

Well, fek, I guess I'm leaving now.

Gösta walked to the stable doors and looked in all directions. He did not see anyone in the gathering darkness, so he had some time before the stablemen woke or someone discovers them. He could hear the cannonades from the gunboats and the Russian artillery units. That should provide some cover for his escape. Escape was the right word since he hadn't joined this army voluntarily. He saddled Popov's horse and rode out of the stables.

If I gallop out of the town, everyone will think I am on some important army mission and think nothing of it.

So, Gösta galloped out of Umeå and took the road west, and no one gave him a second glance.

* * *

An hour later, lieutenant Andrei Davydov cleared his throat behind captain Popov. The captain was standing with several other officers watching the artillery barrage. He turned to his lieutenant and said, "what is it, Andrei?"

"Sorry, sir, your horse is gone."

"What!" Popov cried and then pushed the man aside and strode toward the stables. The other officers, including general major Jerschov, looked his way then turned back to the artillery show. Popov glanced down at a man lying on the floor as he walked to the stall where his horse had been stabled and cursed when he saw it empty.

"Who did this!" Popov yelled.

"It was Gösta." A stableman said. The man sat groggily on a stool cradling his arm.

"Gösta!" Popov cursed, "that son of a dog! What happened here?"

"We minded our own business, doing our work when he went crazy and started swinging those tongs at us."

"He's dead, sir," lieutenant Davydov said. He was kneeling beside the man on the floor.

"What is the problem," general major Jerschov asked. He and several officers had entered the stables.

"Uh, we had a soldier go berserk." Popov said, "killed a man and stole my horse."

"Stole your horse!" Jerschov said, obviously more appalled at that than of a dead soldier.

"I will send some men after him," Popov said.

"Yes, of course. But can we spare any soldiers while we are under attack?" The cannonades continued in the distance.

"Sir, we do have those three in lock up for theft of supplies." lieutenant Davydov whispered to Popov.

"What was that?" Jerschov demanded.

"We have three soldiers locked up after being caught selling grain to local merchants." Popov said, "we could send them after the horse thief and offer a pardon if they succeed."

"What if they run away?"

"Then we will be rid of them, and they will be Sweden's problem."

"Alright, captain." The general major said, "outfit them with Swedish arms and horses; ones we don't need. Now let's get back to the show!"

"Yes, sir."

The next morning, Pavel, Boris, and a corporal, Adrian, were released from the stockade with instructions to retrieve captain Popov's horse. As for Gösta, they had instructions to shoot on sight. The supply clerk gave them confiscated Swedish muskets and horses; horses deemed undesirable by the Russians. Little did they know that one of the horses was far superior, at least in stamina, to any of their showy horses. That horse was Dagmar, Tobias's horse. The other two were old, sway-backed nags. The sorry-looking trio rode through the streets of Umeå under openly hostile glares from the citizens. They breathed a sigh of relief when they left the streets behind them.

32

Two days later, Gösta rode into the yard of the church's parsonage. He had come back to the scene of his crime from those many years ago. He dismounted and strode up to the house and pounded on the door. A barrel-chested man opened the door and demanded, "yeah! What do you want?"

Gösta, in no mood for resistance of any kind, swung his fist at the man, Igor Rasmusson. He was shocked when Igor easily deflected the blow and swung a ham sized fist at Gösta, smashing him in the face with tremendous force. He was momentarily stunned, and his ears rang as Igor loaded up for another blow. Going into full tavern fighting mode, Gösta ducked underneath Igor's swing and threw all his weight into a punch to the gut. He felt his ribs ache when his fist hit what felt like a sack of hard-packed sand. Before he could react, Igor hit him in the side of his head with a roundhouse punch, knocking him off the porch and onto the dirt yard. His horse skidded aside, eyes flaring.

Gösta lay stunned as Igor strode toward him and brought his foot back to deliver a kick to the crotch. Gösta quickly rolled out of the way and came up with his dagger, plunging it into Igor's stomach. Igor bellowed and pulled the blade free. He grunted and staggered toward Gösta with the bloody knife in his hand. Gösta crab-crawled backward in abject fear. Igor stood over him and tried to raise the knife. He had a look of confusion on his face as he stared at his unresponsive hand and then fell forward onto Gösta. Gösta had lifted his elbow and caught Igor on the chin as he landed on top of him. Gösta lay beneath Igor, the wind knocked out of him, and he could not draw a breath with the dead weight on top of him. Gösta began to panic and struggled to get out from underneath the man, pain shooting through his ribs.

"What is going on out here?" Cried a man who had come out of the parsonage. He stopped short when he saw his manservant lying on top of a stranger. The stranger appeared to be struggling mightily and gasping for breath. Seeing someone in distress, the man, who was the church pastor, ran over and pulled his manservant off of the stranger who rolled onto his side, away from him, and gulped air.

"What happened here?" The pastor demanded.

When Gösta got his breath back, he spun around and glared at the pastor.

"Dear God!" The pastor breathed, crossing himself. He staggered back, turned and stumbled into the parsonage, and slammed the door behind him. Gösta sat up and looked at Igor.

Now that was one tough son of a bitch!

Shaking his head, he went and pried the knife from Igor's hand and walked to the door. It was locked from the inside, of course. Going around to the back, he could hear grunting and furniture scraping as something heavy was being moved to block the rear door. Sighing, Gösta walked around to the side of the building to the cellar doors. As boys, he and his childhood friend, Lars Larsson, had been hired to do odd jobs for the previous pastor, so Gösta was familiar with the building's structure.

The doors were near ground level and set in a box that sloped down from the house wall to allow for rain runoff. The doors provided access to the cellar for bringing wood and root vegetables into the lower level without going through the house. Gösta was relieved to see the same flimsy hasp holding the same rusty lock. Sliding his dagger under the hasp, he pried up, and the screws offered little resistance before sliding out of the old wood.

He lifted one door and went down the stairs, lowering the door behind him. He stood at the bottom of the stairs and let his eyes adjust to the gloom. There were two sets of stairs in the cellar, the short set of stairs he had just come down, and another, longer set leading up to the house's main floor. The door at the top of those stairs was sturdier than the outer cellar doors. The dank, dirt floor cellar was windowless and had the smell of soil and something else, like potatoes in the early stages of rot.

He had to be quiet so the man wouldn't know he was down here. He did not want him blocking the door leading into the hallway. He crept toward the stairs from memory. The darkness was absolute. He almost made it when he stumbled over a metal pail and fell headlong onto the packed earth floor. He heard sudden movement through the floorboards above. Gösta gave up trying to be quiet. He charged up the stairs and threw his shoulder against the door. He bounced off the heavy door, lost his footing, and tumbled down the stairs.

Gösta lay at the bottom of the stairs, momentarily stunned. He laid still and took stock of his body. Nothing seemed broken; his ribs ached miserably, but nothing serious. He stiffened when he heard the door unlock. Feigning unconsciousness, Gösta lay still, his hand holding his dagger under one leg. The door opened slowly, and a face peered around it.

"Who." It came out as a squeak. The man cleared his throat and tried again, "who are you? What do you want?"

Gösta lay still, peeking through the slits of his eyelids.

"Are...are you okay?"

He heard the stairs creak as the man slowly walked down the steps. Gösta had to suppress a smile when he saw that the man carried a candlestick in one hand and a lit candle in the other. He forced himself to stay still as a large rat appeared and began sniffing his shoe. *Hurry up!* He yelled internally at the man's slowness.

The rat crept up to Gösta's fingers and began licking Igor's blood that had crusted there.

Hurry!

The man was still four risers up the stairs, not near enough for Gösta to pounce yet. The rat began scraping its teeth against Gösta's skin, trying to remove the blood. He grunted when the rat bit into one of his fingers, drawing blood. Gösta grabbed the rat and threw it at the man, who screamed and began flailing away at the rat, cracking himself in the face with the candlestick in the process. Gösta rose, reached up, grabbed the man's shirt, pulled, and then slammed him to the cellar floor. The candlestick rolled out of reach, the candle went out, and the rat scurried away. Muted light shone through the open door at the top of the stairs, enough for Gösta to discern shapes.

"Now, you little prick!" Gösta growled, his face inches away from the man. "Where is the pastor?"

"I…I am the pastor."

The smell of urine wafted up, and Gösta glanced down, seeing the widening stain on the man's trousers.

"No, the old pastor and his wife, Camilla."

"Pastor Silfersköld?"

"Yes!" Gösta cried, "that's his name!"

"He died two years ago."

"Fek! What about his wife?"

"She, aah, what do you want with her?"

"That is my business. Now, where is Camilla?"

"I, aah, I don't know."

"Now, pastor, it is a sin to lie. Did you know that?"

"Well, not all lies are a sin, take for example-"

"Shut the fek up! Tell me where she is, or I will castrate you right here and now!"

"Aah, she is ministering to the ill. The ones with rödsot."

"Where?"

If I tell him, he will kill her; if I don't tell him, he will kill me.

He will kill me anyway.

"Yea, though I walk through the valley of the shadow of death -"

Gösta slit the pastor's throat and leaned back, away from the arterial spray. Gösta made squeaking noises, trying to sound like a rat, and called, "come and get it!" The rat didn't appear until Gösta picked up the candlestick and walked up the stairs. He rooted around the parsonage, gathering anything silver and what little money he could find. He walked upstairs and went into the bedroom where he had, all those many years ago, raped Camilla and beat her husband, the now-dead pastor Silfersköld. He sat on the bed and relived that long-ago afternoon in his mind.

Sighing, Gösta stood up and went to the dresser. He sorted through the pastor's clothes until he found a plain linen shirt and a pair of grey, woolen trousers. He removed his uniform and tried the pastor's clothes on.

Not a bad fit.

Picking up his sack of silver, he went downstairs and walked out of the parsonage. He stopped on the deck and stared at the spot where Igor had lain. He was gone; blood-stained dirt was all that remained.

What the fek!

Suddenly, a scream pierced the air. Igor slammed into him from behind, and the two of them flew off the deck onto the ground.

They rolled over and over, each trying to gain the upper position, fists flying, and both spat blood from broken lips. Gösta had never been involved in such a primal fight before. Usually, the altercations were over quickly, by knockout or by a knife. As a rule, even when drunk, he avoided tough men. His ribs were still tender, so most of his punches were weaker from that side.

Igor kneed him between the legs and was shocked when Gösta didn't react. His testes had not fully recovered since the incident with the woman in Umeå. They were still there but had withered down to a nearly empty sack. His sex drive had disappeared, which may be the reason for Gösta's constant state of anger. Gösta took advantage of Igor's hesitation and bite his nose hard. Igor bucked mightily, but Gösta hung on and eventually ripped a good portion of Igor's nose off and spat it out. Igor released his grip on Gösta and grabbed the remnants of his nose. Gösta immediately drove his fist into Igor's throat and then wrapped his hands around his large neck, squeezing with all his might, ignoring the pain in his ribs. Igor grabbed at Gösta's wrists, who then slammed his forehead down on the open wound of Igor's nose. Blood covered Gösta's forehead and flowed down his face as he hung on until Igor went still, and then hung on longer. Exhausted, Gösta released Igor, fell over and lay on his back, gasping.

Beside him, Igor suddenly sucked in air and gasped for breath.

"No!" Gösta gasped, "No, fekking way!" He stood and went to the horse, grabbed his pistol, and walked back to the man. He shot Igor between his eyes, silencing him. Gösta stood and watched the man for a few seconds, kicking him once in the ribs. Satisfied he was finally dead, he holstered his pistol and picked up his sack of silver and carried it to the horse. He groaned from countless aches and pains as he swung his leg over the saddle. He took one last look at Igor then heard several muskets cock.

Fek!

He turned his horse to face them, three Russian soldiers on horseback aiming muskets at him. Gösta slowly unholstered his pistol and went through the process of reloading.

"Stop that!" Adrian shouted.

"I thought we were supposed to shoot him on sight?" Pavel, one of the soldiers, said.

"I fought beside him at Oravais!" Boris, the third man, said.

Gösta finished loading, cocked the pistol, and aimed it at the corporal. All guns fired at the same time. Adrian, hit in the chest, flew backward off of Dagmar, who turned and galloped back the way they had come. Gösta felt the punch of a musket ball slam into his shoulder. He turned and kicked his horse into a gallop and, like all wounded animals, sought the safety of home. In Gösta's case, his home was his parent's farm near Överboda.

Boris and Pavel gave chase, but their horses were no match for Gösta's horse, and they were soon left behind. They stopped and turned back to check the corporal's condition.

"He's dead," Pavel said after dismounting and putting an ear to Adrian's chest.

"What do we do, Pavel?"

"I don't know. Let's put these two in the barn. We'll get some sheets to wrap them in from the house."

After they did that, they explored the house for more victims and found the pastor in the cellar.

"Should we take him out to the barn?" Pavel asked.

"Fek that!" Boris was disgusted by the rat that was feasting on the dead man's face.

"It's getting late, Boris. Let's go put the horses in the corral and stay here tonight." Pavel said, "we will figure out what to do in the morning."

Boris, pleased at the prospect of not having to camp outdoors, readily agreed. There was plenty of food in the parsonage, and there were several jugs of wine on cellar shelves.

"Okay, grab some of that wine."

"You get it; you're closer."

"I'm not going anywhere near that rat!"

Pavel shook his head and muttered something that Boris couldn't hear.

"What'd you say?"

"Nothing."

* * *

Gösta rode the familiar trail to his boyhood home. He fell out of the saddle as he rode into the yard. Mårten Nilsson was sitting at the kitchen table in the small, dilapidated cabin when he saw movement out of the corner of his eye. He looked out the window and saw the horse standing in the middle of the yard and then noticed the man lying on the ground.

"Aggie, come look, there's someone out in the yard."

Agneta Sigurdsdotter came over and stood beside Mårten, placed a hand on his shoulder, and bent down to look out the window.

"He's hurt."

"I will go look; load the musket."

"Be careful, Mårten."

Mårten and Agneta were both sixty-five, still active but no longer able to run a farm by themselves. They survived, barely, on the rent they received for their ten-acre field. Mårten rose and walked to the door, picking up a stout branch from the woodpile before stepping onto the porch. As usual, he made sure not to step on the rotted plank. He would fix it someday, whenever he finds a suitable replacement plank.

Mårten cautiously walked toward the man. He lay on his stomach with his face away from Mårten. The horse tried to shy away, but the man on the ground still held the reins.

He must be wealthy to own a horse like that!

Mårten nudged the man with toe, the branch held at the ready. Nothing. Mårten looked back to make sure Agneta had the musket trained on the man.

I hope she doesn't hit me by accident!

He gave a wide berth as he walked around the man. Gösta, who still had Igor's blood on his face, was unrecognizable, even by his father. Mårten, who had not seen his son since he fled the country twenty-six years ago, waved his wife over.

"Take his horse to the corral and tie him to a rail. I will need to do some repairs before we let him loose in there."

Agneta reached for the reins and tried to pull them out of Gösta's hand, but he held tight. She knelt and tried to pry them out of his hand. Gösta's eyes fluttered open, and he whispered, "Mama," before passing out again.

"Gösta?" Agneta's hand flew to her mouth, "is it really you?"

"Wait, I'll tie his horse, and then we'll get him inside," Mårten said.

They lifted Gösta, mindful of his bloody shoulder and carried him inside and laid him on their bed. They took a few minutes to catch their breaths, this being the most strenuous thing they have done in recent memory. Agneta warmed some water and cleaned the wound. The ball had gone through the shoulder, so Agneta sewed up both holes after pouring some of Mårten's homebrew on it. Gösta moaned but did not wake up; he had lost a lot of blood. She then washed his face and then gasped at all the scars and broken nose.

Oh, Gösta, what have you suffered?

Gösta woke the day after arriving at home. Gösta, with many stops to rest and, probably to formulate new lies, gave a glossed over version of everything that happened to him since leaving home all those years ago. To hear him tell it, Gösta had led a chaste and law-abiding life! Of course, Mårten knew better, but Agneta believed her baby.

* * *

It was the second day when Pavel and Boris arrived. They had tied their horses fifty-yards from the cabin and crept the rest of the way. After seeing an older couple who looked like they could offer little resistance, the Russians kicked the door open and stormed into the house yelling.

Mårten and Agneta, both clutching their chests, stared in horror at these intruders waving guns and yelling at them in some strange language. Gösta, hearing the commotion, took his pistol from beside his bed and slipped it under his blankets. He had cleaned and loaded it that morning. Pavel came into the bedroom and grinned at Gösta.

"That was mine." He said, pointing at Gösta's shoulder.

Feeling confident, Pavel lowered his musket and put the stock on the floor. His face dropped when Gösta cocked his pistol, the sound unmistakable through the thin, threadbare blanket.

"You are a stupid man, Pavel." Gösta said in Russian, "tell Boris to come in here."

"Boris, come here."

Boris walked into the small bedroom, his musket in the crook of his arm, pointed downward. Gösta moved the blanket, exposing the pistol.

"Lean your muskets in the corner," Gösta said, waving his pistol toward one corner.

Boris looked like he would try his luck until a musket barrel pushed against the back of his head. Mårten said, "should I shoot him, Gösta?"

"Only if he lifts his musket."

Switching back to Russian, Gösta said to Pavel, "my father wants to shoot you and feed you to the pigs." Gösta didn't know if his father had any pigs, but it sounded good. "Now, lean your muskets in the corner!"

They did so and turned back to Gösta.

"We had to come after you, Gösta; we had no choice." Boris said, "I fought with you at Oravais."

"Did you? I don't remember you."

"You were shooting across the river like a sniper."

"I am a sniper!" Gösta said, "did Popov send you?"

"Yes, we were in the stockade and were promised dismissal of our charges if we killed you and returned his horse."

"If the army is still there."

"What do you mean?" Pavel asked.

"I would not be surprised if the Russians have retreated north again." Gösta said, "you may be trapped here, in uniform, and you can't speak the language. You will be beaten and hanged by the locals!"

Boris and Pavel looked at each other, the possibility of what Gösta said dawning on them. Gösta looked over their shoulders and said to his father, "it's okay, Papa." Mårten nodded and went to the table, setting his musket on top, pointed toward the bedroom.

"You will help me, and in return, I will see you safely to the border." He, of course, had no intention of fulfilling his part of the bargain.

"Help you how?"

"I have a score to settle with someone."

Pavel and Boris looked at each other, and both shrugged.

"Okay, we will help you."

"Good, my father said his corral needs repair."

"Hey, we didn't agree to farm chores!"

"I know, but if you want to eat, you will do it."

"Ach! Okay, Gösta, but there are limits!"

"Yeah, yeah. Go now; I am weary."

33

Dagmar trotted back to the main road and turned east, toward Umeå. Ten miles back, they had passed the road leading to her home. She had tried to turn down that road, but the bad man riding her jerked her back onto the main road. Now there was no bad man to stop her from going home. She assumed her master would be there waiting for her.

The first encounter she had on her journey home was one of the men from the churchyard. The stranger on the tall horse, but he just glanced at her as he passed. The next encounter was two men on a wagon pulled by an old horse. The wagon slowed as they neared each other, and one of the men reached for her reins, but she bolted past him and galloped down the road.

Finally, late in the afternoon, Dagmar trotted into a deserted Öhn farm. She wandered everywhere she had seen her master go on the farm, around the barn, the cabin, and the outhouse. He wasn't here. She drank the stagnant water from the trough, grazed the neglected barley crop, and then stood beside the barn.

The next morning, Dagmar trotted to the main road and turned right. When she entered the Håkansson farmyard, she whinnied a greeting to her friend. From the corral, Agnes responded. Dagmar trotted to the older and taller horse and tilted her head up to meet Agnes's nose.

"Well, look at you!" Eva said. She had been sweeping the front porch when she saw Dagmar trot into their yard. She had walked over to the corral where the two horses stood.

"Where did you come from?"

"Eva, is Johan back?" Israel said as he came out of the barn. He had recognized Dagmar from the time Johan rode him home last winter.

"No, this horse just wandered into the yard."

"This is Toby's horse, do you remember?"

"Oh yeah!"

"That's a ratty saddle. I don't think Toby would own a saddle like this." Israel inspected the saddle more closely and, after seeing a few drops of dried blood, he looked toward the road. "He may be hurt."

Is that Johan's blood? Or Toby's

He led Dagmar into the barn and unsaddled her.

"Give her some water and wipe her down, Eva; after that, put her in the corral." Israel said, "I'm going to saddle Agnes and go see if anyone's laying injured on the road."

"Yes, Papa."

Dagmar was none too happy being put into the corral while her friend rode away. She trotted around the corral with her head in the air, neighing and swinging her head around, occasionally sniffing the ground.

Israel was able to follow Dagmar's tracks in the dirt road. They would occasionally disappear in the center grass strip, but he would pick them up further down the road. He followed the tracks into Tobias's farm and saw how Dagmar had wandered all over the yard. Israel dismounted and called several times, "Johan! Toby!" He went to the door and found it unlocked, which did not surprise him; he himself never bothered to lock his door. The cabin was empty, as was the barn when he looked in there.

Israel remounted and rode back out to the road and continued following Dagmar's tracks. They were a little fainter, and Israel guessed that they were a day older than the tracks he had been following. At the road leading into the Larsson farm, he saw that Damar had gone straight past. Worried that Johan may be lying somewhere injured, Israel did not bother looking in on his neighbors and continued following the tracks. He rode past the Ume River bridge without seeing any sign of Johan or anyone else on the road. He came to a tee intersection and took the road left to Vännäsby. Dagmar's tracks came from that direction.

"What do you think, old girl?" Israel asked, patting Agnes on her neck, "are you up for a few more miles?"

He was not concerned about her stamina; she pulled their wagon whenever the Håkanssons went to the church service in Vännäsby. Of course, she had quite a long rest before the return trip. The pastor usually drew out his sermons to the point where Israel's arse would fall asleep, and he would have to limp out of the church like an old man! Agnes bobbed her head, and Israel steered her to the left.

The tracks were harder to follow in the heavily used road. Israel continued down the road looking on both sides of the road rather than searching for tracks. When he came to the road leading to the church, Israel thought that is as good as any place to give Agnes a rest before going back home. The good thing was, he could take a trail directly from the Vännäsby to Överboda, four miles shorter than the way they had come.

From the moment he rode into the parsonage yard, he felt something was not right. The front door was slightly ajar as if someone had left in a hurry. He also noticed drag marks leading from the house to the barn. Israel dismounted and led Agnes to the well, where he cranked the pail up and lifted it with two hands to drink from, splashing water on his cheeks and down his neck. He set the bucket in front of Agnes and then walked toward the house.

He knocked on the door and then stuck his head in and hollered, "hello, is anybody home?" The house was dead quiet save for the ticking of the mora clock in the parlor. Israel wandered through the main floor, noticing that some of the furniture was out of place, and he could see scratches on the floor where the heavy pieces had been drug to the door and then pushed out of the way. There was a faint odor of sweat and body odor that seemed out of place in this house.

What happened here?

He walked through the main floor and was surprised by the mess in the kitchen.

Someone who shouldn't be here did this.

Empty wine bottles lay on the table and floor, and food scraps everywhere. Israel stood taking this all in and then shook his head.

Pigs! Where is the pastor?

He went upstairs and saw the beds in two of the rooms were in disarray. The body odor was more prominent here. He also noticed someone had ransacked the drawers. Going downstairs, he was going to go outside when he passed the cellar door. He opened the door and smelled blood, earth, and something else. Israel found a lantern, lit it, and descended the stairs. Halfway down, he spotted the pastor's body. Israel shooed the rats away, there were more now, grabbed a linen tarp from a shelf, and wrapped the body. Noticing a shaft of light coming from the other end of the cellar, he found the doors and pushed them open. Israel dragged the body outside and to the barn, where he found the other two bodies, one being Igor, and the other, a Russian corporal with a gaping chest wound.

What the hell happened here?

He understood the blood came from one of these men, but what were they doing with Toby's horse?

Toby can't be responsible for these killings, could he?

With no answer to these questions, Israel rode into town to get the sheriff and, after showing him everything he found, took the trail home. It would be dark before he gets home, but that didn't stop him from giving Agnes frequent rest stops. Of course, the last half mile, Agnes broke into a fast trot, almost a gallop. Israel could hear Dagmar neighing as they turned into the yard. After unsaddling Agnes and wiping her down, he released her into the corral. He leaned his forearms on the top rail and watched the two horses frolic in the twilight.

34

R einforcements were arriving to help push back the advancing Russians. "Johan, they are coming!" Jon yelled. Colonel Sandels led his men into the Swedish northern army's encampment along the Öre River. Johan ran over to where Jon was standing. They scanned the soldiers as they marched by, looking for familiar faces.

"Nils!" Johan shouted, spotting his friend. Nils, of course, whooped and ran over to them, followed closely by a laughing Matthias.

"Get back in formation!" Major Love yelled, then, when he realized it was the Tröger boys, said, "ah, fek it." He watched with a broad grin as the four soldiers hugged and spun each other around like giddy children. Tobias was also watching them. He was less enthusiastic than his younger comrades. He had never fully regained his previous energy levels since recovering from his bout with dysentery. The simple act of marching left him exhausted after only a few hours. More concerning to him was that he seemed to be continually fighting off depression. The thought of the war ending and having to go back to his cabin alone sent him into a dark place in his mind. He was not a man given to sobbing, but he had woken up a few times with tears on his cheeks.

For the next day and a half, the Swedish northern army traded cannon fire across the Öre river with two thousand Russian Imperial Army soldiers. Neither army was inclined to attempt a crossing of the river. And then the cannons went quiet. The Russians seemed to have departed the field. But the Swedes stayed where they were. Johan and Jon were sent across the river to scout the enemy positions. They found the area north of the river deserted. Thousands of soldiers, horses, wagons, and artillery pieces left a clear trail for the scouts to follow. They found the two thousand Russians in a fortified position on the other side of the Ume River, five miles south of Umeå.

"Do you think we could make it back to the camp tonight?" Jon asked.

"Maybe halfway, we can't push the horses any further."

"Yeah, I suppose your right."

"There's no immediate threat to our camp; no sense killing these horses," Johan said.

The next day, in time for lunch, Johan and Jon forded the river and then walked their horses into the encampment.

"Should we eat first, or go make our report?" Jon asked. They did not have breakfast that morning.

"Better make our report now."

They found their captain and relayed what they had seen. The captain then informed Major Öden Love, who found Johan and Jon standing in the lunch line.

"You two, come with me!" He ordered.

Jon's stomach growled as they left the line and followed the major. They were alarmed to see they were walking in the direction of colonel Sandels's tent.

"Colonel?" Öden said.

Sandels turned and said, "yes, major, what is it?"

"Two scouts are here to report on the enemy's position, sir."

"Tell me," Sandels said, looking directly at Johan.

"The road north is empty. The first Russians we encountered were on the other side of the Ume River about five miles south of Umeå."

"Were they on the move?"

"No, sir. They appeared to have fortified their position."

As Sandels pondered the information, Öden said to Johan, "tell the colonel about your encounter the other day."

"Yes, sir. We were scouting and came to an open field about five miles north of here when we encountered a large Russian army. They were on the other side of the field, about three hundred yards away."

"How many, would you estimate?"

"Thousands, between four and six thousand, wouldn't you say, Jon?"

"Yes, more than four thousand."

"Tell the colonel what happened next," Öden said.

"We were dismounted, letting our horses graze; they had wandered quite a way from us when we spotted the Russians. We knew the Russians would run us down with their horses if we ran, and surrender was not an option-"

"Why not?" Sandels asked.

"Our comrade was a prisoner of the Russians; we would not consider surrendering after seeing his condition when he was released, sir."

"Aah, continue."

"We put our bayonets on and march forward, sir."

Öden grinned proudly as Sandels slapped his knee and cried, "two musketeers against six thousand Russians!"

"Yes, sir," Johan said, standing a little straighter. "But before we could destroy them, a rider galloped up to their commander and handed him a letter."

"This commander, what did he look like?" Sandels asked, still chuckling at Johan's bravado.

"We couldn't see his features, but he had no facial hair, and he sat on a tall black horse with a white blaze."

"Kamensky!"

Öden nodded. General Kamensky was the commander of the Russian forces in northern Sweden.

"What happened next?" Sandels asked.

"He shouted an order, and his army turned and left. Then he doffed his hat to us and galloped north."

"Hah!" Sandels laughed, clearly enjoying the story. "I will enjoy retelling this story back in Stockholm! What are your names?"

Öden answered for them, "this one is Johan Sparrman. The other is Jon Emanuelsson, grandson of the Carolean, Olaus Raderman!"

"Olaus Raderman!" Sandels said, "I see where you get your courage from!" He turned back to Johan, "and I remember you from Oravais."

"Yes, we were both there." Johan suddenly reddened as he pictured the officers watching him as he shook uncontrollably after his first attack.

Was Sandels one of them?

Jon's stomach rumbled loudly, and Sandels said, "you boys go get something to eat."

"Yes, sir!"

As they walked back to the cook tent, Jon turned to Öden and said, "sir?"

"Yes."

"How did you know my grandfather's name?'

"I read your file. I was also a friend to your father; I served with him in Pommern."

"But if you know my name, why do you call me Jon with shit on his hands?"

Öden chuckled and said, "do you know how many Jons there are in this army? I need to give each of you a nickname to tell you apart."

"But you know my last name is Emanuelsson."

"Yes, do you know how many Emanuelssons there are in this army?"

"Okay, but why do you call Johan by his first name only?"

"He is Johan; I remember him."

They were quiet until they came to the cook's tent where Öden left them.

"Adjö, Johan Sparrman, and Jon Emanuelsson!" Öden said as he walked away, then mumbled just loud enough for them to hear, "with shit on his hands."

Johan grinned, and Jon scowled.

August 20
Öre River

"Pack your kits; we march in one hour!" A captain yelled just as Johan lit his evening smoke. He could hear the captain and several other officers wandering through the camp, repeating the call. Johan and Jon filled their backpacks and rolled up their blankets. Nils and Matthias had been part of a large group that had crossed the river earlier this day and found ferries upriver to carry the wagons and artillery across the river.

When Johan and Jon arrived at the river, major Love said, "go saddle a couple of horses; you two will scout ahead of the vanguard."

They saluted, said, "yes, sir," and bolted toward the corral. Öden grinned as he watched them run.

I wish I could go with them!

Once mounted, they rode to the head of the column to await the order to leave. They were close enough to colonel Sandels and major Love to hear their conversation.

"About fekking time!" Sandels said.

"Yes, sir." Öden said, "do you think they've landed yet?"

"I hope not, Öden. They'll be up against the entire Russian army while we're sitting here twiddling our thumbs!"

Jon looked at Johan with arched brows. Johan shook his head and shrugged.

Öden turned and noticed Johan and Jon. He nodded and waved a hand for them to proceed.

Johan and Jon rode their horses into the river. The horses had to swim for ten yards in the deepest part of the river. When the horses climbed the bank, Johan and Jon nodded at Nils and Matthias, who were part of the crew handling the ferry ropes.

"You will not die this day, my friends!" They yelled as Johan and Jon galloped north.

August 21
Near Stöcksjö

Johan and Jon had not seen any sign of the enemy throughout the night. They stopped near a large open area, at the edge of a copse of poplars to eat some jerky around noon. They sat with their backs against trees to eat and then closed their eyes to catch a few minutes of sleep. After a few minutes, Johan slumped over and curled up on the ground. It was fortuitous that the side of his face was on the ground as the vibrations woke him an hour later. Sitting up, he saw the dust cloud from the west. He shook Jon's shoulder, waking him.

"Huh? What?" Jon mumbled, sitting up and rubbing his eyes.

"Look," Johan said, pointing to the west.

"Shit!"

"Grab your horse. We need to move back into the trees."

"Fek that, let's get the hell out of here!"

"No, we need to see how many there are."

They stood beside their horses, ready to mount and ride out if they are spotted.

"They're ours!" Jon cried when they saw two scouts come across the field. They mounted and rode out to meet them.

"Hello!" Johan said when they rode up to the two scouts, "who are you with?"

"Lieutenant-general von Döbeln, you?"

"General Wrede. I am Johan Sparrman and this is Jon Emanuelsson."

"Ivar Goransson and he is Arvid Johansson."

"Any sign of the enemy?"

"Nothing, you?"

"I think they may be on the other side of the Ume, about five miles downstream of Umeå."

"Aah, the general will want to speak with you."

When von Döbeln's troops caught up with them, Johan and Jon had dismounted and stood in awe of the great man. After relating what they knew of the Russian position and general Wrede's location and numbers, von Döbeln said, "we're not far from Stöcksjö. Go there with my scouts; we will wait here for Wrede."

"Yes, sir!" They rode to the village and found no Russians lying in wait. So, they returned to von Döbeln's camp to report the town was safe. When they dismounted, Johan was surprised to hear his name called.

"Bo?"

"Johan!" Bo Svärd repeated as he grabbed him by the shoulders, "it is good to see you again, my friend!"

"It is good to see you!"

"Ivar!" Bo called to a soldier a few yards away, "this is the Västerbotten musketeer I told you about!"

"The one who kicked you in the head?"

"Yes, the one and only!"

212

"It is good to meet you, Johan, anyone that kicks Bo in the head is a friend of mine!"

"Ach!" Bo said, then grinned along with the others.

"We had better go make our report, Johan," Jon said.

"Yes, you are right, Jon." Johan said, "I will see you again, Bo!"

Several hours later, general Wrede's northern army arrived. The entire northern army, now four thousand strong, marched toward the Russian fortifications on the north side of the Ume River previously scouted by Johan and Jon.

August 22
Ume River

They arrived early in the morning, having camped a mile away. Artillery crews set up, and the bombardment began from both sides.

"Major Love?"

"Yes, what is it, Johan?" They had to yell over the cannonades.

"Why do we have to be so close to the artillery crews?" Johan asked, "couldn't we move back some?"

Öden thought about that for a few seconds, then said, "I don't know, Johan! It's not like we are firing on them with our muskets. Wait here."

Johan watched as Öden walked toward the general. He watched as the general glanced over at him and then nodded. Most of the musketeers were moved back out of range, while some remained to fire on enemy artillery crews. The bombardment lasted all day.

August 23

Silence.

What is happening?

Johan lifted the door flap and stepped out of the tent. It was unseasonably cold this morning, and fog blanketed the river. He caught the smell of coffee in the air. Following his nose, he found Bo standing by one of the cook's fires, so he walked over and poured himself a cup from the coffee pot.

"It's quiet," Johan said.

"Yeah, I think they left in the night."

They stood drinking their coffee in companionable silence when they saw a shape walking towards them.

"Johan," Jon said, "we have orders to cross the river!"

"All of us?" Bo asked.

"No. just scouts."

"Well, good luck, my friends, I don't envy you crossing the river in this weather!"

Johan and Jon rode a mile upstream before finding a place to ford the river. They rode up the other side of the bank and found the road. It was recently chewed up and had numerous steaming piles of horse dung.

"They passed by here within the hour," Jon said.

"Yes, but there still may be some of them at the river."

They trotted their horses just the same. The fog had burned off, and they had good views of the terrain ahead until they got to the Russian fortifications. They slowed their horses to a walk and watched their ears. The horses will detect noise before they would. To their right, Johan and Jon could see their positions across the river. At this distance, their comrades would recognize their uniforms and not mistake them for Russians.

The place looked deserted. Johan dismounted and walked through the Russian fortifications, while Jon rode to a high point and scanned the area.

That's odd!

Johan saw several logs positioned at regular intervals. He walked over to one and circled it. The log pointed across the river, and the end was blackened.

They tried to make these logs look like cannons!

214

Johan chuckled and then turned toward the Swedish side of the river. He spotted Wrede, Sandels, and von Döbeln standing together looking at him.

"They are gone!" He yelled at the top of his lungs and pointed upriver in the direction of Umeå. He waved Jon over, and the two of them lifted one of the log "cannons" to show their commanders. All three had their spyglasses out, and then he saw them look at each other and shake their heads in disbelief.

"Can we cross upstream?" Sandels called.

"Yes, but it is probably better to follow the river and then cross on the bridge." Johan yelled, "we will continue on this side and report any enemy movements we encounter."

He saw von Döbeln raise his hand, indicating approval.

Of course, the general halted their advance south of Umeå. They would enter Umeå the next day once he was sure the Russians had left. Sandels and von Döbeln were furious at all the delays.

35

Anna could get used to this. Since the barn became an infirmary, she had been responsible for cooking and cleaning the house. Now, Anna had Camilla to help her. And the work seemed to be less dreary when she could talk with someone. Now they were eating a dish of Camilla's creation – shredded potato pancakes!

"These are delicious, Camilla!" Kajsa said, "you must show me how you make them."

"I taught Anna how to make them."

"But it's our secret!" Anna said solemnly.

Kajsa looked at Anna and Camilla.

What an odd pair!

"Papa would have loved these!" Maria said, then immediately regretted the comment as everyone went quiet.

"Yes, he would have!" Kajsa said, "and I know your grandfather would have loved them too!"

"These wouldn't be enough," Maria said, indicating the remaining pancakes, "there would have to be two more batches!"

Everyone laughed, including Camilla.

"Did you know my Papa, Camilla?" Anna asked.

"Oh, yes, since he was a boy."

"Really! What was he like, when he was a boy?" Ollie asked.

Camilla looked at Kajsa before responding, and when Kajsa nodded, she said, "he was more mischievous than you are, Ollie."

"Really?" Maria, Anna, and Ollie said in unison.

"Yes," Camilla looked at Kajsa for permission before she continued. Kajsa nodded with a slight smile. "Jarl, my husband, you may not remember, was the pastor before Samuel Nyselius took over. He and I were coming back from visiting a parishioner one day when we met your father and his friends on the road." She cast another glance at Kajsa before continuing, "they were bare naked!"

Shrieks erupted from the girls, including Magda. Ollie and Petter gaped at Camilla.

"Why were they walking naked?" Maria asked.

"Some young girls saw them swimming in the river and took their clothes!" Camilla said, glancing at Kajsa.

"Mama!" Maria cried, "was that you?"

"Yes, with your aunty Stina, but it was Maria Emanuelsdotter's idea."

"Really?"

"Then what happened, Camilla?"

"Well, Jarl was quite upset about the whole situation, so he punished them in church, made them kneel on the oak plank during service, on their bare knees!"

"They had to take off their pants?" Petter asked, wide-eyed.

"Yes, and one of the boys wasn't wearing underwear!"

There were more shrieks from the girls while the boys sat with gaping mouths.

"So, the boys decided to exact revenge on Jarl." Camilla said with a chuckle, "they came one night to the parsonage and moved the outhouse back several feet. Well, early in the morning, Jarl walked out to the outhouse to do his business and fell right into the hole!"

Everyone laughed hysterically at this.

"Poor Jarl, he was covered from head to toe in poop!" Camilla said, clearly enjoying the telling of the story, "oh! And, the words that came out of his mouth!"

Kajsa laughed so hard that her stomach began to hurt, and it didn't help when a fart escaped Anna as she laughed. Her fart was quite loud, amplified by the hard wooden chair.

Kajsa and Camilla shared her bed, and that night, Kajsa asked Camilla about the day of her attack.

"You don't have to answer, Camilla," Kajsa said. She had, like everyone else in the parish, been curious about the events of that day. Lars had told her about Camilla inviting Gösta into the parsonage while the pastor was away, but that was the last time he saw his childhood friend. Kajsa never did like Gösta; he was always staring at her chest, such as it was back then.

Camilla sighed and said, "I guess it would be good to tell someone about it; I have been keeping the secret too long."

Kajsa waited, anticipating hearing what happened that day. Of course, there had been many rumors, but no one knew for sure, other than Camilla and Jarl, and, of course, Gösta. But Jarl dead and, for all anyone knew, so was Gösta. Kajsa didn't know that Maria and Anna were listening intently from their room directly above them.

"Jarl was older than me, and he would rarely do a husband's duty, in bed." A muffled gasp from above and Kajsa called, "Maria and Anna! Get in bed and stopped listening to us!"

"Maybe I shouldn't tell the story," Camilla said.

"No, no!" Kajsa said, "just whisper."

"Aah, okay. So, I had my needs, and Jarl wasn't seeing to them! Do you understand?"

"Yes, of course. I mean, it was never an issue with Lars."

"No, I suspect not. Anyway, Gösta and Lars were cutting firewood for us, and Gösta had his shirt off, all muscles and sweaty." Camilla sighed again and was quiet for a while.

"Camilla?"

"Yes, sorry. So, I knew Jarl was going to be gone until well after supper. He always planned his visit to parishioners around mealtimes because they always felt obligated to ask him to stay and eat. So, I asked Gösta if he could stay and help me move some furniture in the house. Lars offered to help, but I told him I didn't need his help. I knew he was trying to keep his friend from doing something he shouldn't."

"That sounds like Lars."

"Of course, there was no furniture moving going on, except maybe the bed!"

"Camilla!"

The two women giggled, and then Camilla continued, "well, the parishioners Jarl went to visit weren't home, so he came back early and caught us in bed. There was a fight, and Jarl took a severe beating. Of course, I went to Jarl to help him and told Gösta to leave. He didn't leave; he punched me in the face and then forced himself on me."

"Oh, Camilla, I'm sorry."

"When he finished, he walked out and took our horse and buggy with him."

"Did you ever hear from him again?"

"No, it's like he just fell off the earth. Good riddance, I say."

"Thank you for telling me, Camilla."

"Could we keep between ourselves, Kajsa?"

"Yes, of course. And Camilla -"

"Yes?" Their voices had gradually risen above a whisper.

"You can stay with us for as long as you want."

Camilla was quiet for a while, and Kajsa was beginning to wonder if she didn't want to stay with them until she heard the soft sobbing.

"Thank you, Kajsa; I would like that. Anna has become the daughter I never had."

"Really, well, then you can have her."

"Hey!" A muffled cry from upstairs.

"Get to bed!" Kajsa yelled, then join Camilla's giggling.

36

W hen the northern army arrived in Umeå, the Russians had already left. They had gathered on the parade ground where general Wrede addressed them. He explained that a force of seven thousand men led by general Wachtmeister had left Stockholm aboard Admiral Puke's fleet. They landed north of Umeå in the village of Ratan. The plan was to surround the Russians between the landing force and the northern army.

Wachtmeister's army engaged the enemy at Sävar but had to retreat to Ratan. Upon hearing that, the assembled men voiced their disappointment. General Wrede held up his hand to quiet the crowd. He went on to say that another battle took place the next day at Ratan. This time, it was a Swedish victory! Admiral Puke's one hundred cannons resulted in heavy losses for the Russians but, in the process, also destroyed a large portion of the village. The Russians retreated north to Piteå. Wrede finished up by saying the northern army will march north the next day to reinforce Wachtmeister's army.

"We will not stop until we drive the heathens from Swedish soil!"

The crowd erupted in cheers; the end was in sight.

That evening, Johan sat on the steps of his barracks enjoying the night are while he puffed on his pipe.

"We are worried about Toby."

Matthias and Nils had come up behind Johan in the darkness and stood over him.

"Shit!" Johan cried, "don't do that! Wait, what did you say?"

"Toby, he's been depressed for weeks," Matthias said.

"Yeah, and he found out today his horse is gone, taken by the Russians," Nils added.

"Damn! That horse was a gift from his parents." Johan said.

"What should we do?" Nils asked.

"I don't know," Johan said, "we're leaving in a few hours, as you know."

Johan had talked once with Tobias since Sandels's army arrived. He had noticed that Tobias seemed preoccupied but attributed it to how tired Tobias looked.

"Could you go talk to the major?" Matthias asked.

"Yeah, okay, but what do I say?"

"Something's bothering Tobias, and he gets tired easily." Matthias said, "I am worried he will not be able to fight. He should stay behind."

"Okay."

Johan went to the officer's barracks and found three lieutenants standing outside smoking.

"Hi, I am looking for major Love."

"Yeah, aren't we all!" The other two lieutenants laughed dutifully, although it was obviously an old joke.

"Johan?" Öden said, sticking his head out of an open window, "what is it?"

"Can I have a word with you, sir?"

"Yes, of course."

The three lieutenants looked suspiciously at Johan.

Who is this man?

Öden walked out of the barracks a few minutes later, buttoning his shirt. The three lieutenants came to attention as he walked by them.

"You have your pipe, Johan?"

"Yes, sir."

Öden took out a pouch and filled his pipe. He handed the tobacco to Johan. Johan already had his evening smoke, but he packed his pipe just the same. When he passed the pouch back, Öden said, "keep it. I have more."

"Thank you, sir."

"Let's go find a fire."

The first fire they came to, two musketeers were sitting in front of it.

"Sit, sit," Öden said to the men. Johan took a stick from the fire and held it for Öden to light his pipe and then lit his own.

"Damn, that's good tobacco!" Johan said, blowing out smoke.

"It is from Denmark."

"Denmark, but we are at war with them!" Johan said.

"Yes, I am aware; that's why I'm going to burn their tobacco!"

Johan laughed. The two soldiers stood, stunned at the exchange between a major and a musketeer.

They must be relatives.

"Now, what is on your mind?"

"I am worried about Tobias Öhn." Johan said, "he is depressed and tires easily. And his horse, a gift from his mother, was stolen by the Russians."

"And –"

"And I am asking if he can stay behind when we march north tomorrow."

"Have you discussed this with Tobias?"

"No, sir."

"Okay, I will assign him to some duty here, and I will have the doctor take a look at him."

"Thank you, sir. Damn, that's good tobacco!"

"Hah!" Öden seemed pleased that Johan was enjoying his gift. They parted at the officer's barracks, and Johan started walking back to his barracks when he was startled by a voice.

"His son died at the battle of Revolax last year." A captain stepped out from between barracks and into the light.

"Excuse me, sir."

"His son was killed in battle."

"Yes, sir?" Johan said, puzzled at the exchange.

"You remind him of his son." The captain said and walked away without another word.

Well, that explains a lot!

But it didn't change how Johan felt about Öden. He considered the man a friend.

* * *

August 30
Skellefteå

"Johan Sparrman?" Captain Skarsgård asked.

"Yes, sir?"

"Major Love would like a word, come with me."

Johan followed the captain over to where Öden stood with Wachtmeister, Wrede, von Döbeln and Sandels.

Oh, shit!

"Musketeer Sparrman, sir!" The captain announced.

"Ah, Johan!" Major Love said, "as you have traveled this road several times, we would like you to accompany colonel Sandels to Frostkåge."

"Yes, sir."

Sandels nodded at Johan and then turned back to the other officers, dismissing him.

Shit. Shit. Shit.

They rode out two days later under a flag of truce. The group included colonel Sandels, major Love, captain Skarsgård, Johan, and several musketeers. That evening, they stopped near a shallow river.

"Where are you going, Johan?" Öden asked.

"Down to the river to fish."

"Really? May I join you?"

"Of course, sir."

They walked down to the river, and Johan selected a straight willow and cut it down. He stripped the willow of branches and sharpened the point. He handed it to Öden and repeated the process with another willow.

"There are some shallow rapids downstream."

When they came to the shallows, Johan sat down and removed his shoes and hose and then waded into the river, shivering after the first few steps before acclimatizing to the cold water. He found a good spot in a foot of water and turned to look back at Öden. The major was standing looking at him, "you don't expect me to wade in there, barefoot, do you."

"It's up to you, sir," Johan said, then raised his spear in the ready position and scanned the fast-moving water. Suddenly, he jabbed the spear down and came up with a wriggling trout.

"Whoo, hoo!" He cried and carried the fish to shore. He used a rock to kill the fish, then went back out for more.

"Ah, fek!" Öden said, not wanting to miss any of the action, he removed his shoes and hose. The next hour included missed fish, speared fish, and lots of laughter. When it started to get dark, Johan strung eight trout on his spear, and they each grabbed an end and carried their catch back to camp.

"Do you know the song, 'Little Karin'?" Öden asked as they walked.

"Of course."

"And do you hear, little Karin! Say, do you want to be mine?" They sang, well, more like bellowed, the old song the entire way back.

Colonel Sandels stood watching them come into the camp.

"Oh, that was you, major! I thought it was a wounded bear!" He said when they got close.

"No sir, it was us, and we have fresh fish for supper!" Öden cried, rosy-cheeked and grinning broadly.

"Well done, gentleman!" Sandels chuckled.

September 2
Frostkåge

Sandels, Russian general Kamensky, and their officers met in a hostel to negotiate a truce. Johan and the other musketeers stood outside across from an equal number of cossacks.

"Anyone speak Swedish?" Johan asked them.

"A little." One of the cossacks said, holding his thumb and forefinger an inch apart.

"You are camped in Piteå?"

The man hesitated, then shrugged, "yeah."

"There were two Swedish soldiers that went there to cause some trouble last winter. Did you hear anything about them?" Johan was curious to know what had happened to Klas and Arne.

"I remember when we chased your army out of Tornio and Kalix," he said, "we found two of your soldiers hung in the trees outside of Piteå."

"Ah." Johan eyed their clothing. Their shoes were separating at their soles, and their clothing was almost to the point of rags. They had a tough go, by the looks of it. Blocked supply lines, he suspected. He decided to have a smoke and took out his pipe and tobacco. He packed his pipe and looked around for a light when he saw the looks from the Russians—pure craving.

Ah, fek!

He held out the pouch of tobacco Öden had given him. The cossacks came forward, and they all stood around Johan, filling their pipes. The animosity slipped away, and they slapped Johan on the back, their way of thanking him without having the words to express their gratitude. One of them handed back his pouch, which was almost empty, while another ran around the back of the hostel and came back with a smoldering stick. They all lit their pipes, and the cossacks closed their eyes with pleasure.

"It has been a long time since we had tobacco." The Russian said, "and this is excellent tobacco!"

"It is from Denmark."

"Really? I thought you are at war with them?"

"We are," Johan said, "We plan to burn their country down one pouch at a time!"

"Hah!" He laughed then spoke rapid Russian to his comrades, who burst out laughing.

"Here they come." Someone said, and they quickly moved back to their original positions.

Sandels and Kamensky came out first and walked between them. Kamensky glanced at Johan and then stopped. He studied Johan while Sandels watched with curiosity. He turned and said something to a man behind him. The man turned to Johan and said, "he remembers you."

"Me?"

"Yes, he says you and one other soldier tried to fight six thousand Russians!"

Kamensky laughed and grabbed Johan by the shoulders, and quickly kissed both his cheeks. The look on Johan's face made Sandels laugh heartily. Major Love looked on with pride.

37

October
Nilsson farm

G östa sat beside his father on the porch, smoking their pipes. Still the same, cloying, expensive tobacco he had stolen in Finland and always despised. But he refused to throw or give it away.

Oh well, only two pouches left!

They watched Pavel and Boris cutting firewood. The winter stockpile was growing.

"We will be warm this winter, Gösta!" Mårten said, "last winter, we almost froze!"

Gösta just nodded. His shoulder was healing well, but his arm movement was still stiff and somewhat restricted. He wondered how long he could manipulate the two Russians.

"Huh?" Mårten had been talking to him, but he hadn't been paying attention.

"I said, maybe we need to build a small cabin for the boys."

"For those two?" Gösta asked, "why would we do that?"

"They can't sleep in the barn all winter; they'll freeze!"

"They won't be here for the winter."

"What? Why not?"

"They are Russian deserters." Gösta said, "if the Russians don't come for them, the Swedish army will. For me too." Gösta had told his parents everything that had happened to him since he left – his version of events where he was the victim.

"No one will know they are here, or you either."

"Yes, people will find out, it's only a matter of time, and then you will be in trouble."

Mårten sat quietly thinking, every once in a while, he would take an intake of breath when something occurred to him then, just as quickly, dismissed the idea.

"Shit!" Gösta said, "there, see what I said!"

They could see a rider approaching the lane into the farm through the mostly bare poplar trees lining the road. Gösta ran to Pavel and Boris and herded them into the barn. They grabbed their muskets and watched through cracks in the boards as the man rode into the yard.

"That's the horse the corporal was riding!" Pavel whispered.

"Your right!" Boris added, "how did he get it?"

"Shh!" Gösta hushed them. He sensed their paranoia.

"Hi, Mårten." Israel Håkansson called as he rode toward the house.

"Välkommen, Israel!" Mårten responded, "what brings you here?"

Israel hesitated at the question; it sounded like he was not welcome. Shaking the thought off, Israel asked, "how are you and Agneta?"

"We are fine, come and sit."

Mårten dismounted and tied Dagmar to a porch post. He sat down and noticed the chair was warm.

"Am I taking Agneta's seat?"

"No, no. She's been out back washing clothes all day."

All day?

Who was sitting in this chair?

Dismissing these thoughts, Israel said, "I bring good news. The war with Russia is over!"

"Aah, that is good news!" Mårten cried.

"Yes, my son will be coming home any day now!"

"Well, that calls for a drink!" Mårten got out of his chair on the second attempt and went into the cabin for his homebrew.

He's getting old; maybe I should offer to give him a hand while I'm here. Chop some wood or –

That's odd; how did he get all that firewood?

Israel was staring at the long stack of cut and split firewood running the entire length of one side of the barn. He looked at the barn and thought he saw a flicker of movement. He was about to rise and investigate when Israel came out of the cabin with his jug and two cups.

Great, I have to drink his vile brew; it tastes like dirty socks!

Mårten poured, and Israel took a tentative sip.

"Hey, that's pretty good!"

"Yeah, I, uh, tried something new," Mårten said hesitantly.

"I don't think I had this before; how do you make it."

Mårten tried to remember how Pavel made the homebrew, vodka, as he called it.

"Aah, it's a family secret, handed down for generations. I only bring it out on special occasions!"

"Huh. Well, it is a special occasion!" Israel said, "Johan's coming home, he will marry the Larsson girl, and they will live on my land! But we did lose Finland."

"Ach, Finland! What good did Finland ever do for you or me?"

"Yeah, you could be right." Israel agreed, "you have been busy!"

"Eh?"

"Cutting all that wood." Israel said, "it must have taken a while, cutting all that wood all by yourself?"

"Eh?"

Israel pointed toward the barn.

"Oh, no. It didn't take long at all. I can still put in a hard day's work!" Mårten said a little too aggressively.

"Well, I better get this horse back to Toby. I hear he is back home. I just wanted to give you the latest news and see if you needed anything." Israel drained his cup and stood.

"Thank you, comrade." Mårten laboriously rose out of his chair and shook Israel's hand.

Comrade? When did he ever call anyone comrade? He never served in the army.

Israel mounted and rode out of the yard, glancing at the barn as he passed, and the hairs on neck stood on end. He noticed Dagmar's ears twitching, pointing toward the barn.

Someone's hiding in there.

At the main road, he turned and galloped toward the Öhn farm.

"Let's go!" Gösta said.

"Where?"

"He knows we are in here. We need to shut him up before he reports us."

"He doesn't know we're here!" Pavel said.

"Did you see the way he was looking toward the barn?"

"Let's go ask Mårten what they talked about."

"Okay." Gösta hadn't thought to do that. "But we better hurry! Boris, go saddle the horses!" Boris nodded and ran behind the barn.

Boris doesn't my question orders, not like Pavel.

Israel rode into Tobias's yard, Dagmar galloping the last fifty feet, right up to the house where Tobias had been standing on his porch. Tobias had stepped off the porch, and it was a good thing; otherwise, Dagmar would have galloped right up onto the porch!

"Dagmar!" Tobias cried gleefully, "Where did you find her?"

"She wandered into our yard a few weeks ago," Israel said, dismounting and handing the reins to Tobias.

"I thought she was gone forever!"

Israel kept looking back toward the road.

"What is wrong, Israel?" He was rubbing Dagmar's neck as he talked.

"I don't know, just a feeling I have. I stopped at Mårten's house on the way here, and I had a feeling someone was hiding in his barn. Gave me the creeps."

"Huh, do you think Mårten is in any danger?"

"That's the thing, he seemed relaxed, but he called me comrade."

"Comrade?" Tobias said, "that doesn't sound like Mårten."

"No, it doesn't. I better be getting home."

"Well, I thank you for returning my horse, Israel."

"Adjö, Toby," Israel said as he walked out of the yard and turned toward home.

Tobias took the old saddle off Dagmar and let her loose. He stood and watched her wander over to the area behind the corral to graze.

Bad men are coming, Papa.

Tobias nodded and walked to the cabin, and went inside. He lifted his musket off the wall pegs and loaded it. He laid the gun on top of his kitchen table, strapped his holster and sword scabbard on, loaded his pistol, and then sat in the chair facing the door. "I'm ready, Georg."

Gösta, Pavel, and Boris trotted down the road. Dagmar's tracks were plain to see on the road, but Gösta ignored them; he knew where Israel lived.

"He turned in here," Pavel said.

"What?" Gösta asked.

"The tracks, they lead into this farm."

Gösta turned and walked his horse to where Pavel and Boris sat. He looked down and the tracks.

Why did he go into Toby's farm?

Gösta unslung his musket and held it across his lap; Pavel and Boris followed suit. They walked their horses into the yard.

"Someone's here," Boris said, pointing toward the smoke rising out of the chimney.

"Go see if he's in there, Pavel," Gösta said.

"Me?" Pavel said, "why me?"

"Because I said so!"

"No, this is your fight; you go."

They glared at each other until Boris said, "I'll go!" He dismounted and walked up the steps and across the porch to the door. He knocked and heard someone say, "come in."

Boris turned his head back to Gösta and nodded before opening the door and was blown back across the porch. He didn't hear the musket blast that killed him. Pavel's horse reared, but Gösta's mount was trained for battle and stood still.

Tobias quickly reloaded his musket and walked out the door. Without breaking stride, he shot at Pavel and saw that he hit him. With his left hand, he fired his pistol at Gösta, saw that he missed, and then charged at him with his sword. Gösta shot Tobias and rolled off his horse just as the sword swung toward him. He heard the horse squeal and then stagger before falling. Gösta tossed his musket aside and pulled his dagger out. Tobias had risen to his knees, blood blossomed on his chest, and dribbling out his mouth. He took his dagger out and stood, swaying.

"Toby!" Gösta said. As a boy, he had worshipped Tobias.

Tobias staggered toward Gösta like a drunken man, raised his dagger, and then fell on his face. Gösta holstered his pistol, walked over to Tobias, shook his head, then turned and looked down at his horse. Blood flowed from the large gaping sword wound on its neck. He watched two of the horse's leg kick, getting weaker and weaker until they stopped.

"Fek!" Gösta yelled. He heard a moan and walked over to where Pavel lay. Tobias's musket ball had hit him in the stomach. Pavel looked up at Gösta and pleaded, "help me."

"Okay." Gösta knelt and slit his throat. He stood and looked around for Pavel and Boris's horses. They stood together a few yards away, and he had no trouble catching Pavel's horse, the better of the two. He led the horse to the porch and tied it to a post. Israel was not inside. Gösta mounted Pavel's horse and trotted out of the yard, followed by Boris's horse.

Tobias took Georg's hand in his.

Do you think we can find Mama?

I don't think so, son; she may have gone somewhere else.

Where?

I don't know; come on, they are waving to us.

Okay, Papa. Papa?

Yes?

Those were bad men.

"Yes, they were. Don't worry, Georg; we will never see them again."

Dagmar watched them through the trees until they faded. She had grown used to Georg's presence and was not frightened. She lowered her head walked to the road.

Israel heard the gunshots in the distance. He knew they were coming from Tobias's farm.

I hope I didn't lead anyone to Toby's house!

Israel increased his pace with a sense of urgency, a quick shuffle as his running days were long gone. Over the pounding of his heart, he heard another pounding. Behind him! He jumped off the road and hid in the bushes until a rider galloped by, followed by a riderless horse.

Frida!

Israel went back to the road and ran. He ran as he had run as a young man.

Frida was in the back yard, in the garden plot when she heard the horse. Thinking it was Israel coming back, she walked to the back door, wiping her hands.

I better get supper on.

Her hand was on the door handle when she heard the front door bang open.

"Israel, where the hell are you?"

She stopped short, her hand still on the handle.

Who is that?

She could hear someone kicking doors inside and someone yelling, "come on out!"

The stomping footsteps were coming closer to the back door, so Frida ran, bent over below window level, around the corner of the house toward the front. She heard the back door get kicked open, so she went in the front door and hid in a closet, leaving the door slightly ajar so she could see out. Frida saw a fearsome-looking man go by the house's side windows. Pushing the door open wider, she saw, through a front window, the man walking toward the barn.

After a few minutes, the man came out of the barn and walked back toward the house. Frida quickly pulled the closet door shut and prayed. She stopped her prayer when she heard the horse galloping away. But she stayed where she was and began shaking uncontrollably.

Israel was gasping, and his lungs felt frozen as he ran. Suddenly he stumbled. He tried to recover, his arms pinwheeled, and then he fell through the willows on the side of the road and into the ditch. Israel lay there and gasped for breath, his heart hammered, and his head swam.

I am going to die!

He was still struggling to breathe when the horseman galloped past. Then another horse followed.

Israel rolled onto his belly and worked his way up to his hands and knees. His arms shook as they tried to hold his weight. Eventually, his breathing returned to normal, but his chest felt like a belt pulled tight around it. He stood and shakily climbed out of the ditch, through the willows, and onto the road. Ashen faced and sweat on his forehead, Israel staggered down the road.

He finally made it home. Terrified at what he may find, Israel stumbled toward the house. The door opened, and Frida came running to him. He collapsed into her arms and lost consciousness.

38

The day was warm, and it was time for fall cleaning at the Larsson home. They had cleaned the barn the day before. The influx of dysentery victims had stopped, the barn was empty, and Erik had gone home.

"We may see more illness once the soldiers return home," Camilla said.

"I hope you are wrong, Camilla," Kajsa said, "but we will be ready if it comes to pass."

Kajsa and Camilla were outside washing blankets. Maria was on her hands and knees inside the house scrubbing floors, and Anna was outside cleaning windows. Petter and Magda were carrying water, emptying dirty water, and generally getting underfoot. The doors were open to allow fresh air into the house, and Ollie was in the back yard beating rugs. Kajsa missed her father at times like this. Of course, she missed Lars too, but, on cleaning days, he always found work to do in the barn or the fields. On the other hand, Olof would have been hovering and wandering back and forth, offering suggestions but doing little to help. She smiled at the memory of past spring and fall cleanings with her father.

"What are you smiling at, Mama?" Anna asked. She was washing windows on the same side of the house where Kajsa and Camilla were scrubbing blankets. Kajsa worked the wet blankets on a ribbed board in a galvanized tub full of water and homemade soap while Camilla would hang them on ropes that were strung between trees to dry. Kajsa always loved the smell of bedding after they hung outside in the crisp autumn air. After the cleaning, she would have her best sleep of the year in the fresh-smelling bedding.

"Oh, just thinking about your grandfather."

"Mama?"

"Yes?"

"I don't think about grandpa unless someone mentions him," Anna said. "Is that bad?"

"No, of course not!"

"I used to hear Maria cry at nights after he died, but I didn't cry."

"Maria and your grandfather were close. You were close with your grandmother, remember."

Anna looked up and said, "yes! I cried when grandma died!"

"Okay, now get back to work."

"Yes, Mama." Anna turned back to the window and sloshed soapy water on it.

"Do a good job, Anna. Don't leave soapy streaks behind."

"Okay, Mama," Anna said. "Mama?"

"Yes, Anna?"

"I'm hungry."

"We just started!"

"Can I have a snap?"

"No. Maria's washing the floors."

"Oh, I don't have to go inside," Anna said, dipping a soapy hand into her apron pocket and coming out with a ginger snap. Kajsa just shook her head and sighed. Anna smiled and took a bite, and then made a face when she tasted the soap.

Ollie came around the corner carrying a rolled-up rug over his shoulder. He carried it to the open front door and called, "can I bring this rug in?"

"Leave it by the door!" Maria said. She came into the living room to inspect the rug and nodded her approval. Ollie walked out onto the porch and sighed loudly, "aah."

"Where?" Anna asked.

"Where what?" Ollie said.

"Aah."

"Eh?"

"You said, aah…, Johan."

Kajsa laughed and shook her head. "You two."

"Did someone say, Johan?" Maria asked; she had popped her head out of the open front window.

"Johan's not here yet, Maria," Kajsa said. Johan had written that he would be discharged from the army any day now and would be coming home.

"Oh," Maria said, obviously disappointed. "Hey, why didn't you tell me we were taking a break?"

"We're not taking a break," Kajsa said.

"I'm hungry," Anna said.

"Is the kitchen floor dry, Maria?"

"Yes."

"I will go make lunch," Kajsa said, drying her hands on her apron.

"I'll help you," Camilla said.

The man arrived after lunch. Maria was sitting in the outhouse and saw him through a crack between the door boards. He was holding a pistol.

Gösta was at a loss on how to find Camilla. He decided to visit his old friend Lars; maybe he knew where he could find her. Of course, Lars had a part in Gösta's troubles those many years ago; the arsehole should have stopped him from going into the parsonage.

He had scouted Lars's farm to make sure no soldiers were lying in wait. Gösta circled to the side of the house and came in through the trees behind the line of blankets. He weaved his way through the blankets and stood looking at a woman in profile. She looked familiar.

"Kajsa?" He asked, startling her. "Is that the little brat that stole our clothes when we went swimming?"

Kajsa spun around and then moved around the tub, putting it between them.

"Who are you; what do you want?" She said it loud enough and with enough distress for her children to hear her and hopefully stay hidden inside.

Gösta didn't bother to respond. He held his pistol steady on her and said, "where is Lars?"

"Lars died from the rödsot."

"Aah, that's too bad. He was your husband?"

"Yes."

"Where's Olof?" Gösta asked, scanning the farm in search of the old soldier.

"Rödsot."

Gösta nodded. "How many children do you have?"

Kajsa caught movement behind and to the left of the man. It was Maria slipping quietly out of the outhouse and sneaking behind the building.

"Fi – four."

"Do you know where Camilla is; pastor Silfversköld's wife?"

"No."

"Call your children."

"What happened to you, Gösta?" Kajsa asked, playing for time.

241

"Call those kids? Get them out here!"

"They are in the house. They can stay there."

"No, I want them out here. Call them now!" He leveled his pistol at her.

Kajsa hesitated, then called, "Ollie, Anna, Petter, Magda, come out here."

Anna slowly walked out of the house, followed by her siblings. When they were twenty feet away, Ollie stepped around Anna and leveled his father's French carbine at Gösta. The barrel shook considerably.

Gösta pointed his pistol at him and said, "put the gun down, boy."

"Ollie, put the gun down!" Kajsa cried.

Ollie hesitated for a few seconds before Anna put her hand on the barrel and looked him in the eyes. Ollie lowered the gun and set it down on the ground.

"Come here," Kajsa said, opening her arms and waving her children to her.

"I haven't seen Camilla in days, Gösta," She said, "you need to leave, now."

"Tie them up."

"What?" Kajsa said, not believing what she was hearing.

Gösta walked over to one end of the rope clothesline and cut it where it wrapped around a tree. Kajsa looked on in dismay as the blankets fell to the ground. He walked to the other end and cut again.

"Put them in a circle, back-to-back, and tie them securely. I will check." He tossed the rope at her feet.

Kajsa slowly picked up the rope and grouped her children in a circle. She looped the rope around their waists tied it, secure enough without hurting them. Anna whispered, "where's Maria?"

"Shush! Where is Camilla?"

"She snuck out the back and is going for help."

"Stop that whispering! Now, back up," Gösta said, waving his pistol. Kajsa backed away toward the carbine. If Gösta noticed, he didn't give any indication. He checked the tightness and the knots.

"That will do. I wouldn't try it, Kajsa."

Kajsa had been inching toward the carbine but stopped short a few feet away.

"Now what?"

Gösta walked toward her, forcing her to back up. He stooped and picked up the carbine.

"This is a nice gun! I think I'll keep it." He glanced at the boy and was pleased to see him scowl at him.

"Now, you tell me where I can find Camilla." He turned the carbine toward the children.

Camilla stumbled onto the road and looked both ways. She saw a man walking from the north and ran awkwardly toward him.

"Camilla!" Johan said, "What are you doing out here?" He grabbed her by the shoulders to steady her.

"Gösta; he is holding Kajsa's family hostage!"

"Gösta! Hostage? What are you talking about?"

"He's crazy; he tied them up and is waving a gun around. He's looking for me!"

"Go to my father's house and tell him what is happening!" Johan said.

"Okay." Camilla hurried down the road, "be careful, Johan, he has a gun!"

At Johan's discharge from the army, he was allowed to keep his uniform, as worn as it was, but nothing else. As he neared the road into the Larsson's, he looked through the bare poplar trees as saw them grouped on the south side of the house. He would have to circle and come through the trees undetected to have any chance against a man with two guns.

Is that Lars's carbine he has, the one Lars showed Johan almost every time he visited?

243

How do I do this with no weapon? The tool shed?

He changed direction and headed for the tool shed. There should be something in there that he can use as a weapon. Johan moved as fast as he dared, circling through the bush, putting the house between him and the group. Once out of view, he ran through the bush and across the open yard to the crib. The door opened with a squeal of rusty hinges. Johan stopped and held his breath, watching the corner of the house. He let his breath out and slipped inside when no one came around the house. It took a few seconds for his eyes to adjust to the gloom. Lars did have, or had, a lot of tools. Johan selected a hatchet and a hand scythe. He crept out of the tool shed and ran to the house. Through a window, Johan could see across the house and out a window on the opposite wall. He could see a man's head moved in and out of view as if he were pacing.

Johan ran around back and crept to the corner. Peaking around it, he saw Petter, Magda, Anna, and Ollie sitting on the ground, tied up. Kajsa was standing a few feet from the man.

Where is Maria?

"Now, you tell me where I can find Camilla." The man said and then turned the carbine toward the children.

No!

Johan yelled his battle cry and ran at the man. Kajsa dove at Gösta, but he hit her with the carbine's stock, knocking her down. He turned, aimed the carbine at Johan's chest, and pulled the trigger. Nothing happened. Petter, Magda, and Anna, Ollie yelled, "Mama!"

Johan threw the hatchet on the run and saw it hit the man's raised arm. He lifted the hand scythe when Gösta shot him with his pistol.

Johan felt the punch of the ball hit his chest and drive him backward. He lay there looking up at the cloudless sky. He saw geese flying high above him in a vee formation. Johan smiled when he remembered Olof asking him if he knew why one side of the vee was longer than the other. Johan couldn't think of a reason, and Olof said, 'because there are more geese on that side!'

Why am I thinking about that now?

The man's face came into view. He should be scared; the man had a scary look, and he was reloading his pistol as he stood over Johan. The man's left

244

forearm was bleeding badly where the hatchet hit, but he did manage to load the gun.

Johan watched him as he cocked the pistol.

I can't move.

Suddenly, the man jerked, a shocked look on his face, and then jerked again. The man dropped the pistol and fell to his knees. His eyes appeared to glaze over, and blood trickled out of the side of his mouth. Maria's face came into view. She grabbed the man by the hair and said into his ear, "you hurt my family!" Then she pushed him over. Johan saw two arrow shafts sticking out of the man's back as he went down. Then darkness.

39

March, 1810
Umeå church

Israel, Frida, and Eva rumbled into the churchyard in their farm wagon. Israel was still recovering from his heart attack, so Frida drove. Johan rode beside them on Dagmar. He had recovered from his wound. The musket ball had hit Johan high in the chest, breaking a rib but missing vital organs and major arteries.

Johan dismounted and tied Dagmar to the wagon and then helped his father down. Johan heard a familiar yell behind him, actually two yells, as Matthias and Nils ran toward him. Nils lifted him in a bear hug, and Johan grunted.

"Sorry, I forgot about your injury."

Johan could tell it was killing the Trögers not to bear hug him, so he grabbed Matthias and hugged him, then Nils. A stout woman in her fifties was making her way toward them.

"This is our Mama!" Nils cried, "Mama, this is Johan!"

She held out a large hand and said, "I am Tova; thank you for taking care of my boys."

"I don't know if I took care of them or if they took care of me."

She squeezed his hand and smiled, "a little of both, I suspect."

Johan flexed his hand after she released it.

"Johan!"

Johan turned to see major Love ride up on a tall stallion. He dismounted with a flourish and strode up to him, "congratulations, my boy," he said before embracing him.

"Careful, he has a wound," Nils said, "sir."

"Oh, sorry, Johan!"

"It's okay, just a little sore. I didn't expect to see you here, sir."

"I wouldn't miss it!" Öden said, he handed Johan a wrapped package and winked, "your wedding present, from Denmark!"

"Thank you, sir!"

"The colonel sends his regards."

"Really? I am surprised he remembers me."

"How could he forget - and who is this lovely lady?" Öden asked, seeing Tova behind Johan.

"This is Tova Tröger." Johan said.

"The mother of the Tröger boys?" Öden said, taking her hand, "the bravest warriors of the Swedish army?" He bowed and kissed her hand.

Tova blushed and smiled demurely while Nils and Matthias stood behind her with their chests puffed out.

Jon came over, nodded at Öden, and then said to Johan, "we should go inside before Maria arrives."

"Okay." He turned to his friends and said, "I will see you in there."

Johan and Jon walked to the church where Erik Kiällberg was helping Israel up the stairs. Just then, an older couple riding in a fancy carriage pulled by two horses that looked similar to Dagmar arrived. Riding alongside the carriage was a Sámi woman on a magnificent mare. What was more striking was twelve armed Sámi men flanking the carriage. Two riderless horses trailed behind the carriage.

"Who are those people, Erik?" Johan asked.

"That, my friend, is Pehr Raderman and Lovisa Öhn," Erik said, "the woman on the horse is Toby's sister, Dárjá."

"Why do they have all those Sámi men with them?" Johan asked. He recognized Nikko and Kálle and lifted a hand in greeting to them.

"They are guarding Pehr. The Swedish army wants him for desertion."

"No!"

"I doubt if the army is still looking for him, and I believe Pehr is innocent, but the Sámi are taking no chances."

"They must think highly of him."

"They think highly of Lovisa," Erik said.

Johan walked into the church and up the aisle and stood beside Jon at the altar. He smiled nervously at friends and relatives in attendance.

When Pehr, Lovisa, and Dárjá entered, a hush fell over the church's older people, followed by excited whispering. As the trio walked down the aisle looking for a place to sit, several older women reached out to shake Lovisa's hand, and some embraced her. Lovisa had presided as mid-wife at many of their births, and they still held her in high esteem. The older men shook Pehr's hand; very few had known him before he left to fight the Prussians half a century before, but they all respected him. Several people moved to make room for them, one couple giving up their seat to them and then standing along a wall.

The doors opened, and Kajsa, Anna, Petter, and Magda walked toward the pews in front. Camilla stayed back at the farm to prepare the wedding meal. Kajsa cried out when she saw Lovisa and squeezed past people to go to her. They stood and hugged, Kajsa alternating between sobbing and laughing. Many of the women watching dabbed their eyes with handkerchiefs. Kajsa told Lovisa she would visit with her after the ceremony and made her way back to the aisle.

"Hi, Aah!" Anna said to Johan when they got to the front pews.

"Hush!" Kajsa said.

Everyone looked to the door as Ollie walked his sister down the aisle. Audible gasps from the Trögers caused a few giggles. She was stunning in her wedding dress. Johan felt his knees almost give way. A loud crunch and Kajsa glared at Anna, who had bitten into a cookie. She grinned and put the rest of the cookie back in her dress pocket.

After the ceremony, the newlyweds stood beside Kajsa at the church's door, accepting congratulations and gifts from the guests.

"Maria, Johan," Kajsa said, "this is my uncle Pehr and my good friend, Lovisa Öhn."

"It is an honor to meet both of you!" Johan said, "I have heard so much about you."

"Our wedding gifts are tied to the back of our carriage," Pehr said.

"And we want you to ride home in our carriage," Lovisa said.

"But, how will you get there? You are coming to celebrate with us, aren't you?" Maria asked.

"Of course, min älskling!"

"And your friends are also welcome." Johan said, "I know Nikko and Kálle."

"Yes, they won't leave Pehr's side until we get back to Norway," Lovisa said.

Maria wondered how she would get Pehr alone to ask him if he would finish the story Erik told her about him.

After everyone left the church, Johan went over to have a smoke with major Love before getting into the carriage. He told him Pehr's story.

"Ah, that explains the armed guard." Öden said, "Johan, I will speak with Sandels and see if we can clear his name."

"Thank you, sir."

"Call me Öden, Johan."

Johan watched Pehr and Lovisa untie the two horses from behind the carriage and walk them over to where Eva was standing with Dagmar.

Lovisa stroked Dagmar's neck as she spoke to Eva. Eva squealed and embraced Lovisa.

I guess she can keep Dagmar.

Pehr and Lovisa swung up onto their horses with ease.

They are seventy years old!

Maria poked her head out a window of the carriage and called, "come on, Johan, let's go home!"

Yes, home.

A NOTE TO THE READER

Although Sweden fought in two wars simultaneously from 1808 to 1809, the Finnish war and the Dano-Swedish war, this story focuses on the soldiers fighting in the Finnish war.

The dysentery epidemic in Sweden, during both wars and for a few years after, resulted in the death of approximately 50,000 people.

Please turn the page for a preview of the next
Sandberg novel coming in late 2021

THE EXECUTIONIST

1

July 1840
Västerbotten County
Northern Sweden

G ustav Andersson was surprised to see two children emerge from the woods alongside the dirt road. They were a hundred yards away, and they turned and began walking towards him. They had not spotted him yet. Gustav was eighteen years old and had spent the last two years traveling the county doing odd jobs wherever he could. Most of the work was on small farms but also with sawmills and a glass factory. Gustav has been saving the money he's earned for passage on a ship to America.

There, they see him.

The children did a double-take and stopped walking. Gustav raised a hand in a friendly wave to put them at ease. They were still a few hundred yards away.

What were they doing in the woods?

"Hello!"

"Hi." The boy, who appeared to be about twelve or thirteen, replied.

"Hot day."

"Yeah."

"I am Gustav."

"Carl. This is my sister, Maja."

"Would you know where the Höglund farm is?"

"Yeah, it is close to five miles from here." Carl said, "the Umeå road is three miles or so and then go right about a mile and a half."

"Thank you. Were you picking chantarelles?"

"No!" Maja giggled, "it's too early for chantarelles!"

"Yeah, you are right." Gustav stared at them, but no further explanation seemed forthcoming. "Well, I must be on my way."

"Adjö, Gustav," Carl said, taking Maja's hand and walking past him.

"Adjö, Carl and Maja."

Maja turned her head and waved to him.

Nice kids.

Gustav kept an eye on the spot where the children had emerged from the bush and slowed his pace when he neared the area. He walked past it, stopped, and then turned around; the children had disappeared around a bend in the road. Gustav scanned the brush but did not see a trail.

It must be here!

He walked back the way he came, never taking his eyes off the brush. There! He spotted the faint trail between two large spruce trees. He hopped over the shallow ditch and took a giant step over the grass so as not to leave any trace of his entry. A faint trail weaved through the bush around trees and willows before suddenly ending at a large clearing. And in the middle of the clearing was the beginnings of a small log building.

He ducked when he heard a wagon go by on the road and then felt embarrassed when he realized no one could see him through the trees from the road. He turned back to the logs and noticed they sat on an ancient rock foundation. Looking around, Gustav saw a small dip in the ground about four-foot square.

That must be the old well. I wonder when this place was abandoned.

As the sun was low, Gustav decided to sleep here and arrive at Höglund's farm in the morning. He built a small fire inside the foundation and heated water for tea. The mosquitoes, for some reason, were none existent in this clearing.

I better mark that old well, so those kids don't fall in. I bet there is only a thin layer of moss over rotting boards covering the well.

After his tea and jerky, Gustav gathered spruce boughs for his bedding – there were many boughs where the kids had trimmed the spruce logs. Laying his blanket down, Gustav settled in for the night. It was getter cooler at night as the summer was coming to an end but still comfortable enough to sleep outside with a single blanket. He drifted off to sleep, thinking, as he always did, about going to America.

When he woke in the morning, Gustav built a fire and made some tea. He dreamt of being robbed of his savings – his greatest fear.

Can I trust Arvid and Bengt?

No, I can't.

I had better hide my money and then pick it up after I finish working for Arvid.

Gustav's eyes settled on the stacked stone foundation. He crept on hands and knees around the exterior of the foundation, looking for a loose stone. Gustav found what he was looking for; a stone about four inches in diameter wobbled when he pushed it with a finger.

Taking his knife out of its sheath, Gustav worked the rock free. There was a gap big enough for his sack of coins. He removed his coat, cut the seams he had sewn below the armholes, and removed a cloth sack from each side. Gustav stuffed the bags into the cavity and pushed the stone back in the hole. He took some sand from the inside floor and packed it around the stone. He looked around and found a short branch. Gustav sharpened one end and then pushed it into the dirt in front of the stone as a marker. He sat back and inspected his work.

Perfect.

＊ ＊ ＊

Is this the farm?

Gustav thought back to what the men in the tavern had told him about the farm. They had sat down uninvited across the table from him as he ate his meat pie, a rare splurge for him. He had worked hard that day, and he felt he had earned the treat.

The men, local farmers Arvid Höglund and Bengt Nilsson, who looked to be in their late fifties, struck up a conversation with him, and the talk eventually turned to Gustav's dream of traveling to America. Arvid and Bengt expressed their admiration for his courage to venture across the ocean all by himself.

They heartily congratulated him when he bragged about having saved most of the ticket price. Sure, it was only steerage, but Gustav has slept in worse places than the hull of a steamship. If all goes as planned, he will celebrate his nineteenth birthday on the ocean crossing.

So impressed were his new friends with Gustav's determination that Arvid offered him a job on his farm. At first, Gustav was dubious of the two men. They were dressed in threadbare clothes and had the look of hard men, but so did many of the farmers Gustav had worked for in the last couple of years. Because he was so close to his goal, and no other offers were forthcoming, he agreed to work for Arvid.

That was two days ago. Today Gustav stood in a light drizzle at the entrance of a rundown farm. *Is this the farm? Can I trust this man to pay me for my work?*

"Hello!" A voice called.

Gustav looked around but didn't see anyone. Then he saw them. Arvid and Bengt were standing in the gloom of the barn's door. The barn's red paint had mostly flaked off, exposing aged, cracked boards. Some boards were missing, and grass covered at least two feet of the barn's bottom. Rusty tools and implements lay scattered in the yard.

What am I getting into here?

"Come on; we'll show you what you will be doing and your sleeping quarters." Arvid waved him in.

For a few seconds, Gustav felt the overwhelming urge to flee. Flee as fast and as far as he could from this place. Then it passed. Sighing, Gustav walked toward the barn.

A couple of weeks, and then I will have enough for my ticket.

"Come in out of the rain, Gus." Bengt beckoned with a wave and a semi-toothless smile.

Rain trickled down the sides of Gustav's face and spine.

I can always leave if I don't like it here.

Gustav followed Arvid into the barn, and Bengt followed after shutting the door. Gustav stopped to let his eyes adjust to the dark interior when he felt a shiver run up his spine. Shaking it off, Gustav was about to step forward when something crashed into his skull. The blow stunned him, his ears were ringing, and he felt wetness on his scalp.

"Let's put him in that chair and tie him up."

"Check his pockets," Arvid said as he tied the knot at the back of the chair.

Bengt rooted through the unconscious man's pockets.

"Nothing!" He cried in disgust.

"Let me see," Arvid said, brushing past Bengt.

He patted the coat, shirt, and trousers.

"Shit!" Arvid said, "where's all that money he was bragging about?"

They sat on a bench and waited for Gustav to wake up.

"Light a fire," Arvid said.

"It's raining outside."

"Light it near the door; use those boards."

"Why do we need a fire? It's not that cold?"

"No, it's not, but we have to convince him to tell us where he hid his money."

"Ahh," Bengt said, grinning and nodding his head.

Gustav regained consciousness slowly. His head ached, and a wave of nausea surged over him. Blinking to clear his vision, he saw the two farmers sitting on a bench in front of him.

"Where's the money?" Arvid asked.

"What money?"

"Don't bother lying to us, Gustav; it will prove painful for you." Arvid turned and repositioned the iron poker in the glowing coals. Gustav watched this, not comprehending the significance of the gesture.

"I have no money."

"Bullshit!" Bengt cried, "we found the ripped open pouches sewn into your coat! Where'd you hide the money?"

"I'll never tell. You may as well give up; I won't say anything about this."

Bengt looked at Arvid and nodded. Arvid turned and took the poker out of the coals while Bengt stood and ripped Gustav's shirt open. Arvid stood in front of Gustav and put the glowing poker tip near Gustav's eye. Gustav could feel the heat emanating from the poker.

"Last chance."

Gustav shook his head, and Arvid lowered the poker and pressed it to Gustav's chest. Gustav screamed as his flesh sizzled and smoked.

"That's enough, Arvid!" Bengt cried, disgusted at the smell.

"Shit, it's stuck!" Bengt reached over and, between the two of them, managed to rip the poker, and a chunk of skin, from Gustav's chest. Mercifully, Gustav passed out again. Arvid, too impatient to wait, placed the poker back in the coals and went outside to get a pail of water. He threw it into Gustav's face.

"Tell us, or it is going to get worse!" Arvid yelled at him when Gustav opened his eyes.

Gustav shook his head again but changed his mind when he saw the red-hot poker moving toward his right nipple.

"Okay, okay!" He cried, "I will tell you."

Arvid put the poker back in the coals and looked at Gustav, "in case you change your mind."

"Now, where is the money."

"I hid it in the woods," Gustav said, "on the other side of the Ume."

"Where in the woods."

"I will take you there."

"No, you will tell us exactly where it is, and then you will take us there."

"No."

Arvid looked at Gustav and then said, "wait, I'll be right back." He went out of the barn and returned a few minutes later. He walked over to Gustav and slapped the burned flesh; Gustav screamed and then clenched his teeth.

"What was that?" Bengt asked.

"Salt." Turning to Gustav, he said, "now, tell me where the money is, or it is the poker again."

"In the woods between the bridge over the Ume River and Sörfors, on the left. There's an old homestead with a well. It's down in the well, just above the water." He was purposely deceitful, thinking he could escape before they got anywhere near the money.

"There, that wasn't hard now, was it?" Arvid said, walking behind him and picking up an axe. He brought it down on Gustav's head, splitting the scalp and killing him instantly. Blood and brain matter splattered Bengt's face.

"What the hell!" Bengt cried and wiped his face, "what if he was lying?"

"Huh, I never thought of that." Arvid said, "I guess there's only one way to find out."

"What do we do with him?" Bengt asked, disgusted by the gore.

"I thought about that. If we dump the body in the river, it will wash out to sea."

"You think so?"

"Yes, once, I didn't tie my boat securely, and the next day, it was drifting out in the bay."

"He is not a boat."

"No, but the current will take him." Arvid countered, "do you have a better idea?"

"We could bury him."

"And if he is reported missing, and if he told someone where he is going? No, we will throw him in the river and, if anyone asks, well, we will say he didn't want the job and left."

"Okay, but let's wait until dark," Bengt said.

"Good idea! Now, let's have a drink."

ABOUT THE AUTHOR

Albert Sandberg is a retired civil engineering technologist living in southern Manitoba, Canada.

Also by Albert Sandberg:

The Radermans Part 1 • *The Radermans Part 2*

Manufactured by Amazon.ca
Bolton, ON